FAT BLACKMAIL

BRUCE KENNEDY JONES
AND ERIC ALLISON

First published in Great Britain 2009 by Old Street Publishing Ltd,
40 Bowling Green Lane, London EC1R 0NE, UK
www.oldstreetpublishing.co.uk

A CIP catalogue record for this book is available from the British Library.

ISBN13: 978 1905847 80 8

Typeset by Martin Worthington.

Printed and bound in Great Britain by J. F. Print, Ltd.

10 9 8 7 6 5 4 3 2 1

FOR AILSA AND SID

FAT
BLACKMAIL

1

I swept up a pinch of wet soil and dropped it onto Monty's coffin. It hit the polished wood lid with a dull thud and the thin spears of rain mixed it to mud in a couple of seconds.

I thought of my old mate lying there in the box, hands resting on the little leather wallet I'd watched his Japanese wife Noriko place there earlier that morning. It held six sovereigns.

'He told me he was sixty,' she sniffed at me now. 'I only found out he was seventy-one when they gave me the death certificate. Did you know?'

She tucked herself into my body against the November drizzle and her long, black-painted nails dug into my arm.

'We used to call him the face who nicked ten years off his age,' I said.

There was a knot of mourners waiting on the gravel path. Middle-aged armed robbers, one or two north London gangsters posing in black shades, a couple of young lads already making their name on the pavement and come to pay their respects to a legend. A few had umbrellas up. None of them were sharing.

I felt the shift of Noriko's body as she turned to follow my gaze. 'Why did he do that?'

'I guess they were his to nick.'

We watched as a guy with long grey hair pulled back in a ponytail came across to say his piece. Others trailed over, all wanting words with the widow.

'Do you want to talk to them, Noriko?'

'Uh-huh. It's OK. I'm fine. I'll see you at the car.'

'All right.' I nodded at the line of faces, snapped up my collar and stepped away.

Off the main path, the rain had turned the grass to mud and mulch. It sucked at my shoes. A few yards on I stopped at a new plot, glancing down to take in a couple of pots of fading flowers and a washed-out wreath. A soggy card lay open against it, with *Love you Daddy* spelt out in six-year-old's handwriting. I imagined a little boy squeezing the pen hard as he wrote the letters. Maybe his mam sat over him as he did it.

None of this was fair.

Monty flicked through my skull: lying on his back, arms folded, eyes closed, nose a few inches away from the wooden lid of his coffin. His final cell, with six feet of earth between him and the outside world. He was supposed to be at rest, but I could see nothing peaceful in this picture: just cold and darkness and absence.

I threw a glance over my shoulder. There was a loose group of dark coats and Bogart macs forming itself around Noriko. She seemed to get smaller as they moved in. I turned away, thinking about her dead husband.

I'd met Monty about fifteen years before while I was doing a bit of bird in HMP Manchester, better known as Strangeways. The first time I saw him, he was bounding up the stairs between the landings two at a time and roaring out the back end of a joke at the geezer puffing along behind him. With spiky grey hair cropped right back to his nut and powerful broad shoulders he was a ball of energy, bouncing down the wing to vanish into a cell with a yell of greeting. Prisoners and screws alike stopped what they were doing and took notice. You always took notice of Monty.

I started to get to know him a couple of weeks later. It turned out he was at the back of what he called 'a very civilised three years,' for a bit of pavement work. An armed robber almost from birth, he was old school and a proper straight face – an honest criminal. He was more than thirty years older than me but we got on well, and working together over the years he taught me a lot about the business of being a villain. If I needed help, he was there. He got me out of grief more than once. Now he was gone.

The old guy had known he had cancer, but it was a heart attack that got him in the end. Noriko came in the door of their Chalk Farm flat to find him already cold on the carpet, eyes wide open and hands like claws. The doctor said he'd probably collapsed and died a few minutes after she split for her dance class. She called me later that day. I'd known he was ill, but we hadn't spoken for a while. He'd blanked me for months, hadn't returned my calls. 'It wasn't personal,' said Noriko. 'It was the cancer. He just wasn't himself.'

And this is where it ended. Highgate Cemetery on a wet Thursday in November, surrounded by illustrious corpses.

The service that morning had been Salvation Army. We crammed into a small chapel in Archway, all light wood and the smell of Alpine Domestos. The place was packed by half eleven. Villains, wives and girlfriends, and a few of Noriko's Japanese friends dressed and painted like it was a fashion show sponsored by *Undertakers Weekly*. The address was given by a tall thin geezer with bins called Major Tim. He went on about how Monty was now with 'the Lords,' ignoring the head-shaking of some of the chaps in the pews.

It finished with Monty's favourite song, the one that had been playing in the bar the night he met Noriko about ten years before. Peggy Lee singing 'Is that all there is?' The old guy had been on his way home when he walked past a club on Oxford Street and heard it coming out the street door. Thinking the place was kosher he slid in, only to find an ironic easy-listening joint popular with students dressed up in cardigans and suede boots. Up on a tiny stage was a geezer swinging in a big white frock, several inches of make-up and a ton of costume tom, looking more like Peggy Lee than Peggy Lee ever did. Noriko was alone at the bar and they got talking. They were wed about six months later.

We filed out and the people who weren't going on to the cemetery shook themselves down to split. I had a few words with little Jonny Jones, a face from Catford. He was short with about a week's stubble just turning into a beard.

'It was a good service.'

'The padre was a bit different, anyway.'

Jonny smiled briefly, then nodded to where Noriko was standing with a couple of her pals watching Monty's coffin being gently manoeuvred into the waiting hearse. 'Will you be looking after the girl, now? I know you and Monty were close.'

'Noriko can look after herself. But I'll make sure she has what she needs.'

'Well, she might need it. From what I heard, there won't be much left.' He caught my look and pulled up. 'Poor guy,' he added. 'He lost it a bit towards the end, with the cancer. Well, let me know if there's anything I can do.'

'I will. Thanks for coming, Jonny. Be seeing you.'

People shuffled around outside the chapel and chatted. One or two smoked, fags cupped in hands like sentries. Someone nudged me and nodded across the main drag. There were a couple of Old Bill parked up in a silver saloon, filming the outflow from the chapel. They always do it for a serious face. They like to see who's come to the party, who's mixing it with who. Sometimes they'll be hoping for a villain on his toes to turn up and say his farewells.

Now we were on the move. A few of the lads waved at the camera and gave the cops their good side, but mostly people piled into a hearse or one of the other motors for the short buzz up the hill to the cemetery. I rode up in a well-polished stretch Bentley, crushed between a Battersea face called Ken Crago on one side and a Japanese funeral Barbie on the other. Noriko sat in the back with a friend either side. A string of motors behind us, and the coffin in a hearse up ahead – wreathes, white lilies and MONTY spelt out in yellow carnations.

Sometimes five minutes can feel a lot longer. The woman beside me didn't speak any English. I glanced over my shoulder to see Noriko staring blankly through the rain-spattered window, dry eyed. Ken Crago spoke only once, when the driver went into third. 'Feel that,' he muttered. 'Smooth as butter.'

'Please God,' I thought. 'No traffic.'

The traffic was thick and we made the cemetery a year later. Some guy in a puffy grey jacket appeared and opened up a pair of iron gates. The line of crow-black motors pulled up behind; doors opened like wings and faces slid out. Monty's casket was hoisted onto a quartet of frock-coated shoulders and the four undertakers carried it up a flag-paved path to a plot in the far corner.

We followed in a procession, Noriko and I at the head, her arm threaded through mine. We went past the Pocklington family, the family Muncey, a cluster of salmon-pink graves in Polish, Mavis Barnet (1920), A.H. Boney (1919), some young lads (1914–18), then the man who invented Hovis. Ten foot of stone with Karl Marx on top, and a Celtic cross for two grandparents. This had a framed picture of the duo on it, arms clasped round each other's shoulders and smiling into the camera. A porcelain bell swung gently on a green ribbon from a stump of rosebush at the foot of the cross.

There was a tall fence up ahead and next to it an open grave. We gathered round, three deep in dark coats and black dresses. Some quiet sobbing from Noriko's pals. Then Major Tim said a few words and they lowered Monty into the ground.

Now it was half an hour later and I was still standing in the cemetery and it was still raining. I squinted back up the slope to see how Noriko was doing with the line of well-wishers. She looked tiny and frail in her black dress and pillbox hat, a crescent of lace across her face. She raised the veil as a young lad in a sharp mod suit stooped to shake her hand and kiss her on the cheek. From nowhere, I felt a shiver across my back as his lips brushed her face. I snapped up my collar and watched while she held the lad's paw as they spoke for a moment; then she flicked him the tiniest of *thank you* smiles and let it go. She looked over at me and I tried a smile of encouragement. She didn't return it.

I moved down the slope and drifted onto the gravel path. There was a sudden gust of wind and drizzle swung across my face like a curtain. I noticed three figures stood a few yards up the hill on my right, where the trees and vines got thicker. There was a young woman in red, another in a grey duffle coat and a gangly lad in baggy strides, geek glasses and long hair, tapping a water bottle on his lower teeth. They'd just lit thick white candles in blue glass holders and the trio were now making the sign of the cross. At this distance – glimpsed through the trees and bushes – it looked like their gestures were slightly exaggerated, as if they were being filmed, or taking part in some kind of drama they were improvising on the hoof. I stared at them for a while as they continued in this dumb-show. A few minutes later they turned and disappeared into the trees.

My mind went back up north to Manchester and the Crown Court. Today was day one of Casey's trial, and it wasn't looking too good for my friend and fence. A receiver and seller of stolen goods, the big fella had been lifted on charges of handling a stolen painting. I was trying to help him out by nobbling the jury. I had someone sitting in the public gallery at the court right now, spotting which of those twelve honest citizens might respond to the suggestion – and a few quid – to go against the Crown. It could make all the difference for Casey.

I looked at my watch. They might just be coming out for an early lunch. I dialled a number and got voicemail. I didn't leave a message. You never know who might hear it.

It stopped raining as I reached the front gate. Lighting up a fag, I turned and saw the mourners moving back up the path in a loose knot. Most were walking slowly, but one geezer in a dark green topcoat was making like he had to be somewhere else. Well over six foot tall, he had long wavy black hair and a couple of days' stubble on a jaw like a paving stone. He took long strides through the gates and nodded at me as he passed, as if we knew each other. His face meant nothing but I nodded back anyway, then squinted past him down the path for Noriko.

I clocked her a good way behind, talking to a guy in a cheap-looking brown mac. He was in his late fifties, about five and a half foot up and fat with it. Straggly moustache and a long untidy barnet, suspiciously black. Even from here he looked sweaty. As they got closer, it seemed like they were arguing. Noriko's face was screwed up in irritation and she walked faster to pull away from him, then turned off the main path and disappeared. I flipped my fag away and pushed through the bodies as they came through the gate, half skidding down the muddied slabs. She was a few yards down a side path, standing under a tree and sobbing.

'Noriko –'

She looked up and just shook her head, then buried her face in my chest, crying silently. I wrapped myself around her, feeling the jerks of her breath and shoulders as she sobbed. I may have cried as well. I don't remember.

'It was about money,' said Noriko.

'It always is,' I said. 'Thank you.' I took the cup of tea she was holding out and she perched on the edge of the sofa. 'No villain ever died without some unfinished business.'

It was about half three and we were sat in her and Monty's flat at Chalk Farm. There'd been a few people round for drinks after the cemetery. Last to split had been Ayumi, one of Noriko's Japanese friends. She'd left reluctantly, promising to call Noriko in the evening. They spoke in English, for my benefit.

'He said Monty owed him money,' said Noriko, 'and did I know anything about it.'

'And do you?'

She snapped a glance at me. 'I never knew any of the details. About his business.'

I'd heard something about Monty fucking a few faces for dough over the last few months. I'd had a call from someone we both knew. This lad had said Monty was into him for a few grand and the old guy had gone AWOL. That wasn't like Monty. Maybe he had been plotting some final coup for his last days, to balance the books. If he had, it was too late now.

'What was his name? The guy who was bothering you?'

'Bob something. I've never met him. Don't even know how he came to be at the funeral.'

'Probably just heard the news. Monty was quite famous. In certain circles.'

'I know.' Noriko sighed loud enough to rattle the windows. 'But you know what? I don't have any money. Mine or his. Monty left me with virtually nothing. The flat's in my name, so the council will have to let me stay, but that's about it. We spent most of his savings on doctors.'

'I wouldn't know,' I said. There was an uncomfortable silence. I filled it by knocking back my tea. Then I stared into the empty cup. After about a month, I asked the question.

'Why was Monty blanking me, Noriko? One phone call in January to tell me he had the cancer, then nothing.'

A beat. 'You weren't the only one,' she said after a moment. She was looking away from me and I could see the tension in her neck and shoulders. 'He just didn't want to talk about it.'

'All the times I rang,' I said. 'I lost count.' I nodded at the answer-phone in the corner. 'Did he get my messages?'

'Sometimes. And sometimes he'd see the light flashing and just wipe the tape.' She sniffed and rubbed her eyes. 'He started to get very weird. Up all night, asleep all day. And he disappeared a few times, two or three days. Wouldn't tell me where he'd been.'

'Maybe he was working.'

She shrugged. 'He certainly came back with money a couple of times.' She ran her fingers through her hair. 'We went to America, you know. Some cancer clinic. They said they could do something.'

'I heard.'

'It was a complete fucking waste of time,' she snapped. 'And it cost a fortune. A load of half-science, new-age bullshit. I couldn't believe he went along with it.'

This didn't sound like Noriko at all.

'They wanted him to stop taking his drugs. But he wasn't that stupid.' She sighed again, and her face fell. 'I really love him, you know,' she said.

Still using the present tense. 'We both did, Noriko. Look, if there's anything I can do. Money, help, anything –'

She said nothing.

'If anyone else starts asking about money, give them my number,' I said. 'I can tell them how it is. And there might be some chancers swimming round in the next few weeks. People trying to take advantage, thinking you might believe them if they turn up with a tale of cash outstanding. It happens.'

'Yeah.' She stood up. 'I need to get out of these clothes. Could you excuse me for a minute?'

I nodded and she made for the bedroom. I heard the door click shut behind her, stood up and went over to the bookshelves on the far side of the room.

Monty did have some money that I knew about, and I was looking at it right now. The old guy was into collecting books. Early editions, most of them children's classics. He had an 1871 *Through the Looking Glass*, also an early *Alice in Wonderland* and a couple of obscure Lewis Carroll jobs called *Sylvie and Bruno* and *Sylvie and Bruno Concluded*. Not first editions, but certainly early. Might be worth a few thousand between them.

I laid my cup down on a heavily carved table. It was solid mahogany, the one bit of Monty's past life with his first wife Elspeth that he'd hung on to. Each leg was an elephant's head, with the trunk curling down to the floor for a leg. I wondered vaguely where Elspeth was now, or if she'd even heard the old boy was dead. They divorced after a brief marriage thirty-odd years ago, and he rarely spoke about her. Maybe she was dead as well.

I ran my finger along a shelf and stopped at an edition of something called *The Family Reunion* by T.S. Eliot. I slid it off and it fell open where the binding was weak. It was a play in blank verse. Swimming in the middle of the page was a stage direction underlined in pencil. Twice. 'The Eumenides appear.' What the fuck were the Eumenides? I flipped to the front and saw it was published in 1940 and called itself a second impression. Well-known author, early edition, got to be worth something.

'They're not worth that much.'

I turned to see Noriko, changed into a simple black dress and gold ballet pumps.

'I think some of them are,' I said.

'Not as much as Monty thought. Anyway, I can't bring myself to sell them. Not just yet, for sure.'

I slid the play back into place. Noriko was still standing in the doorway, holding a long white envelope in both hands, the front out towards me like a tiny shield. Her long painted nails looked very black and shiny against the paper. Then she took a couple of steps into the room and stretched her arms straight out at me like she was acting in some ritual and this was the big moment.

'This is for you,' she said. 'From Monty.'

I took it. No name, just PRIVATE AND PERSONAL in thick black ink on the front.

'He wrote it for you the day he came back from the hospital in August,' she said. 'It was the day they told him there was nothing more they could do. He told me to give it to you. When he died.'

She seemed oddly composed. Uncomfortable, I slipped the envelope into an inside pocket. After the months of radio silence, I was surprised.

'Thanks, Noriko. I'll look at it later.'

I saw fear and sadness wash across her face and moved towards her. She stepped back, waving *no* with her hands.

'I'm all right, all right, really.'

She didn't look it. I reached into my pocket and drew out the grand in twenties. 'This is for . . . for exes,' I said. 'I owed Monty a few quid, as it goes.'

She took the money and looked up at me.

'No,' she said. 'I don't think you did.'

I got a cab across town to Gower Street where I was flopping in the Chimes Hotel. The sign on the front wall had been screwed on half a century ago and gave the gaff's sometime telephone number as Museum 5676. The owner looked like Hattie Jacques and there was an early Christmas tree with flashing lights in reception. A notice warned guests about noise after ten at night. My room smelt of the fifties. The carpet was a flock nightmare of black and purple. Red velvet curtains dropping from ceiling to floor and curled up on the deck in an ill-tempered, dusty fold. I could have paid for better, but the gaff suited my mood and my memories of Monty. He was old school: his personal clock had stopped a long time ago, and it was the sort of gaff he'd have liked.

Pulling off my coat and tie, I moved to the window and stared out. There was a bookshop on the corner across the road, windows full of red and green lights and celebrity memoirs for Christmas. The pavements were busy. Car lights, noise, the usual buzz of the city. A coffee kiosk on the main drag was sending up clouds of steam. There was a woman in her twenties wearing a bright-green coat framed in its light. She peeled a white lid off her drink and took a sip. I imagined the heat on the tip of her tongue, the cold on her ears.

Then I remembered the letter, turned back into the room and fished it out of my jacket. It felt thick and serious. I looked at PRIVATE AND PERSONAL scrawled on the front in proper black permanent ink from a bottle. Strong downward strokes and then double underlined.

For a moment I thought of the old guy writing out the words, nib scratching the paper. Knowing that I'd be reading it one day when he was gone. Did he think of this in his last moments? That second you know it's all up, the moment you find out it's all been a big joke and there's nothing to come? Or did he feel himself falling, spinning towards Christ and nod that it was going to be OK after all? As long as I got his letter?

'Why did you blank me all this time, Monty?' I said aloud.

I dropped the envelope on the desk and went to take a bath. This was the wrong place for letters from the dead. I knew where to go.

The India Club was down on the Strand, near Covent Garden. It took me a while to find it, tucked away between a baker and a travel agent. If you weren't looking, you'd miss it, like one of those streets that vanish in a fairytale. It took me two sweeps past before I found the sign, with its menu tucked behind thick yellow plastic that made it impossible to read. Monty brought me here once, and it was the first time I'd been back. Nothing had changed.

The stairs up to the club pulled me into something that looked like a movie set. It had a black and white diamond floor and old black and white snaps of Raj action lining the walls left and right. Tables in school rows, all busy with a pre-theatre crowd: students, suits, professional shoppers, twentysomething lads in shiny shirts worn outside the belt, trim-faced birds checking their make-up. A young guy in a cream tunic appeared at my shoulder like a magic trick.

'Just me,' I said.

He smiled and gestured to an empty table. I sat with my back to the window, not watching the door. Not tonight. I ordered a yoghurt drink, a ruby and a couple of side dishes. Then I took the letter out and laid it on the cloth in front of me.

And stared at it, running my finger along the edge.

He wrote it for you the day he came back from the hospital in August. The day they told him there was nothing more they could do.

'OK, Monty,' I thought. 'What's the deal?' I slid a finger under the flap, tore down the edge and tugged out four sheets of flimsy A4, the sort they used to do carbon copies on. All of them covered with Monty's big bold handwriting.

Hello mate,

I'm writing this sat on a bench in Russell Square. Actually, it's THE bench, if you remember that caper we had with Jimmy G a few years back. The place where we sat while we were waiting to go into the Imperial at the top of Southampton Row for that meet. I can see the gaff clearly from here, I can even see the window of the room we met Jimmy in.

Well, enough All Our Yesterdays. To business. If you're reading this then I'm dead. The doctor's just given me six months, maybe a year, without the option. Up till now there's been a bit of hope. But not now. That's it. Time to sort myself out for the other country.

It's lung cancer, of course. Sixty a day for sixty odd years.

I should have known, but then you never think it's going to happen to you, do you? Death is crap, mate. Get pissed on me sometime soon. You're alive, and I'm dead.

Well, that's what this letter is all about. I need a favour.

It's about money. The girl's going to need some now I'm not around. She hasn't worked for years. She'll get a job, I know, and I'll put the flat in her name now, so the council can't take it off her, but there's a bit more to it than that. I've got a bit of a long stocking stuck away, and I need you to sort it for me.

It's a good few quid, and it's all for the girl. She's all I've got for family, as you know. And I love her, mate. I really do fucking love her. Looks fucking weird writing those words on paper, but when you know the end of the road is in sight it doesn't matter much.

I need you to sort the prize for me. It's a big ask. You'll need to do a bit of running around, but I know if there's anyone in this world I could trust to do this for me, it's you. Sorry to put this on you, but that's the way it is. I'm desperate, mate. I hope you can understand. You're the only one I trust.

You need to go and see an old friend of mine, a bird called Jenna Pleasing. She's got a bunch of stuff to give you from me. It's all the details you need to unlock the prize.

Thanks mate. For this and everything else.

Be lucky.

M.

Apart from a mobile number at the bottom of the page, that was it.

I folded up the letter and stuffed it back in the envelope as the waiter showed with the food. Then I ate quickly and left to see Jenna Pleasing.

2

I came out of Finsbury Park tube and turned right up the road. It was all closed up at this time of night, but I could see it was rag-trade land: dozens of shops and warehouse down each side, all the windows stuffed with mannequins in low-rent gear.

I'd called Jenna Pleasing from outside the restaurant, saying I was a friend of Monty's and could I drop round? She gave me the address and directions. Now I was passing the church at the top of the road, hitting some numbers on my phone as I went. Three rings and Casey picked up, sounding on edge.

'How did it go, Casey?'

'Not great. Hang on.' A creak as he sat down. He'd be in his dining room, case papers and laptops spread out the length of the ten-foot table. 'The judge is some character called Chipchase. Know him?'

'I've never been up in front of him, if that's what you mean. But I've heard the name.'

'And?'

'Face I know vaguely called Bill Clack was in his court a couple of years ago. Told me Chipchase was planning a holiday and wanted it all sacked in a fortnight. Despite that, Chipchase spends most of the mornings telling anecdotes and sharing a joke or two with counsel. Pissed the time up the wall and then put Clack and his crew right under the thumb.'

'And all that means . . . ?'

'Clack's QC announces midway through week two he has to be in the Smoke the next day for the Court of Appeal. He and Clack want an adjournment because otherwise the QC's junior will have to cross-examine the police witness. Chipchase says no, the junior fucks up, and Bill Clack goes down for a five.'

'Which he shouldn't have done, I take it?'

'With a good grilling, the copper in the box should have been shot to pieces.'

'Fuck.'

'What happened today?'

'Chipchase doesn't like me, I can see that. He's coughing and spluttering all over the shop, some kind of bug. But he sneezes at me whenever he gets the chance.'

'I'm sure you're imagining that, Casey.'

'And Stella left this morning. Taken the kids to her sister's in Didsbury.'

This was bad. 'Is she gone for good? Or just the trial?'

'For good, I think, if I'm sent down. Oh bugger all this.'

There was a long pause. I let him take it to the end. Then, 'I'm not used to this, mate. All the papers, the publicity, Stella. She's not a villain's wife, she can't handle all this shit.'

Casey had been a wrestler and a Commonwealth bronze medallist back in the seventies. Later he'd gone professional, fighting on Saturday afternoon telly for a few years. He'd been a bit of a local hero, which meant his nicking made the *Manchester Evening News*. First time he'd been pulled, and Stella didn't like it.

I could have said it was out of order for her to dump on him right now, well out of order. Casey had a good reputation among the chaps and he made good money at the fencing game. Stella never complained before, but this is how it often happened. Sweet when the money's around, sour when it comes on top. I could have said all this. I kept it to myself.

'Have you spoken to the other lad yet?' Casey was talking about Marcus, the guy who was sitting on the jury for me. Marcus and Casey went back a long way as it happened, but there could no contact between them while the trial was on. Not safe, obviously.

'Not yet. It'll be all right Casey, really it will.' Casey didn't sound like he was coping too well. And I wasn't that confident we could get a result either. Bending up a trial takes time, and we didn't have much of that. 'Try to get a good's night's sleep. Stay alert tomorrow. Are you making notes?'

'Yeah. Keeps my mind off it all, if nothing else.'

We hung up as I turned into Jenna Pleasing's street.

The lady's home at number 18 was a three-storey Victorian pile. Five steep steps up to the front door from street level and lights on in the basement kitchen below. There was scaffolding up to the second floor. I pushed the bell. No ring from inside the gaff. I tried again and was rewarded with a distant drilling sound, old, worn out, a bit of kit about to die. I waited for some action inside, heard nothing and was about to push again when a two-watt bulb came on behind the frosted green glass. Two squeaks of bolts being pulled back and the door was opened by a grey-haired woman in her sixties.

She gave me a right coat of eyes up and down, like I was applying for a job. 'I suppose the old bugger's dead, then.'

'Jenna Pleasing?'

'I know who you are, hey? Monty told me all about you. Come on in.'

She stood back and pulled the wood open a few inches. I got the impression there was something jammed behind it. I squeezed through the gap and paused for a second.

I couldn't see much, but I could nose the gaff well enough. It was the smell that means someone round here never throws anything away, just sticks it in a cupboard or under the stairs, then crams some more in after it. Three bikes were dimly outlined at the foot of the staircase. Then she turned on another light and I saw piles of books either side of us, stacked up to the ceiling, cardboard boxes on top of more books, ancient kids' board games jumbled together, five years' worth of *Vogue, Harper's Bazaar, The People's Friend* and an untidy heap of something called *Reveille*. The stairs were used for storage: each step was taken up with piles of bills, letters, phone directories, computer manuals, files, cables and kettle leads. The end banister was covered with a mound of clothes, like someone had hung up everything they'd worn in the last fortnight.

'It's a little untidy,' Jenna Pleasing said from behind me. 'Let's go down to the kitchen. We can talk there.'

Somehow she managed to slide past me and led the way down to the basement. Both sides of the stairwell were covered with leaflet racks like a travel agents, all of them crammed with papers, brochures, leaflets. Some looked like they were produced on an old Gestetner, or photocopied and stapled together by an enthusiast. I glimpsed some of the titles: *Conspiracy vs Conspiracy in American History, Why Ronnie Biggs and city financiers have a lot in common, Corporate power in Thatcher's Britain, The Change Cuba Needs, You and Your Yurt . . .*

I stumbled on a pile of rubble at the bottom of the stairs and half fell into the kitchen.

'Mind the rubble,' she said. 'Oh – too late! Never mind. Have a seat.'

The room was cluttered with plates and food from dinner. And, by the look of the bacon rinds in a saucer on the side of the sink, breakfast as well. There was a stool in the far corner by some French windows. It was the only surface in the gaff that wasn't covered with stuff. I perched. Jenna clicked on the kettle and then turned and smiled warmly at me.

It was the first time I'd seen her clearly. She was about five foot with big red Elton John glasses and a mop of grey hair folded up on top of her nut. She was dressed in a brown poncho with a black and white fringe and looked like the sort of woman who'd have a couple of drags of your cigarette because she'd given up smoking years ago. She was speaking.

'So he's dead, hey?'

'Monty died a few days ago,' I said. 'I'm sorry.'

She busied herself with mugs from a cupboard and spoke over her shoulder.

'Cancer got him in the end,' she said. 'Always telling him to give up. I packed it in years ago. Tried to get him to do the same.'

'It was a heart attack. But the cancer would have got him soon enough.'

'I knew he had it,' she said. 'Tumour in his lungs, then the secondary tumour in his neck. There was a bit of hope till then. Not after. Hang on.'

The kettle clicked off and she poured water over heaped spoons of instant.

'How did you and Monty meet?'

'Ah.' She handed me a mug, went into a fridge and brought out milk. She tipped the bottle at me, I shook *no*. 'Montague Lee. Met him a long time ago on a demo outside Wandsworth nick. Half a dozen of us there protesting about some chap who was about to be deported, and Monty wandered up to ask me what it was all about. Think he'd just been in to see someone on a visit. Anyway, we kept in touch after that. Got to know him pretty well. I used to do quite a bit of prison visiting, running one visitors' centre or another. So we had similar interests.'

'I didn't know Monty was much of a prison campaigner.'

'Oh, you'd be surprised. He was a good man, despite what he got up to sometimes. I took him along to a meeting once – something to do with prison reform. He didn't go down too well. The middle classes like their villains properly reformed and going straight. Monty of course was quite the reverse. He always went back for some more.'

'He's quite a legend. Among the chaps. Well, the older ones.'

There were footsteps somewhere up above. I glanced up.

'My husband,' she said. 'My son's around somewhere as well. Did you go to the funeral?'

I took a swig of the coffee. 'Today, at Highgate.'

'I told him I didn't want to go, last time I saw him. That was a few months ago. He knew the game was up then. How's Naoko taking it?'

'Noriko,' I said. 'Pretty well,' I lied. 'Do you know her?'

'No. I only heard about her from Monty. He seemed to do all right there.' She sighed loudly and smiled at me like she was encouraging a child who'd barked his knee. 'OK. I know what you're here for. It's upstairs, come on.'

Back up past the leaflet racks and the rest and then off the hall into another room. The door had a poster for a play tacked on it: a screen-printed black and white image of a line of police with riot shields, waving batons. But wearing the normal button-boy uniforms, not the full riot gear. WORKERS FOR THE UNWAGED THEATRE COMPANY PRESENTS 'THE CUTS' the poster read. A TWENTY-FOUR HOUR

CYCLE OF IMPROVISED DRAMA ABOUT THATCHER'S BRITAIN AND MAGGIE'S MILLIONS. £1.50 AND 50p UNWAGED. It sounded like a threat, not a show.

'This is my study,' she said from inside. I snapped out of it and stepped in after her. The room was about twenty feet square and fifteen foot high. And it was entirely crammed with paper. Massive stacks of paper and files from floor to ceiling, all the way round the room. Two creaky old brown wardrobes were pushed up against the wall on the left, doors jammed open by an overflow of junk with a hill of newspapers on top. There was a patch of space just inside the door and a few square feet of brown carpet between me and a computer on an untidy desk. Behind that was a sea of paper, stuffed brown envelopes and waves and waves of old files and bills and Christ knows what else.

Jenna Pleasing was looking at the wall of junk behind the desk like it was a library and fiddling with her puffy grey bun.

'Monty gave me an envelope for you,' she said.

God help me, I thought. 'How long ago?' I said.

'I do know where everything is,' she said. 'Why don't you sit down for a moment?'

There was a stool, the twin of the one in the kitchen. I leant on it, wondering how long I was going to be here.

'So how did you meet Monty,' she said, riffling a section of stack. 'He talked about you a lot, but he never told me where he met you.'

'Strangeways,' I said.

'On a demo?'

'On the wings.'

'I was joking.' There was a creak from upstairs and she shot a glance at the ceiling. 'My husband's getting restless,' she said. 'I'll have to go up and see to him in a minute. Alzheimer's. He's only sixty. How about the desk?' She pulled a box over and squatted on it, going through the drawers one by one and talking over her shoulder at me as she went.

'He was a good man, Monty,' she said. 'A good man. I'll miss him. Ah! Here we are.'

She plucked out a thick brown A4 envelope with PRIVATE in Monty's thick black ink on the front.

'Here we are. And, there's something else – let me come behind you.'

I stood off the stool and she edged behind me to the wardrobe. 'Here.' She swung round, her bust now about two inches from me. I took a step back and came up against the desk. 'Don't worry,' she said. 'I'm not going to jump you.'

I took the second envelope she was holding out. It was unsealed and stuffed with sheets of paper.

'That's his as well,' she said. 'He gave it to me years ago to hold onto. He was going inside at the time, I think. Then he forgot all about it, but still. You might as well have it. You're obviously a good friend. Or you wouldn't be here.' Suddenly she looked very tired. 'I'd better go and see to Gerald. I'll show you out.'

I tucked the second envelope inside my coat with the other. 'Thanks, Jenna. I'm sure he was grateful.'

'Well, well.' She prodded me with a thumb. 'I hope they bring you luck.'

I walked for the tube punching Marcus's number into my phone. He answered before it had rung once.

'Marcus.'

'Just calling you. How was the funeral?'

'A heap of laughs. I'll tell you later. How was court this morning?'

'I don't know yet, mate. The twelve of them sat there like they'd scored front row seats at *Les Mis*. All of them with notebooks, all of them hanging on the judge's every fucking word.'

'This is Chipchase, right?'

'Yeah. He's got a streaming cold, pissing germs all over the QCs, sneezing and coughing everywhere.'

'Casey said.'

'How is he?'

'Not good. It's all new to him and not very pleasant. All he can think of is the three years he'll get if it all goes reels.'

'Well, give him my best tomorrow, eh? And are you still all right to look after the shop on Saturday?' Marcus owned a secondhand-stroke-repro furniture joint down by Manchester Victoria.

'Behave yourself. Thanks for today Marcus. Speak tomorrow.'

We hung up and I found I'd walked past the tube and out onto the main drag. Across the lines of traffic, I saw a couple of fat, stubble-faced men in donkey jackets march down the pavement, almost in step. The fattest broke his stride and pushed open a door into a brightly lit shop front. The other guy followed. My eye slid up to a neon sign: *Finsbury Sauna and Mass*. The last three letters were dead, then they suddenly flickered – and started to blink *age* at me, off and on. I grunted and turned back for the tube.

An hour later I was sat on my bed at the Chimes picking through the contents of the first envelope and reflecting that Monty must have trusted Jenna Pleasing as much as he trusted anybody. I finished a tumbler of red wine and refilled my glass, then stood looking at the papers spread out on the bobbled counterpane.

'Congratulations, Monty,' I raised my glass, 'on a very decent piece of work.' I pulled a chair across to the bed and spread the contents of the envelope in front of me to tell the story.

Main exhibit was a letter from Monty. Same thick black ink, same powerful strokes. This one told me that back in May, Monty and two others had successfully robbed a cargo plane at Heathrow airport and got away with four million quid in large denomination Swiss banknotes. I remembered the news reports. The chaps' gossip was that it was a bunch of ex-soldiers because no one had heard of the money moving about, or anything connected to it at all, in fact. The police had got nowhere, despite a four-hundred grand reward. That's more than enough to turn so-called straight faces into grasses.

Monty had worked with two others. One was a villain called Bob Devorty, the other – fuck me – was called Frank Korda. *Detective Chief Inspector* Frank Korda. Even bigger surprise was the reference Monty gave the rozzer: *You can trust him, mate. He's been tested more than once, and never been found wanting. So take it from me, he's one-hundred per cent.*

There were two snaps in the bundle. One had *Korda* written on the back, the other *Devorty*. Korda's smudge made him big and powerful with a copper's stock-issue moustache. And Devorty, well . . . Devorty was the guy who'd been arguing with Noriko at the funeral. That explained his chat about the money Monty owed him. I stared at Devorty's photo. Of the two, he was the easiest to distrust from looks alone. He looked out of condition and sweaty, like it was an effort to hold for the camera, even for a couple of seconds.

I turned back to the letter. The dough had been laid down in a safe deposit box in a bank in Zurich, said Monty. It was all in Swiss francs – and thousand-franc notes at that. This had made the prize too hot to change up – at least by August, the time Monty had written the letter. The SP might be different by now. After the launderer had done his bit and taken his twenty-five per cent, there would be three million quid to draw, in dollars and euros.

This was absurd money. More than most people saw in a lifetime. I took another swig of the booze and came to the strangest bit. The cash could only be accessed by Monty, Korda and Devorty showing up at the bank together. No one got his share till they all got their share.

'Someone didn't trust somebody else, eh Monty?' I said aloud. 'Wonder which one of you it was?'

Monty's letter gave me the first four figures of the code number to access the box. Korda had the middle three, Devorty the last three.

None of us know the other's numbers. You need all the numbers to get at the money. The complete set of ten numbers is a combination to open the strongbox.

<u>*On no account*</u> *must you let Korda or Devorty know my numbers until the moment you take control of or transfer the money.*

'After the reference you gave Korda, it must be Devorty you don't trust, Monty,' I thought. 'Or maybe they don't trust each other?'

The trio had talked about appointing successors. One each in case they were nicked or died suddenly. Monty's death sentence meant he'd actually gone ahead done it. This was part of my game.

I'll tell them who you are, mate, but there are a couple of extras to identify yourself. The first is a question and response, like you get in the movies. You say 'I've got toothache,' and they should respond 'then you better not fight today.'

There was also a torn section of a postcard – one of three, Monty said. The picture showed a Tutankhamen-style death mask.

I flipped it over again and saw a bit of barcode, no other clue where it came from. Korda and Devorty had the other two sections, which I assumed showed the rest of a sarcophagus – an Ancient Egyptian coffin. The idea was to match up the pieces so you knew who you were talking to. Christ, this was complicated. Still, it was Monty's money, so it was Monty's rules.

The old guy asked me to contact Korda and Devorty – there were addresses and phone numbers for both – and get hold of the money. His share, of course, was to go to Noriko – minus fifty grand for my own expenses, which would come in handy. He'd leave it to me how I'd get the dough to his widow. She knew nothing about the Heathrow job, apparently.

I stood, scratched a fag out of the packet on the desk, lit up and moved to the window. I wondered what had stopped Monty and the others laying hands on the cash before the old boy died.

'Why didn't you just call me up, Monty?' I thought. 'Then we could have met and talked, like pals. Instead it's letters and numbers and bits of postcard. Your head must have been right up your arse.'

That he hadn't cut me in on the coup was up to him, but I still felt a slight pang of jealousy. I shrugged and picked up the second envelope Jenna Pleasing had given me, then let it drop back on the desk. I'd already glanced inside. It seemed to be two or three short stories Monty had written a long time ago on a wobbly old typewriter. And a few snaps and other bits and pieces. Not important for the matter in hand, but a nice keepsake of the old guy.

It was gone midnight and I'd been up early that morning for the funeral. I wrote down Monty's numbers on a scrap of paper and memorised Devorty and Korda's addresses. Then I took both letters to the bathroom, burnt them over the toilet and flushed away the ash.

3

Nine o'clock Friday morning and I was sitting on the bench in Russell Square where Monty wrote me his letter. It was cold, the fountains were off and the café in the corner hadn't opened yet. Apart from a few straightgoers striding through the park on their way to work, I had the place to myself. I sat for a few minutes, looking at what the old boy looked at when he wrote to me. The park, the skeletal winter trees, the Imperial Hotel, a couple of buses chugging up the bus lane. Then I slipped out my mobile and dialled Bob Devorty's number. He answered sounding like I'd woken him up.

'Bob Devorty?'

'Who's this?'

'A friend of Monty's. I think we could do with a meet.'

Silence. Then, 'Oh yeah?'

'I've got something for you. A postcard the old boy sent me just before he went.'

Devorty's tone changed immediately. 'A postcard. I think I've got one of those.'

'Well, that's nice. How about half ten at your place?'

'Fine by me. Could you do us a favour and pick up a pint of milk?'

A beat.

'Skimmed?' I said.

'Full cream. Cheers.'

I hung up and schlepped across the square, wound my way through a bunch of side streets and came out at King's Cross. I bought a roll from a café by the station and hopped on a number 73 bus. Monty had done his bit and given me full story and pictures for getting to Devorty's gaff. He lived in Stoke Newington, past Newington Green and opposite a parade of shops.

Stoke Newington had changed a bit since I'd spent a few months flopping there in the early nineties. Then, most of the houses along Albion Road had been pretty rundown, with gardens full of household junk and the odd crapped-out car up on bricks. Now, most of the gaffs were smart and the gardens had well-mown lawns or neat little flowerbeds. A couple more minutes and my bus pulled up outside a shop with an old advert for sweets taking up half the front wall: WIN HER AFFECTION WITH A1 CONFECTION. I jumped off, nipped into the newsagents for a pint of blue-top, then crossed the road and looked for 132a. The flat was above a betting shop, a dull-grey metal door to the right. Three bells, no names. I pushed the lowest and Devorty's voice crackled over the intercom.

'Milkman,' I said, and he buzzed me in. He was standing at his open front door when I reached the landing, wearing a blue robe over purple track pants. He stuck out his paw and we shook.

'You were at Monty's funeral yesterday,' he said. I nodded and stepped inside. Devorty gestured me down the hall into a black and chrome eighties nightmare of a living room. Fat, low-slung leather sofa, black ash coffee table and a couple of canvas-sized prints of Audrey Hepburn twirling a cigarette in *Breakfast at Tiffany's*. This was a room sparse of taste.

'Sit yourself down.' Devorty went through an arch into the kitchen and starting brewing up. He was a big man with a big waist. Close to, the moustache looked very thin and straggly and I could see the grey roots coming out from his skull. He clearly dyed his hair black. His nails were too long for a man and dirty with it. There was a line of grime around the collar of his robe. He felt my eyes on him and looked up.

'Before we go any further,' I said. 'I have to tell you that I've got toothache.'

'Sorry to hear that.'

'No, I've got toothache.'

'You looking for a dentist, what?'

'Not looking for a dentist. I say, *I've got toothache*, and you say . . . ?'

'Oh, sorry, fuck it. Hang on.' He turned round and rooted in a cutlery drawer, then pulled out a scrap of paper and read it. 'Then you better not fight today.' He looked at me. 'All right?'

'And there's this.' I pulled out my chunk of postcard and laid it on the work surface, dead face up. He nodded, rustled around some more and fished out his section. I slid the two together. Two thirds of an Egyptian sarcophagus. I flipped his chunk over and read: 'King Sety the First. 1279 BC.' Taking the mug he offered me, I slipped my bit of card back in my pocket and sat, feeling the sofa relax as my backside sank into it. He slid into a puffy leather armchair and stood his mug on the deck.

'You were arguing with Noriko yesterday.'

He looked up, guilty. 'Yeah, sorry about that. We had some . . . business.'

'No,' I said coolly. 'You didn't. Noriko knows nothing about this. So don't talk to her again. And at the old guy's funeral – that was out of order.'

'I'm sorry. I just got a lot of money grief at the moment, you know how it is.' He paused. 'I'm glad to see you now, though.'

'You knew about me?'

'Monty told us you were his successor. He showed me a photograph a while back, in the summer. You and him in the Lake District some-where, big lump of stone in the background.'

I remembered the day. 'We were doing a bit of hiking.' I rang the lip of my cup for a moment. 'I've known Monty a lot of years, Bob. No disrespect, but I can't remember him ever mentioning you before. Had you known him long?'

Devorty shuffled in his green plastic sandals and looked embar-rassed. 'A little bit for quite a while, just to let on to. That sort of style. We didn't quite work in the same worlds, you might say.'

'What was your game?'

He shuffled again. 'I used to . . . bring people together. Organise entertainment, that sort of thing.'

'Entertainment?'

'Party girls.'

'Call girls?'

'Nothing like that. I'd make a few introductions and then, the next day or the next week or when they got back from Dubai and so and so, the girls would send their phone bill or their Visa card round to be set-tled up by their . . . new friends. Or whatever.' He caught the look on my face. 'No one was forced to do anything. They all made a good living.'

Some of my best friends are prostitutes. It's the pimps I can't stand. What I said was: 'None of my business how a man makes his living, Bob.'

He looked at me defensively. 'I brought the knowledge on the Hea-throw work, all right? I came to Monty with it in January and he was happy to have me on the firm. You're his successor. No one's asking your opinion.'

I finished my coffee and stood it on the table. 'All right,' I said briskly. 'Let's get on. I haven't seen this Frank Korda yet. I knew Monty could buy knowledge from the filth, I didn't know he was that close with them. Before I go, what can you tell me?'

'When are you going to see him?'

'Soon as. I've got his address – he dwells in Manchester. If I can pull him today or certainly before the weekend, the three of us can make an arrangement to get across and unlock the cash. Noriko needs her portion, apart from anything else.'

Devorty was looking at me like I was a cash machine that had just taken his card off him. 'Oh fuck it.'

'What?'

'You don't know, do you?'

'Know what?'

'Frank Korda's in Strangeways. He was nicked in October for taking bungs. He's on remand and he's not going anywhere.'

'Fuck.'

'You've said a mouthful there.' He wiped his lips with the back of his hand. 'I thought you'd come here to tell me he'd got bail or they'd dropped the charges or something. Why do you suppose we hadn't got the money out yet? Because we were giving up being rich for Lent?'

'Monty's letter didn't say anything about this.'

'When did you get it?'

'Just yesterday.'

'And when was it written?'

'August some time.'

'There you are. He wrote to you before Korda was lifted.'

'What's Korda in for?'

'Sold some information off the police national computer. As a result, one of the witnesses in a big case got shot by some pals of the crew he put away.'

I'd been away a lot in October, otherwise I'd have known this. Copper being lifted on matters corrupt would have made the local news at least. This was a bastard. 'And that's really down to Korda?'

'So says the Crown.'

Devorty picked his mug up by the rim. As he stood, his robe fell open and I noticed a grease stain the shape of India on his crotch. 'I'll get you some more tea.' He slapped into the kitchen and flicked the kettle. 'It was a fucking pisser, I'm telling you. I was looking for my retirement there.'

'Has the money been laundered yet?'

'About four weeks ago. We got word. And then the next day, Korda was nicked. Slung into the Big House.'

I went and leant on the arch. 'And?'

'Monty said Korda reckoned he could beat the rap. And walk. Or at least make bail.' He emptied the teapot and dumped the bags in the bin under the sink. 'Turns out, he was wrong. Then Monty went and died. I was asking myself, "who the fuck's going to fix this fucking mess now?" – and look. Here you are.' He flicked me a nervous little smile.

'Why was the money locked away so complicated?'

'I wanted it that way. I took the original knowledge to Monty, he pulled Korda in on the coup. I knew what plane the money was coming in on, but I couldn't supply the stand it would go to when it landed. Only the airport knows that, usually an hour or so before the plane lands. Korda had a contact somewhere in Heathrow. I wasn't too keen – Old Bill is Old Bill – but Monty said he was OK. I still insisted on the cut-up being abroad, though, and only when we were all there.'

The kettle clicked off and he slung water into the pot.

'In any case, it was far too hot to handle over here. There was quite a scream. So we met this guy Monty knew in a field near Dover and gave him the prize.' He spread his arms and mimed lifting a bag. 'Thousand franc notes, it wasn't that big. Decent-sized sportsbag.'

'And then?'

'He got into his plane.'

'He flew?'

'Flew himself. Little single engine job. Took off and dropped over the white cliffs. Apparently the trick is to fly just above the sea at forty miles an hour. Then you show up on the radar as a motorboat.'

Another bit of Monty's world I knew nothing about. But if the launderer was Monty's man, he could be trusted. One-hundred per cent.

'So why didn't he just fly it back when it was clean?' I said.

'He told us it would take a while to launder up, even abroad. So he stuck it in the safe deposit and sent us our numbers separately. Said he would clean it when it was safe. The idea was that the three of us would go out together and take control of the dough. Monty wanted to spend his last days travelling with Noriko, so he was in favour. Korda had put his papers in.' The kettle clicked off. 'But by the time it was safe, he was nicked. So it never happened.'

'Have you heard from Korda since he went away?'

'*Niente*. More tea?' I shook *no*. He shuffled back through the arch and eased himself into a padded black leather recliner. There was a flat red cushion which he slid up and stuck behind his head, then tipped the seat back a few inches, slopping some of his brew down his front. 'As I said, I thought you were here because you had some knowledge.'

'No, sorry.' I scratched my chin. 'Any idea when the trial is?'

'Next year.' He shrugged. 'Spring. He's gone *no* all the way, so . . . '

I drained my mug and stood. Devorty followed. 'Maybe he's got plans to nobble the trial,' I said. 'Or maybe the prosecution case isn't that strong.'

'Except he hasn't got bail, has he?'

I moved for the door. 'I'll see what I can find out, Bob. Maybe there's a way out of this. Didn't Korda appoint a successor too?'

'If he did, we haven't heard from him.'

'But you knew about me already.'

'Monty knew he was ill. The copper didn't expect to get nicked.'

'Well, that's the first thing to find out. I'll get back to you.'

'Well, good luck.' He followed me to the door looking dejected. 'It's in dollars and euros now. Three million quids-worth in small notes.' He plucked at his grease-stained robe and gave a sad little smile. 'All that money, and we can't get at it.'

I made Noriko's just after noon. I hit her landing to find her in a black mini-dress and boots and talking to the old girl who dwelt in the flat next door. Well into her seventies and bent at the waist like a rusted hinge, she was leaning on a zimmer and going on about her son. Noriko introduced her as Rose and nodded me inside. 'I'll be with you in a second, yeah?'

Indoors, I laid my coat on the elephant table, switched on the kettle and started going through Monty's books. Which of them would get a decent price? The two *Alice*s were worth something. Maybe the other two Lewis Carrolls. I flipped them off the shelf one by one, checked the spines and the dust jackets, then laid them on top of my coat.

'Rose was asking for Monty,' said Noriko. I turned as she closed the front door and came into the living room, heels clicking loudly. 'She doesn't seem to realise he's dead.' She sank onto the sofa like Mary

Quant: knees touching, feet and ankles far apart. 'Not sure I do yet. What are you doing?'

I thumbed at the shelves. 'I just thought I'd get a few things valued for you. Not to sell for now, just so you know. I'm not an expert, but I reckon some of these are worth a couple of grand each.'

'All right. Get the prices. But don't sell any of them. Not yet.' She sniffed. 'Oh – I had two guys round here this morning. They said Monty owed them.'

'Who were they?'

'I didn't ask, and I didn't let them in. We spoke on the intercom. They sounded like they were Russian or something. I just told them to come back next week. I'm going away for a few days, tonight or tomorrow. I've told Ayumi and the girls. Give me a chance to sort myself out.' She sighed deeply and seemed to fold into her own body, somehow shrinking a little. The kettle boiled in the kitchen and clicked off. 'How much fucking tea have I made in the last week?' she said abruptly.

'I'll do it, Noriko.'

'No, leave it.' She stood, straightened her skirt and went out. A couple of seconds she was back, waving a sheet of paper at me. 'You see this?'

'What is it?'

'It's a list of all the creeps I asked to the funeral. Apart from my friends from Japan, do you know how many of them have been round to see how I am? None, that's how many. My ears are burning, the phone's ringing off the hook with well-wishers.' She shrugged. 'Sorry, I don't mean you.'

'Don't worry about it.'

She shook her head again. 'Look, I'm not really feeling that great. I just want to lie down, have a little sleep. Would you mind going?'

'Is there anything I can get for you –'

'No. Just stop being so bloody nice, all right? Just take the books and go. I just need some rest.'

I hooked my coat over my arm and picked up the Carrolls. 'I'll give you a call, eh? On your mobile. You'll leave it on?'

'Yeah yeah yeah.' She hustled me out to the front door and opened up. Then she put one hand on each of my shoulders and kissed me fiercely on the cheek. A second and she snapped back, licking her fingers and rubbing the lipstick off nervously. 'There.' She rubbed harder. 'Now no one will know.' She nodded and I stepped out into the hall. Then she raised her hand, wiggled her fingers and closed up.

I was on the train out of Euston by three and the carriage was quiet. Too early for the Friday rush hour. I'd managed to annexe two double seats and a table, and I was looking through Monty's second envelope. It had a number of stories packed into it, plus a few newspaper clippings and some photographs.

Most of the newsprint came from late 1962 and early 1963. An A3 sheet from the *Melody Maker* had a picture of two women in skinny jeans and straw boaters and the caption, *How can trad jazz fans expect us to take them seriously if they insist on dressing like this?* Then there was a big piece about some artist called Ruskin Spear and the painting he'd just exhibited for the first time – a portrait of the comic Sid James – flat cap pulled down over his nut and looking pissed off. 'He's got me looking very miserable,' said Sid. 'I don't know what Hancock will have to say about all this . . . '

I looked at the photographs. One was a black and white snap of a little boy with a round face climbing up some wood trellis on a white-washed wall. He was wearing shorts and big heavy boots and looking back over his shoulder at the camera. I flipped it over and read *Monty, aged 5* in faded black ink. I smiled and picked up the next one. This had two young lads sitting on a sea wall, boots swinging. They had the same cropped hair and the same nose. I turned the snap. *Monty age 12*, it said. *Ted age 10*.

I leant back in my seat. I knew Monty had a brother called Ted. He'd told me one night, when he was drunk, though there wasn't much to tell. When Ted was 17, he got a job on a boat. A few months later, Monty got a letter from Gibraltar and that was it. He never heard from him again, and Monty never spoke about him again. I knew not to ask.

I turned to the short stories. Flimsy typewritten sheets, proper old school: mistakes were XXXXX-ed out, or painted over with Tippex. The longest was about four pages. There was no title, just a date. This is what I read:

Bradford 1962
So there was me, Joey, Bill and Wal. All sat in
that pub with 'Little Bitty Tears' playing out
the jukebox and this South African bird called
Cricket next to me. She sat there twisting the
filters off the tabs before she lit them up and
then she had two or three puffs and stuck them
out. She was seventeen, only a couple of years
older than me, but she seemed more. Especially
when she was talking about places she'd been —
Spain, Hong Kong, Rhodesia.
Then Wal was calling me over and I got up and
went over where he was standing with Joey and
some other lad I never saw before. They were

talking about some money that Joey and Wal owed
– about five pounds. Their man, he wanted it
tonight or else. Wal reckoned he knew where he
could get some.

Then there seemed to be a page missing. Turning over, the quartet was now outdoors, apparently chugging through dark backstreets on scooters.

We went past the Springheeled Jack just as they
were chucking out, then on up Marston Road to
the corner where we stopped.
Here was his house, the little guy. I heard Wal
say this was it, Mr Desai lived here. Then he
told me to stay with the scooters. We're going
up, have a word with Mr Desai. Just stay put
with the scooters.
The other three went inside. I saw a blue light
flickering at the top of the house, whiter lights
in the rest. I just stood by the scooters,
feeling sick.

The rest of the page was torn off. The next sheet had a couple of paragraphs scored out with thick black marker pen, I couldn't read them. Then:

There was movement up the street. But it
always happened when I wasn't looking. I'd see
something whip round a corner or going in a door

or dissolving behind some bedroom curtains. I didn't want to be on the street any more. I wanted to throw up again, but instead I went inside looking for the rest.

I could hear a telly from up above. It was showing This Is Your Life with Eamonn Andrews, doing Acker Bilk. I could hear the lads too – not shouting, just raised voices. I started to climb, one flight, then the next. I got to the top floor. The TV was getting louder. All the words running around and chasing each other.

I was at the top. Blue light dancing everywhere. I rounded the corner and looked in. I saw the telly first, playing away. Joey, Bill and Wal were stood there, looking down at the carpet. The only light was from the TV. Acker was up on a stool talking, there was clapping from the audience. Then I looked down. The little man was lying on the floor. I could see a big lake of black spreading out from under his body, soaking into the carpet. The three lads heard me and looked up. Wal shook his head. I think he dropped something on the floor, I saw a flash of metal.

I knew Mr Desai wasn't going to get up again. He wouldn't be walking down to his shop tomorrow morning, opening up at five and taking in the papers and the milk. I knew he wouldn't be

And that was the bottom of the last page. Some of this rang a bell. That night when he was drunk, Monty had said Ted had been mixed up in a stabbing when he was a kid. I rooted through the rest of the papers hoping to find the ending. Nothing.

I hit Manchester at half five and went straight to Marcus's second-hand-stroke-repro shop. The doors were still open onto the pavement, jammed back by a pair of big brass pigs. Inside, I schlepped down a corridor formed by lines of wardrobes and tallboys, turned left at six marble birdbaths and made for the office past a row of life-size plaster statues: Joe Louis, Las Vegas Elvis, a cow, Guy the Gorilla. I pushed open the little door and found a youth wearing a tight-fitting grey suit and knitted brown tie. His feet were up on the desk, squeezed into old-school winkle pickers. His hair was long, wiry and backcombed, and despite being indoors he was wearing big wraparound shades.

'I was just hanging on for you,' the youth said as he unfolded from behind the desk. 'Marcus called to say he'd be along about six and you were to make yourself at home.'

'Thanks.' I dropped my bag on the desk. 'Has anyone ever told you that you look like John Cooper Clarke?'

He unhooked a shaggy Afghan coat from the back of the door. 'I hope so, I'm a fucking tribute act.' He gave me a quick blast of the Salford whine: *'I'd like to do one of me poems about unemployment . . .* see you later, mate.' He split, and I heard him echoing out through the store. *'When I woke I was gagged and bound . . . for Majorca.'*

I slipped my coat off and made tea. Just as the kettle boiled, Marcus showed.

'You been here long?'

'Ten minutes. The Bard of Salford just left.'

'Oh aye.' Marcus was wearing a thick black coat, woolly scarf and a flat cap. As I brewed up, he hooked an electric fire from under the desk with his foot and turned it on. Fishing a fan heater out of a filing cabinet, he plugged it in and stood over it so the hot air went up his trousers.

'It is fucking cold in those courtrooms,' he said.

'No it isn't,' I said, shrugging off my jacket and unbuttoning my shirt. 'You're always fucking cold. Was anyone else dressed for Ice Station Zebra?'

He took the tea I passed across. 'Well, I suppose not. Now you mention it.'

The sweat was already building up on my shoulders. I flapped a bit of breeze onto my face with a receipt book.

'So what happened?'

'No guarantees,' said Marcus, 'but I reckoned there were a couple of likely candidates. I pointed them out to the two lads on standby out front. They had orders to follow them as far as they could. All the way home if they got lucky.'

'That's a good start. How did Casey look today?'

'Very low. Just sat in the dock staring at his hands. He was taking notes, but he looked pretty defeated, to tell the truth.'

'And he's got the weekend to get through. I'll go see him tomorrow. Let him know the news.'

'Aye.' He sat down on a swivel chair, rubbing his hands over the heater like he was Captain Oates about to step outside. 'You still all right to look after the shop for a bit tomorrow?'

'No worries.' I stood, did up my shirt, pulled on my jacket and coat and picked up my bag. 'About ten, yeah?'

'Please. I've got the gas coming round. Heating at home's a bit fucked.'

I said nothing, just waved my hand and split. Out on the pavement, the cold air slapped me around the cheeks and made my ears sing.

When I got back to my gaff I rang Casey and made a meet for tomorrow. Then I took the slip of paper with Monty's numbers and hid it, along with the scrap of postcard, in my copy of *Through the Looking Glass* – at the part where Tweedledee and Tweedledum have their fight.

I whipped up a quick omelette and sat at the computer while I checked my emails. There was one from my daughter Lou. She was in America with her twin brother Sam and Sara, my ex. They'd been there for a couple of days and were planning to stay another three weeks. Lou had sent me a couple of pictures of the pair of them. *We're on the Staten Island ferry going out to see the Statue of Liberty,* she wrote. *Mum took the pictures.* They were leaning on a rail, with New York spread out behind them. Sam was still a bit of a schoolboy, but Lou was a young woman now. Her hair pulled back in a ponytail, she was wearing a long red coat and knee-high boots. They were both smiling and waving at the camera. Just turned eighteen, the pair of them. Only seemed yesterday we brought them home from the hospital.

I sent her a brief reply and was about to switch off when a message popped up from Naples – englishteacher68@libero.it. It was the first time I'd heard from her in weeks and I'd been wondering what was up. Turned out her father was in hospital after a heart attack. *I think he will be OK, but I don't know,* she wrote. *I'm not sure if I'll be able to come and see you in the New Year. I'll call you in a few days when we know how he's doing.* I wrote back, then switched off and lay on the sofa, thinking about Monty, Noriko and the copper Frank Korda.

After a while, I pulled Monty's stories out and started to flick through them again. There was one set at a gig sometime in the sixties. Monty described young lads in straight-legged strides and V-neck jumpers bouncing round the dance hall and trying to keep up with each others' moves. One of them spun big on his heels and toes, trying to catch the eye of some mini-skirted dollybird stood smoking by a pillar. She stared right through him for a while, then turned and walked away.

4

Casey opened his door to me the next morning, looking puffy and drained in a white robe. He'd shaved his beard off for the trial and his face looked naked.

'How did you sleep?' I didn't need to ask.

'Not well.' He stood back and gestured me down the corridor to the dining room. I sat down, noticing crumbs and grease on the table he'd not bothered to clean up. Through the kitchen door I could see a bin overflowing onto the deck. The house felt empty. His kids were seven and eight and Saturday mornings normally meant running around all over the shop and watching cartoons on TV. Not today.

'I'll get some tea going.' I watched his six-and-a-half-foot frame disappear into the kitchen. He looked diminished today and his hair stuck up at the back of his head where he'd forgotten to comb it. He was back in a few minutes.

'What's Marcus got to say?' he asked.

'He sent the lads after a couple of likely bankers last night. Don't know how far they got.'

'And after that?'

'We'll have to see. Nobbling a jury is not a precise science, Casey. It might take four or five nights to get them all the way home, picking them up at a later spot every day. Then it depends what area they live in. If it's the right corner of the world, you can ask the question.'

'And then you're still *hoping for the best.*'

'I always told you that.'

He creaked back in his chair and folded his arms. I could see he was staring down three years without the option.

'The guy who stuck you in for this –'

'Dicky Eden.'

'Yeah, Eden. Tell me why he did this again.'

'He owed me money. The painting was to repay part of the dough. Only he'd set me up with the filth, as we now know.' Casey had met Eden in a hotel in Salford to pick up the merchandise. Turned out matey boy was wired up and the filth were on site in the room next door.

'Do you think Eden might be leant on?' I asked.

'You'll have to find him first. The Bill have got him safely tucked away. When he comes to give evidence, which is due a week Monday or Tuesday, it'll be armed filth a-go-go all over the court and precinct.'

'Difficult. Listen, Casey, the best thing I can tell you now is that we *should* be able to turn this one around for you. We'll do everything we can. In the meantime, try to get out this weekend, do something to take your mind off it, eh?'

'I'll try. The house feels like a mausoleum without the kids.'

'Well, why don't you give Stella a ring, drive up and see them for tea or something? Where are they again?'

'Didsbury.'

'There you are. There's a couple of decent four-stars round there. Take them out this afternoon. Go on. Give Stella a ring.'

'OK.' We stood and he saw me to the front door.

'What's prison like?' he said, as I stepped outside. I turned and looked at him. 'Not much fun,' I said. 'But if that's where it ends, you'll be all right. You're big, you can take care of yourself. And I can get you sorted on top.'

He tapped his forehead. 'You can't do anything about this, can you?'

'No. You have to look after that yourself. Sorry, mate.'

I was at Marcus's to mind the shop at ten. John Cooper Clarke let me in and then left to audition for the TV talent show that was in town. 'I didn't get as far as the judges last year,' he said. 'All I got was two minutes in front of a couple of producers. Mind you, I was doing Phil Oakey that time.'

'Good luck,' I said, and picked up the phone to ring Noriko. The landline went to answerphone, her mobile did the same. Today was Saturday: she had said she was going away for a few days. I wondered for a moment where she'd gone. Then a shuffle out front reminded me that I was the sales guy today. I spent half an hour with a young couple who wanted a cheap dining table that looked more expensive than the hundred and fifty they could afford. Another bloke was after a plan chest; then I sold a student a school desk for her bedsit.

It was nearly one by the time I was back in the office brewing up and thinking about the meet with Bob Devorty the day before. I didn't really trust him, and my brain ran through people to prop about him. A name jumped up pretty quick – I should call Harry, a brass I knew up in the Downs. We were close, although we hadn't spoken for a while. I punched in her number.

'I thought you were dead,' she said.

'Well I've been away. You know.'

'And how was Italy? Naples, wasn't it?'

'Yeah, Naples. All right, it was all right. And you?'

'The usual. Just working. You know.' A beat. I could hear her brain rolling down the line. 'So . . . you calling to chat, or do you need something?'

'Yeah, I do. Listen, Harry – I know this is an outside chance, but have you ever heard of a face called Bob Devorty?'

She snorted down the line. 'That creep. Everyone knows Bob Devorty. Well, a lot of us do, anyway.' Her doorbell buzzed in the background. 'But I can't talk now. Customer. Come round later, we can catch up.'

'Three o'clock?'

'Fine. OK, I got to go. Bye.' She hung up and I went to attend to my next lot of punters.

By the time John Cooper Clarke got back, I'd surprised myself by shifting two Afghan stools and a repro Victorian desk. The lad was in a bad mood. Apparently the production people were too young to know who John Cooper Clarke was.

Harry opened the door to me dressed in a black leather jumpsuit and spiked dog-collar. She'd grown about four inches. Flicking my eyes south, I sussed the pin-sharp, skyscraper-heeled, patent-leather boots laced from ankle to knee. She was holding what looked like a big table tennis bat covered with sharp silver studs.

'I came for some information,' I said. 'Not correction.'

She rolled her eyes. 'Funny. You know where the living room is.'

Over her shoulder the bedroom door was open. I glimpsed a pair of naked buttocks – someone on all fours, head out of sight. Harry caught the glance and prodded me across the hall.

'I'll be along in a minute,' she hissed, and shut the door firmly.

I'd known Harry for about ten years. She was Thai and her real name went on for a couple of yards, so we called her Harry for short. She was a tom, but she worked for herself, no pimp. She did all right.

I crossed to the window, pushed it up and fished out my smokes. I was just stubbing out my fag when she showed again.

'S and M pays better,' she said. 'But the dressing up is a total drag.' A beat. 'There's a joke in there somewhere.'

'If only we could find it.'

She chucked the tennis bat onto the leather sofa and followed it down. Stretching out her pins, she licked a finger and rubbed at something just below the knee. 'It takes me ages to get into these,' she said. 'All the laces. But at least I can charge someone to take them off.'

I sat on the sofa opposite her. 'What's with the Madam Sin routine?'

'More money, like I said. And I don't usually need to have sex with the client. They just do what I tell them. There's a guy in the bedroom cleaning my shoes. With his tongue.'

I stretched for the tennis bat and studied it. 'What's this for?'

'What do you think? It's a paddle. For punishment. A whack on the buttocks with the rubber side if they're a bit naughty and a whack with the studs if they're very naughty. The one out back gets it if my shoes aren't nice and shiny.' She relaxed into the cushions.

'Very good.' I slung the paddle back onto the sofa and smiled at her.

She was eyeballing me now. 'So. How was Italy? And your friend?' There was the slightest inflection there, on *friend*.

'It was fine. She was fine.'

'Glad to see you, was she?'

Time to move on. 'Bob Devorty,' I said. 'You told me you knew him.'

'Your Bob Devorty – is he short and fat with a crappy moustache and dyed hair?'

'Unmistakeably him. When did you meet?'

'Hmm. Late nineties, in London.' She reached for the paddle and spun it on her finger. 'I'd only been in England about six months and I was working in a massage parlour in London. West Hampstead. No FPS, just HR.'

'No what just what?'

'FPS is full personal service, which is sex. HR is hand relief, which is –'

'All right Harry, I get the idea. Go on.'

'We were called Beverley Hills Health Studio or some crap like that. It was run by quite a nice couple, actually, but they sold it to a crew headed up by Bob Devorty. The mattress money went up immediately –'

'Mattress money?'

'All the girls in a massage joint pay rent for working there. I don't know what it is now, but it used to be thirty quid a shift. On top of that, you pay the house about a third of what you charge the punter. Devorty banged up the nightly rent, plus he started questioning the punters about what service they had when they left, to check he was getting his portion.'

'Breaking up the happy home.'

'Yeah. Also he liked to try out new girls when they came for interview. That's not unheard of, but it's still out of order. Pig. So a lot of us left, me included. That's when I came up here.' She spun the paddle again, then let it drop. 'Manchester's far more tolerant, anyway. There's half a dozen big, well-known brothels up here. Open twenty-four hours, dozen girls on duty, good websites. Police don't seem to care as long as there's no trouble.' She stood up suddenly.

'Won't be a minute. Just need to see how my slave's getting on.'
With a squeak of leather and polished PVC, she split.

I lit up again out of the open window. I'd got halfway down the smoke when she was back.

'Moving on to the strappy sandals now. How weird is that? And I see pretty weird, I'm telling you.'

She flopped back on the sofa and stretched. I noticed something on her right wrist I'd never seen before. It looked like a tattoo.

'What's that, Harry?' I flicked my fag out the window and came to sit opposite again. She looked down at her wrist.

'This? You remember I'm going to retire at thirty-five?' I nodded. She stretched her right arm at me, pale underside up. I saw it was a neat little rose, in blue outline only. 'Well, this is my line in the sand. I had it done a couple of months ago, but it was so painful I couldn't bring myself to have it filled in. So I left it until I retire. Then I'll get it coloured and it will be the start of the new life.'

'I see. Nice idea.'

'I'm about ten thousand quid away from my target. Which I should make next spring, worst way. And then that's it. House paid for, PGCE paid for. And then I reinvent myself. Go back to college and emerge two years later as a teacher. Or something. But not a whore.' She twisted her wrist and rubbed it. 'This is to remind me.'

'Do you have a place at college yet?'

'Not yet. I'll apply next year. So . . . tell me more about Naples?'

A very abrupt change of subject.

'It was fine. I didn't do much, just loafed around for a few weeks. Then I hired a car. Did the Amalfi coast, slowly.'

'No swimming?'

'Too cold.'

She stood up and went across to close the window I'd opened. 'You didn't call me when you came back,' she said. 'A couple of texts to say you're back in the country, but they don't really count. You avoiding me?'

'No. I kept myself to myself for a few months. After all that business with my nephew and Leon, I . . . well, I don't know, I fancied a bit of a change. I was in London quite a bit.'

'Really? We might have run into each other.'

'Why?'

'I've started seeing someone. He lives in London. I try to go most weekends. He knows the score about the job. It makes it easier that I'm giving it up, though.'

I felt uncomfortable. 'Well, that's great news, Harry.' I looked at my watch. 'Better be going, got something to do.'

'OK.' She led the way to the door. I glanced over her shoulder, the bedroom was closed. She opened up, then stretched and pecked me on the cheek. 'Don't be a stranger now,' she said. 'You know where I am.'

I nodded. 'Thanks Harry.' I heard her lock up after me as I went down the stairs.

I slid behind the wheel of my motor. It was cold, so I switched on the engine and let it idle while the heater warmed the car up. Harry used to have it with a copper called Dave Craze, a sergeant in the Greater Manchester Police. Or rather, he was a regular client with licence to run over time. I'd never quite understood the nature of their relationship, but I remembered she'd been cut up when she couldn't see him again. I wondered if he was back on the scene. 'Not unless he's transferred down south,' I said aloud. Oh well, at least she'd found somebody to make her happy, whoever he was. For now, I had work to do. I pulled out, pointed my BMW in the direction of the city centre and drove.

It was gone five by the time I made the bank in King Street and the roads were drying up. The Saturday shoppers were off home to get sorted for their nights out. I pulled a baseball cap over my nut and walked confidently up to the front door, checking the bank's lit windows as I did so. I knew the different combinations of lights that meant 'open for business', 'shut but full of workers' and 'everyone out'. The last thing you want to do when you're a villain and you're at it is to stroll in and find some over-keen employee putting in a spot of overtime. Just now, the picture was right – the bank was empty. I slipped in my twirl and pushed open the heavy plate-glass door.

This bank was my main bit of work at the moment. I'd been looking at it for months, ever since I got into a cashier who worked in the gaff. He played chemmy at a casino I went to; he'd been losing hard for a while and was well in debt. His wife knew nothing about his gambling. A man with secrets is much easier to corrupt and he'd sold me plenty of knowledge on the gaff – alarms, security checks, all the rest. So here I was.

Inside, the foyer was carpeted and in half-darkness. It was shared between the bank and a couple of other businesses upstairs. There was a camera up in the corner, but I had the cap well down to cover my boat. And no one would be watching, anyway. Not unless there was a kick off. Crossing the thick brown pile, I pulled on a pair of turtles and unlocked the door into the bank itself. This door also belonged to us. We'd fitted it by taking the original mechanism out and removing the barrels so that any mortice key – including those held by bank employees – would open it. We'd done this in broad daylight a few months before. It's amazing the authority a pair of brown overalls gives you. Two guys stripping the lock and no one's asking any questions. Just as it should be.

There was no alarm to worry about in the banking hall. Banks only stick clangers where there's money. And all the money here was downstairs in the basement strongbox. Up here, you had cleaners in and out every day. Any touch pads or sensors this side of the tellers' windows and you'd have Mrs Mopp setting them off every ten minutes. Or forgetting to reset them when she split. So it was just the cameras upstairs, and the baseball cap took care of them — amazing what a good-sized peak does to hide your mug from CCTV. A balaclava or similar would be favourite, but then you might just run into a cleaner or worker out of hours. And a geezer with a bally over his face was a nailed-on bandit — three nines would be dialled. But with the cap and a bare face, there was half a chance to talk your way out of it.

As for the cameras themselves, my inside man told me all the images were stored on a hard drive off site and linked to the gaff by cable. No one would look at the film unless there was trouble, he said. And the film was dumped every three months, anyway.

All this knowledge made me feel pretty safe as I moved across the hall, taking in familiar sights — seats, sofas, ads on the wall for savings and kids' accounts.

I'd spent a lot of time in here after hours, working out how best to get at the prize and I knew the gaff well. Today's trip would be the last — I was here to check everything was in place for the pounce.

I hit the other side of the room, a door at the end of the cashiers' windows. I took out a bunch of keys and slipped one in the lock. The levers slid into place smoothly, just as usual. Same style for a door at the back, and I stepped into a corridor.

The keys had come from Roman, the boss of the cleaning outfit who spruced the gaff up every evening. My bent cashier had given me the company name, and I'd made Roman an offer he didn't refuse. He handed over a set of twirls, and from then on it was open house.

Along the corridor to the lift. I took it to the basement. Roman told me his staff never used the stairs. Good enough for them, good enough for me.

The lift slid open onto a narrow corridor. I flicked a glance round in the dim half light. Vault at the end, two other doors. Toilets, male and female. Their being here was a right stroke of luck. Privacy laws meant no cameras. Which meant no cameras on the strongbox.

I took the twelve steps to the gated vault doors. They looked powerful and strong, just what you'd expect from a bank which took delivery of half a million pounds of 'fit' money – meaning cash for the ATMs – every other Monday. Busy city centre like Manchester, those ATMs got through thirty or forty grand a day, easy. Then there were the boxes in the vault – cash, gold, jewels, who knew? A decent bonus, whatever there was.

I checked the most important bit. The cleaning cupboard, directly opposite the vault gates. It was unlocked, as normal. And there was still enough space in among the clutter for two people.

Now I was done. I took the stairs up and strode out into the foyer confidently. No one loitering outside as I opened up and slipped out. There were two women walking side by side about ten foot down the street, all shopping and shoulder-bags, their backs towards me. I walked after them, making for the motor.

I got home via the corner shop and ate a dreadful pizza lying on the sofa in front of something with Bruce Forsyth in it. Around nine I turned off the box and stared at the ceiling, thinking about Bob Devorty and how I thought he was holding back on me. Then there was the copper Korda, banged up in Strangeways. Who could I get to slip a message to him?

I was considering an early night when there was a gentle tap at the flat door. Opening up, I found Mr Wesson, the retired guy from upstairs.

'Ah, you're in,' he said. 'Tried you earlier, you must have been out.'

'I was out most of today,' I said. 'Are you well?'

'We're both fine. Here.' He held out a white padded envelope at me. 'This came this morning, mixed up with our post. Meant to put it through your door earlier but I forgot.'

I took the package. It was A5 size and thick. 'Thank you.'

'No problem. Hope it wasn't something you were waiting for. Completely forgot about it. Must be age. Goodnight.'

'Goodnight, Mr Wesson.'

I closed up and went into the living room, turning the letter over. I didn't recognise the handwriting but it had a London postmark. I don't get much post. I don't have many friends and even fewer know where I live. I tore the envelope open and upended it over the coffee table. Something square fell out, wrapped round and round in tissue paper and sealed with parcel tape. I picked at the tape until the package ripped and its contents fell out.

A square of card and a slip of paper. The first was a Polaroid photograph, face down. I scratched at it between thumb and forefinger and flipped it over. Then I stopped breathing.

It was a photograph of Noriko. She was wearing the same black dress I'd seen her in yesterday. Her eyes were screwed tight shut and there was a man standing behind her – you couldn't see his face because the camera had cut it off. He was squeezing her into him, pinning her arms behind her back. Her dress had been torn across the breast. He was holding a knife at her neck. It looked like he'd just cut the skin – there was a thin trail of blood running down her throat.

Oh Christ.

The slip of paper was typed.

Monty owed us money. We have his woman and we want his prize. We will be in touch. Fat Blackmail.

I was out of the flat in seconds and driving for London.

5

I made Chalk Farm about two on Sunday morning. The road was quiet, no traffic up or down. Just me and the wind. All the lights in the building were off as I pulled on a pair of turtles, slipped across the street and loided the Yale on the street door. Taking the stairs two at a time up to Monty and Noriko's flat on the second floor, I pushed against the woodwork and felt only the Yale push back. The other locks weren't thrown. Out came the plastic again and I was inside.

I stood in the hall for a moment, letting my eyes adjust to the dark, then walked on the balls of my feet to the living room and paused. The curtains were drawn back and the yellow from the street picked out the elephant table on its side and a couple of other objects lying on the deck. Stepping carefully across the room, I pulled the curtains closed and switched on the light.

Aside from the overturned table, there wasn't much to report. A few ornaments scattered over the floor, a vase under the coffee table. A small grey rabbit – one of the soft toys Noriko collected – had rolled out of its place in the fireplace with a bunch of other soft toys and was lying face down by the fire irons.

I made for the kitchen: a single plate in the sink and the box from a ready meal on the side. The fridge hummed quietly in the corner. Back across the living room and hall to check the bedroom. The bed was neatly made up, with a teddy bear dressed as a Beefeater and a purple dragon in shades staring at me from the bright yellow duvet cover.

They took her on Friday, after I left, probably in the afternoon, I thought. The door hadn't been forced, it was somebody she knew or somebody she thought Monty knew. She wouldn't have opened the door to a stranger after dark. Maybe they'd been sitting on the flat, saw me leave. Maybe she thought the ring at the door was me.

I checked in the bathroom: neat and tidy, two toothbrushes in a mug. No clues in the hall cupboards either. I went back into the lounge and noticed a sheet of paper lying under the coffee table. I picked it up. It was the list she'd waved at me, the list of names she'd asked to the funeral. I pocketed it, then went to the window, twitched back the curtain and looked out over the street. A couple walked up the other side of the road, arm in arm. She was wearing high heels and they clacked into the pavement noisily then died away. Just the sound of traffic from the main drag.

Turning back, I went into the kitchen for an ashtray, then sat in the lounge and sparked up. The tension was crackling up and down my spine, but I pushed it down and tried to think.

Someone calling themselves Fat Blackmail – whatever the fuck that meant – had kidnapped Noriko, because Monty owed them money. Monty owed a few people money – that I already knew – so the list of suspects was going to be long. *We have his woman and we want his prize.* That had to mean Heathrow. But how had Fat Blackmail heard about Heathrow? Even I didn't know about that. I pulled out the funeral list and looked over it. About sixty names in all. Was Fat Blackmail one of these? Some of them I knew, some of them I knew to let on to. Many of them I'd never heard of, but I'd probably know someone who could point me in the right direction.

I felt in my pocket for the Polaroid. It didn't tell me much, but it told me one thing. At least two men: one to hold Noriko, another to take the photo. How many would you need to lift her? One, probably – she was tiny. Six stone wet through. I glanced across the room, imagined her backing away from some geezer into the elephant table, knocking it over, gasping as he clamped a paw over her mouth, hitting out at him with her tiny little mitts.

Oh Christ.

I stared at the trickle of blood where the knife was pressed to Noriko's throat. To show they meant business. And then they send it to me.

I stood and clicked off the light, then sat again, heavily.

They sent it to my home address. Not many people had that. More to the point, they knew about the Heathrow prize. And all this must have been organised in the last week, since the old guy died; I'd only heard about the prize on Thursday night. And how did they know I was Monty's successor? Who else knew? Devorty and Korda, of course. Who had they told? How fucking big was this crew? How well got? Their knowledge and confidence almost overwhelmed me. And the one person I'd normally turn to right now was gone. Monty was dead. And Noriko . . . her life was literally in my hands.

A cold wave swept over me, the chill crackling from the top of my skull down to my toes. Christ, what a fucking mess.

I lit another fag and forced myself to calm down. Think.

If Fat Blackmail knew about me, he almost certainly knew about Devorty and Korda. Maybe he knew about me *because* of them? Korda was locked up and out of the way for now. But what about Devorty? What was that he'd said? 'I've got a lot of money grief.' Maybe this was a bit of private enterprise on his part to hurry things along. Or maybe not – but he was a link. Either way, I had to go and see him. Then I'd better get back to Manchester sharpish. If Fat Blackmail was contacting me at home, then I needed to be there. But Devorty first.

I punched in his mobile: straight to voicemail. His landline just rang out. I let it go for a couple of minutes, pressed off and checked the time: ten past three. Maybe he'd got lucky for the first time in twenty years. Either way, the prick wasn't answering. I could go round and bang on his door, but if he wasn't in I'd just be making noise for no reason.

I stood and pulled my jacket off. Then I gave the gaff a more thorough spin, looking for any stash Monty might have on site. I went across every inch of skirting board, looking for a chunk that might slide out. Then I tapped my way around the rest of the wood surfaces, pulled up the carpets at the edges and checked the floorboards. I found a torch in a cupboard off the hall and checked all the light fittings and sockets for one that might lift out. Then I went all over the place again, just to be sure. Nothing.

Around six, I kicked off my shoes and lay on the bed with the Beefeater bear and the dragon. I imagined Noriko laying the pair of them on the pillow like the woman-child she chose to act sometimes. I lay on my back with one toy on each arm and waited for sleep.

Sunday morning. Three days after Monty's funeral. Three days after the old guy's last request from beyond the grave, and about forty hours since I'd last seen Noriko. She'd kissed me on both cheeks and then rubbed the lipstick off. 'There,' she'd said. 'Now no one will know.'

I stared up at Monty's bedroom ceiling for a few seconds. Then the image above me slotted into what I understood and I sat up. Just gone eight.

I washed in the bathroom, cleaning my teeth with a Japanese brand of toothpaste Noriko must have picked up from some specialist joint to remind her of home. I made black coffee and tried Devorty. Voicemail, and the landline rang out again.

Older people are often up early in the morning. They don't seem to need as much sleep. Must be meant as compensation, the closer we get to the end. When I rang the next-door bell a few minutes later, I could already hear Rose clattering around. It took a while for her to open up and then she was out of breath, leaning on her zimmer.

I was about to say *hello* but changed my mind. 'Do you need to sit down?' I asked instead.

'Would you mind?' I followed her into the flat and waited till she settled into a high-backed chair at the window. I sat on the daybed next to her.

'I think I saw you the other day,' she said, nodding at me. 'I was talking to Noriko. You came up the stairs.'

I didn't want to worry her, so I just said I'd come to pick Noriko up but she wasn't in. Rose took the bait immediately.

'The last time I saw her was Friday afternoon. I thought she was leaving with you.'

'Are you sure it was Friday?'

'Completely. I get the meals on wheels Monday to Friday. They don't come at weekends. I always sit in this chair about lunchtime waiting for the van to arrive. That's when I saw her go. There was some man with her. I thought it was you.' She squinted at me curiously. 'They were walking very close, he had his arm round her shoulders.'

'Did you see his face?'

'No, no, no. Back towards me. They got into one of those people-carrier things. My son has one. Do you think she's forgotten about you?'

'Apparently so. I'll put a note under her door. Thanks for your time, Rose. I'll let myself out.'

I took the stairs two at a time and drove east for Devorty's gaff. I made his front door just after nine. He was opening up, clutching a bottle of milk. He hadn't shaved.

'I called you this morning, Bob. Where were you?' He jumped, twisted round and nearly dropped the bottle.

'All right, mate,' he said. 'What are you doing here?' He looked edgy. 'I was out with a bird.'

'I'm sure you were. Inside. Now.' I hustled him up the stairs. Once we were inside the flat I took the milk off him and slammed the prick up against the nearest wall, fist under his chin.

'What's all this, what the fuck's going on?' He was dribbling, squirming against the plaster, eyes flicking all over.

'You tell me, Bob. Who else knew about Heathrow?'

'What the fuck . . . ?'

I tightened my grip, pushed harder and felt him go onto the tips of his toes. 'Noriko's been kidnapped, you prick. Now, who else knew about Heathrow?'

'What do you mean she's kidnapped?'

'I mean she's been fucking kidnapped, you moron. What do you know about it?'

'For fuck's sake, nothing. Now let me go. You're choking me.'

I dropped him and pulled his jacket straight. I'd gone too far and I knew it. 'Sorry, Bob.' I stepped back, slipped out the Polaroid and handed it across. 'I got that in the post last night.'

Devorty took the snap and stared at it. Then he half-staggered a couple of paces to the sofa and collapsed. Somewhere in the leather cushion, I heard an air vent exhale as his weight sank down. 'Oh Jesus.

Oh God.' He looked up at me. 'Was this all there was?' I showed him the slip of paper. He read it.

'What does Fat Blackmail mean?'

'No idea. Thought you might know something.'

'How the fuck should I know? Have you been round to the flat?'

'I have. Reckon she must have known whoever took her. She opened the door to him. Or them. The lock wasn't forced.' I sank into a chair, my anger ebbing away. 'Whoever Fat Blackmail is, they know about the prize, they know about me. They know where I live for Christ's sake. That means they knew Monty or they knew you.'

'Or they knew Korda.'

'Or they know Korda.' I chewed a thumbnail. 'Someone must have got wind of your plans, Bob. And they know I'm Monty's successor.' I looked at him, he was looking at the smudge. 'Are you sure you haven't let anything slip, Bob?' I asked quietly.

'Yes.'

I didn't believe him. I stood and took back the Polaroid and the note. 'You better watch yourself, Bob. Someone out there is very well connected.'

'I never trusted him, you know.' He looked small, round, and scruffy. For a moment I felt sorry for him. 'Korda, I mean,' he said. 'Never.'

'Whoever it is, Bob, you better watch your back.'

'Do you think this is serious?'

The anger flashed back. 'He's kidnapped Noriko, Bob.' He looked up then, nodding hastily. 'There's a million quid in it. People have died for less.' I made for the door. 'Keep out of sight. I'll call you when I know anything.' He stood to show me out and I split.

*

I drove north for Manchester thinking of Fat Blackmail with his arm round Noriko, probably a knife or a gun stuck in her gut and Rose watching mildly from the window, waiting for her meals on wheels. He'd have had someone waiting in the motor, I thought. Someone to keep control of Noriko, to tape her mouth and eyes shut so she didn't know where they were going and couldn't scream.

Plans and half plans formed in my nut. I had to wait for Fat Blackmail to contact me again. He'd demand the prize, but it was tightly locked away as long as Korda was in Strangeways. Logically, that meant that neither Korda nor Devorty were involved in this. They'd have known from the start that I couldn't get at the prize.

So I'd have to get the dough together myself, or some flash money. Either way would cost, but I could take them at the exchange. But I didn't know when or where the exchange was going to be, so how could I plot it up? And how was I going to get a million quid in flash money together, fake or otherwise? What did I have, what could I borrow? I knew a few faces who had hundreds of thousands tucked away. I could go round with the begging bowl, but that would take time and no guarantee they'd say *yes*.

Or I could take the other route. Try and find them. If word about the Heathrow caper had got out – and it had, otherwise they wouldn't have come after me – the chances were that someone else knew something about what was going on. Maybe the funeral list was a place to start – but there were too many names. Even if I got lucky early on it would take days. I didn't have the time.

I hit Manchester about one and drove back to the flat to get freshened up and check for a message from Fat Blackmail. Nada. I lay down and dozed fitfully for a couple of hours, then headed back out. I needed information.

Marcus was in the shop alone when I turned up. The office was a furnace as usual. I pulled my jacket off and hung it on the back of the door.

'Where's Cooper Clarke?'

'He doesn't work Sundays. Cup of tea?' He caught the look on my face. 'Or was there something else?'

'Noriko's been kidnapped.'

His hand was going for the kettle. It stopped and hovered in mid-air. 'Fucking hell, mate.'

I gave him the full story. After I'd finished, he was silent for a full minute. Then he opened a drawer like he was looking for something, closed it, sat down at the desk and lowered his forehead onto his fingertips. Another beat and he looked up.

'What are you going to do?' he said.

'I don't know yet, but these cunts are not going to get away with this.'

'Go to the police.'

'No.'

'Go to the police.'

'People like us don't go to the police, Marcus. No fucking way. That's not part of the game.'

He leant across his desk towards me. 'You cannot deal with this on your own, mate. You said yourself you don't know how big this crew are. And they know what they're doing. *You* don't. Go to the police.'

'I made my choice a long time ago. I thought you had, too. In any case, they'll think it's two villains arguing over a prize. They won't take it seriously.'

'For God's sake –'

'Or if they do, they'll fuck it up. They always do. Look what happened to Leslie Whittle when the Black Panther kidnapped her.'

'That was a long time ago –'

'He was one man and he still ran rings round the filth. And the poor girl died.' I thought of Noriko: the big dark eyes in that pale face. Then I took a breath, steadied myself. 'And in any case, if I start dialling three nines now and the Bill start crawling around, it will fuck up any chance of getting a result on Casey's trial. And you know that's true.'

Marcus tapped a small pile of papers that was sat on the desk. Then he lifted them by the corner and let them drop again, one by one. There was a long beat. Then he said: 'What do you plan to do?'

'I don't know yet, mate. I don't know enough. But there's a piece missing . . . or a person, any rate. I could use your help.' Marcus nodded, his eyes on me. 'Can you ask around, see what you can find out about this Frank Korda? He's a detective chief inspector with the Greater Manchester Police, though he's been in Strangeways since October.'

'I'll see what I can do.'

We stood and I left, pulling on my jacket as I walked out of the shop. Outside, I crossed the road to the car park at Victoria station where I'd left the Beamer, fired it up and pointed it towards the Alex Park Estate.

Benny opened up his front door to me about twenty minutes later. He wore a United shirt and about three days' stubble. He leant heavily on the woodwork and squinted at me through bottle-top specs.

'You all right?' he wheezed.

'Yes, thanks Ben.'

He nodded me in, then bolted up behind us. I knew where to go and moved down the corridor. The old guy was getting slow these days, so I went into the kitchen and made a brew while he shuffled into the living room and made himself comfortable. I came in with the mugs and stood one in front of him, brushing some lumps of dope out of the way to make space.

'Ah, great,' he rattled, then gestured at the dope. 'You here to buy?' There were half a dozen cubes spread out on a sheet of newspaper on the table between us. There was also a penknife and a nine bar of resin.

'I will, but there's something else.'

Benny didn't get out much what with his chest, but he had plenty of lads and others in to buy. He'd been a big enough man in his time and was still pretty well connected. All this made him a good source of knowledge. I asked him about Frank Korda. He lit up a spliff and considered for a moment.

'This is the lad from the GMP who went away for being bent, sometime last month? In the Big House right now, yeah?'

'That's him. I need anything you can dig up for me, Benny.'

'Like what?'

'He's screaming *no* all the way. What's the word on whether he did it or not? Is he likely to get bail? And come to that, anything else you can find out: family, friends, enemies. Who's he on the take from? How bent was he?'

'I'll see what I can do, mate.'

I bought half an ounce and split for home.

The traffic was thick for a Sunday and I didn't make it to my front door till six. I got inside and checked the answerphone first thing. The light was flashing. Christ. I hit play. It was a recorded message, a muffled voice. It was from Fat Blackmail.

'*This is Fat Blackmail,*' said the machine. '*Text the number that follows. Do not call.*' I scribbled down the number, then sat at the desk and sent the text.

Fifteen minutes and nothing had come back. I sent the same text again and sat staring at my phone, willing it to ring. Finally it lit up and buzzed at me. I pressed answer. The voice was male, crackly and distorted.

'*This is Fat Blackmail* –'

'Let me speak to Noriko –'

'– *We have the woman.*' The geezer carried on talking and I realised it was a recording. Someone was playing a recording down the line. '*She is unharmed. We will now let you speak to her.*'

There was movement in the background and Noriko came on. I imagined her being dragged across a room, then the handset jammed under her chin.

'Noriko?'

'They want me to tell you I'm OK. I'm all right. They're –'

'Noriko, I will get you back –'

There was scuffling at the other end of the line and she'd gone. In the background, I thought I heard movement across a wood floor, a door being opened and closed. Then there came a metallic click against the phone and another tape.

'*We want one million pounds. We know Monty had this money. He fucked us over and he owes us. You have ten days to get the money or his woman dies. This phone number will not work again. We will be in touch to arrange the exchange.*'

The line went dead. I dialled the number – no dialling tone, nothing. I took off my jacket, turned off all the lights in the flat and lay down on the sofa. I didn't want to move. I lay in the yellow from the street lamps and stared up at the ceiling. I smoked three spliffs and thought of Noriko frightened, locked up somewhere, men pushing her around and roughing her up. And cutting her body to show me they were serious. I went through all the options, all the plots I could think of.

At five past one, I decided what I was going to do, rolled off the couch, went to the bedroom and stripped. I slept immediately.

6

I was already up when the alarm went off at six. I'd packed a bag with Monty's writings and the books I'd taken from Chalk Farm. I took an unused but charged-up prepay mobile from the desk, drank a cup of black coffee and split.

Marcus was always in early, even if he wasn't open yet. His shop was dubbed up but I could see light coming from the back. I banged on the woodwork and he let me in. I was folding my jacket and sweater over the back of a chair as he joined me in the office two minutes later.

'Why the alarm call?'

'We're going to have to sack Casey's trial for today, Marcus. I need your help for something else.'

He was reaching for the instant. His back was towards me, but I felt his expression change.

'And what would that something else be?' he said.

'Noriko. I need to pull a stroke.'

Marcus turned, wrapped his stocky little frame round his knuckle and bit it. I could see the anger coming up.

'Casey and me go back years,' he said. 'Long before you appeared on the scene. What gives you the right to come into my shop and start telling me what I do for my friends?'

'Marcus, this has to take priority. Fat Blackmail contacted me again last night, I've got ten days to come up with the money or else –'

'And Casey –'

'Casey will have to grow up and wait.' I was almost shouting. I dropped my voice a couple of rungs and went on. 'I'll talk to him. Listen Marcus, I am not abandoning the big man, but if I don't make a move today, Noriko could end up dead.'

'You take that seriously?'

'Look at what they've managed to do so far. This is a serious, organised, connected crew. Whoever they are.'

Marcus turned on the kettle and stared at it. Sideways on, I saw his jaw was set and his top teeth were tearing at his lower lip.

'You told me Casey was right on the edge.' A beat. 'What have you got in mind?'

'I need to get into Strangeways and see the copper Frank Korda. And then I'm going to bust him out.'

'Oh for fuck's sake –'

'It's the only way I can get hold of the prize and get Noriko back. You don't find that sort of money lying around in the street. Marcus, I need your help.'

He made himself a cup of coffee. After a couple of beats, he said, 'I hope you haven't lost it completely. What do you need?'

'Someone with a lock-up garage, someone we can rely on to help scam the police.'

There was a long beat. 'I know someone with a few garages. I'll give him a call.'

'Can you bring him on for a meet today?'

Another long pause. 'I'll try.'

He sat down behind the desk, nursing his cup. I scribbled down the new prepay number on a scrap of paper and pushed it across. 'My new work number. From now.'

He scarcely looked at it. 'Will you call Casey and tell him?'

'Yeah.'

'They start at ten. Make sure you call him before then. Please.'

Outside, I wove my way across the road, got behind the wheel and nudged out into the thickening rush hour traffic, heading for Cheetham Hill and Laurie's car shop. It was coming up to eight. First set of red lights, I dialled Harry's landline, hit loudspeaker and dropped the phone on the passenger seat. Her answerphone kicked in.

I waited for her message to end. 'Harry, it's me,' I said. 'Can you pick up, it's important. Harry –'

Clunk, rustle and then, 'Can't a girl get any peace? I didn't get to bed till two this morning.'

'Sorry for the wake-up call. Listen Harry, I need a favour. I need to hire you for a couple of days.' There was a beat, then I heard movement like she was sitting up in bed. 'I don't think that's a very good idea,' she said softly.

'I meant as a companion. To be seen with.'

Another beat.

'Of course you did.'

Moving quickly on. 'I need you between three this afternoon and tomorrow evening, about six. Can you do it?'

'I've got a regular booked for an overnight tonight. It's six hundred and I can't afford to lose it.'

'I'll make up the difference.'

'No. I'll see if he can shift to tomorrow first. Let me call him now, between home and work. Then he'll be able to talk. Are you coming round?'

'About ten.'

'I'll definitely know by then.' I gave her the new number, hung up and headed for Cheetham Hill.

Laurie ran a small car hire outfit on the corner of an industrial estate. Well, it called itself an industrial estate but it was more like ten acres of waste ground with a bunch of prefab units on it. Laurie's two Portakabins and the chunk of tarmac where his cars were normally parked up had gone. So had the chainlink fence that used to go round the lot and sing in the breeze. I slid out from behind the steering wheel and started to punch in his number.

'Are you looking for the car hire?'

It was a tall slim woman with curly brown hair and an accent I didn't recognise. She was swinging a clipboard and hard hat and wearing an orange hi-vi vest.

'Laurie's car hire,' I said. 'Yes.'

'We've just moved him. Shall I show you?'

I pinged the BMW's locks. 'Thank you.' She smiled and led me up a rough gravel path.

'I don't recognise your accent,' I said.

'English people always want to know where you come from,' she said. 'And what you do. I'm a surveyor and I'm working for the company that's building some permanent structures here. And I'm from Lithuania.'

'I've never visited.'

'Not many people have. If English people know anything of Lithuania at all, it's because they think we spend all our time supplying prostitutes to British escort agencies. I'm Ivy, by the way. Zivile to my Lithuanian friends. Who, naturally, are all people traffickers.'

'John Drake,' I lied. Some habits are hard to break.

'Well, John Drake, here we are.'

We rounded a tin-coloured warehouse at the top of the slope and there was Laurie's empire – moved piece by piece like London Bridge.

'Nice to meet you, John Drake,' said Ivy/Zivile. She turned and went back the way we'd come. I watched her orange-striped back for a second, then made for Laurie's place. He was loitering in the front office and saw me moving across the tarmac. He loped out onto the front steps and waved a handful of flimsy green forms at me in hello.

'Aha! Nice surprise for a Monday morning. Long time, long time.' He stuck his hand out. He was six foot tall and three steps up. I had to stretch.

'You coming in?'

'Yeah.' I followed him through the outer office.

'You found us, then,' he said. 'We had to move, landlord's redeveloping. He says we'll get the same space back, but I doubt it. Now then, now then. Nice cup of tea?'

'Please,' I said.

Laurie's long fingers trailed along a shelf of mugs in his tiny kitchen area. He chose one with 'FBI' stamped on the side for himself. I got a mugshot of Tom Baker as Doctor Who with a caption that read *The Guv'nor*.

'Now then,' said Laurie. 'Hit me with your rhythm stick.'

I had no idea what he meant but I didn't follow it up. Instead, I laid a tall order on him: 'I need four cars, Laurie.'

'Off the book?'

'*Well* off the book.' I gave him my needs. One motor for that afternoon. It would end up in the hands of the police, I said. And I wanted three more for Thursday – three days' time. Of that trio, two would not be coming back. 'Can you help me, Laurie?'

Laurie played it straight, but he was actually as bent as a nine-bob note. 'Got a stolen motor you can have for today. It's been rung and comes with a moody tax blob. Will that do?' he asked.

'It will. Thanks.'

'Thursday's motors I'll have to farm out.'

'Can you manage them all?'

'I know a chap with a pool of stolen motors. It's never been a problem before.'

'When can you let me know?'

'Couple of hours, probably.'

I gave him the new work number and split. It had started to drizzle outside and there was a wet breeze. Ivy had gone.

I got behind the wheel and saw the dash clock said nine thirty-one. I couldn't put it off any longer. I lit a fag and tried to find the words but they weren't coming. Feeling like shit, I punched in Casey's number. It went to voicemail and I hung up. Fuck. Then the phone rang and it was the big man.

'Just got a missed call from you. Anything wrong?'

'Casey,' I dragged on my fag and exhaled slowly. 'I'm real sorry mate, but we'll have to hold off on the business today.'

'What? What do you mean hold off?' It sounded like he was in the street. And he was nearly screaming at me.

'Casey, where are you? Calm down for Christ's sake.'

'I just parked up. I've got a meet with the brief in two minutes, at the court. What are you fucking around for?'

'Casey, something came up and it's big, I can't say over the dog. I'll explain when I see you, soon as I can –'

'Christ. This fucking trial is set down for two more weeks, max. We don't have fucking time. You promised me, you promised me –'

'I did, and I will. But this won't wait.'

'Oh, fuck off.' He hung up.

'That went well,' I said aloud, and turned the ignition.

I drove for Harry's, ringing train enquiries on the way and getting times for the Glasgow rattlers that afternoon. She buzzed me in a few minutes later wearing a blue housecoat and a face naked of make-up.

'Don't hear from you for months and suddenly you're all over me like a teenage first-timer.'

We went and sat in the living room. Harry took a couple of seconds to tuck her feet away underneath her.

'My regular can do tomorrow,' she said, 'so I can do tonight for you. But I need to be back here by eight in the evening. So . . . what's going on?'

I told her I had to deal with some shit flying around over the next couple of days, so I needed a rock solid confirmable alibi for that evening. 'There's virtually no chance you'll be pulled into it, Harry. But if it comes to it, would you be prepared to give a statement saying you were with me tonight?'

'Will they believe a whore?'

'Will they know you're a working girl?'

'I've never been raided or pulled, so I guess not. Not officially, any-way.'

'Six hundred for the night?'

'I'm not going to fuck you. So two hundred will be enough.' There was a pause you could have driven an HGV through.

'OK,' I said, avoiding her eye, 'here's the SP. You need to pack for a night away, two changes of gear. I've checked the trains. There's one leaving Manchester Piccadilly for Glasgow this afternoon at three-eleven. I need you to be on it. You get in at six forty-five. Do some shopping or whatever. Then meet me on the station concourse, at the John Menzies, at quarter to eight. We'll be back on a train tomorrow afternoon. And that's it.' I paused, patted my jacket. 'No money on me, I'm sorry. I'll have to settle up with you this evening.'

She stretched her bare feet out in front of her and flexed her toes. They were painted bright pink. 'I can manage the fare, don't worry.' A beat. 'Are you going to explain all this to me at any point?'

I looked at her. 'Some of it,' I said. 'Call me if there're any problems.'

She stood and waved me across to the door. 'There won't be,' she said. 'But I will.'

I split. It was ten forty-five. I had a train to catch by four and too much to do before then.

Sitting in the motor, I called the Cameron House Hotel by Loch Lomond in Scotland. Using my own name, I made a reservation for two people for that night. 'Do you have a suite available?' I said. The jock at the other end smelt money.

'Not tonight, sir,' he purred. 'But we do have an Enhanced Executive Double. Superking bed and a specially big room with a large living area and separate en-suite bathroom.'

'I'll have that,' I said. 'We'll be checking in about half eight.'

'Look forward to it, sir.' I hung up and shut my eyes for a moment. Not enough sleep. Too bad. I shook my head, nosed the Beamer into the traffic and pointed it towards Moss Side.

Georgie Manning opened his front door to me at ten past eleven. He was big, he was Jamaican and he was an armed robber. He stretched down a paw and we shook.

'Good to see you, friend. Early to see you, but still good.'

Two minutes later we were in the kitchen and Georgie was feeding his local strays. He opened the back door and rattled a metal bowl with a spoon. A couple of seconds later, a huge ginger cat appeared along with two smaller beasts, one tabby and one black and white. They shot over the back wall like kids on a water slide and skidded into the kitchen, squawking in chorus. The big ginger tom stood on its hind legs and pawed the air as Georgie emptied out a couple of tins of cat food into two dishes. He clanked them down and the animals fell on the food.

'I've never seen a cat like that before,' I said, thumbing at the ginger one. 'Why's he so big?'

'He's a Maine Coon, friend,' said Georgie. 'American breed, they act like a dog. And they're valuable. Fuck knows what this one's doing on the street.' He bent his own huge form and stroked its tufty ginger ears. 'Good boy.' He straightened. 'Now. You here about King Street or just passing through?'

'It's not about the bank job,' I said. 'But it is business. And it's quite a tall one, Georgie. I need a clean gun and some shells. And a pair of number plates. By this afternoon.'

'A clean gun costs . . . ' He turned and reached into the drawer behind him. Out came a couple of number plates. 'But here's something I made earlier. Come back at one, I'll have the gun for you then. Two grand the lot.'

'Thanks,' I said. 'Be seeing you.'

'And you.'

Out in the car I felt for the keys, then the planet slowed and stopped. The street went quiet. I ran my palm along the dashboard. Looking up, I stared over the bonnet. There was an old ambulance a few yards down with a hippy changing the front wheel. The motor was painted in psychedelic patterns and the back doors were open. It had been converted into a neat little sleeping area inside. I sensed batik, dreads and henna tattoos. And travel. Me, I was headed for a cell in Strangeways tomorrow night. Right now, I wouldn't mind changing places with the fabulous furry freak brother. The hippy stood and ferreted in a toolbox.

Yeah, like that was going to happen.

The street started up again. I drove for Amy's.

Amy was born Agnieszka in the old Czechoslovakia. She was knocking on for seventy and she dyed her hair black. She liked bingo, *Strictly Come Dancing* and Rynka, her Jack Russell. She was also my safe house. No one knew about her: not Casey, not Marcus. Not even Monty. She felt particularly safe now.

I rang her doorbell and heard the dog bouncing off the walls with excitement. Amy opened up, pulled me inside and kissed me on the cheek three times. 'You here for breakfast? Breakfast is no problem. Come and eat, *zlatko.*'

Amy didn't normally drop into Czech, but I knew she'd made a trip home a few weeks before. 'A cuppa will be enough, thanks Amy. What does *zlatko* mean?'

'Actually Slovak. Means sweetie, maybe darling. You want to see your uniforms?' Amy was helping out with the bank job by stitching together some moody security guard clobber for the coup.

'Not today, Amy,' I said. 'Just my other stuff.'

We moved down the corridor with Rynka yapping away a few feet in front. The hound continued to bounce around the kitchen as I shifted its bed, rolled back the carpet and pulled out the canvas bag under the floorboards.

How much would I need? Laurie, Georgie, Harry — who else? I'd asked Marcus to sort me a lock-up — I'd need to pay his man as well. I counted out ten grand. Fuck, this was slicing into my long stocking. I only had twenty large left. Suddenly I got the fear, that wash of panic that always freezes up my gut when I can see the end of the money. I still remembered seeing my mam sitting at the kitchen table sobbing because we'd run out of dough, slumped across the top, weeping hopelessly and not caring who saw her. From then on I decided: everyone got to eat.

This was not the time. I got a grip, pulled out the Asda bag with Monty's bits in it and tucked them behind a joist. Then I stuck back the boards, flopped over the carpet and slid back the dog's basket. I straightened up as Amy stood a mug on the kitchen table for me.

'Your tea, come on.'

'Thank you, Amy.' I stayed and chatted with her for a few minutes. I needed the breather.

My new work phone rang as I left. It was Laurie. He could organise all the motors for the price of fifteen hundred sovs. For today's capers, he'd sorted 'a silver Nissan saloon.' I told him where I needed it. He said a lad would drop it off at half two and it would be clean of prints.

The phone rang again the minute I hung up. It was Marcus, saying his guy would do the business.

'He's got a line of lock-ups in Failsworth. Can you get across for half past?' I could. He gave me the address and I drove. The place was called the Gasworks, off a side road and well tucked away. There was a line of garages, space for a few cars and a small grey prefab. I saw Marcus locking up his red Merc as I swung onto the tarmac. He waited for me to park up, then came across and shook.

'The guy's name is Eddie Box,' he said. 'Don't let him put you off, he's sound.' He shivered, though it was warm for November. 'Let's get inside, come on.'

Eddie Box met us at the door. He was the old scrote's old scrote. Snow-white hair, black leather jacket and fedora, and huge black wraparound shades, the sort the NHS give out for people with eye problems.

'All right?' he said. 'Come on in, gents.'

He moved back into the office and he moved very slowly. Glancing down at his feet, I saw he was wearing blue beach shoes with the laces loose and flapping. No socks. After about an hour, he made it to his desk, easing down onto the chair like he was sitting on a landmine. Marcus and I pulled up a couple of hard chairs and sat opposite.

'I've given Eddie the broad outline,' said Marcus. 'I told him you'd fill him in on the rest.'

Eddie turned his head towards me. I saw two reflections of myself in his goggles. I looked tired. Eddie Box, on the other hand, looked like he was about to keel over.

'OK,' I said. 'This morning, around ten, a man called you up and asked to use one of your lock-ups. You had one free, so you said yes. Someone will turn up around five this evening. As far as you're concerned, he's the guy that called you. He'll pay for a few nights' use of your garage, you take the money off him, put it through the books, give him a receipt, all the rest. He leaves his car and he splits.

'You'll get a visit from the police tomorrow morning, pretty much first thing. They'll show you a photograph of me. All *you* have to do is identify me as the man who dropped off the car. But tell them that on no account will you stand up and say that in court. When the filth have gone, ring Marcus. You happy with that?'

Eddie coughed solidly for about a minute, phlegmed into a square of kitchen roll and wiped his mouth. 'Court or not, you turning me into a grass, then?' he said.

'No one's going to know,' I said.

He nodded. 'Marcus said there'd be a few quid in it . . . ?'

'Monkey. Half now, half later.' I fished out five fifties and laid them on the blotter in front of him.

'That's lovely,' he said. 'Hang on lads, I'll be right back.' Leaving the cash on the desk, he stood and slid his feet slowly across the deck, then out of the room, shoelaces dragging.

When he'd gone, I turned to Marcus and hissed, 'Marcus, I asked for someone reliable. You bring me someone who might die of shock if his gas bill came in.'

'He's all right, mate. He's sound, don't worry.' We sat in silence for a few minutes.

'What's he up to?' I said.

'He's a diabetic. Has to use the toilet more than most.'

Another couple of minutes dragged by. 'Is he having a piss or suffering a stroke in there?' I said.

Marcus had his mouth open to reply when Eddie showed in doorway. 'Sorry about that, lads,' he said. 'Age and the kidneys, you know.'

The goodbyes went on till New Year, but we made it outside eventually. I stopped by Marcus's Merc. 'I'm going to need someone to impersonate me,' I said.

'I'll do it.' Marcus's reply was quick and decisive.

'There'll be a gun in the boot. And the car's hot.'

'I'll do it,' he repeated. 'Just tell me where.'

I took him in for a moment. The tight coat wrapping him up like a boiled sweet, the long greying hair with the beanie hat jammed down on top. We'd argued earlier, but he knew what was right.

'Thanks, Marcus. It's a silver Nissan. Keys on the front wheel. Three o'clock, Cheetham Street off Oldham Road, up near the playing fields. Got that?' He nodded. 'One more thing, mate. Could you make the moody call to the filth tomorrow?'

'I assumed I was going to anyhow. Speak to you later.' He got into his motor and left. I gave him a couple of minutes and then drove, waving goodbye to Eddie Box who'd come to stand in the window.

One twenty. Georgie Manning rang just as I was nosing out onto the main road. He said come round, so I headed south for the Moss. Georgie opened up and we schlepped into his back room. The ginger cat was there, stretched out on the rug. He flicked his tail on the deck as he saw me. I must have been interrupting his kip. George went to the sideboard and pulled out a bin liner. He laid it on the table and unwrapped it, being careful not to touch what was inside.

'It's a Glock,' he said. 'Never been fired. That's why it's expensive, friend.'

'And the shells?'

He pointed to a small white box in a fold of the plastic. 'Twenty-four. Do you need a spare clip?'

'No, thanks.' I handed over the cash. 'How much for the plates?'

'Freemans,' he said and stuffed the dough in his back pocket. 'Good luck, whatever it is.'

*

I had an hour till the drop off. I cruised out of the Moss in the direction of Oldham Road looking for a chemist. There was one in Clayton, next to a small café. Pulling up, I slid in to buy a packet of condoms, then went next door for tea. I sipped at it in the car, utterly exhausted.

I woke up. The tea was on the dash and it was cold. The clock said two ten. I'd lost about half an hour. Blinking and rubbing at my eyes, I drove north.

I parked up at the playing fields just as a lad in a dark blue tracksuit and high red DMs got out of a silver Nissan a few cars down. I watched him walk round and leave the keys on the front wheel. Then he turned and strode up towards the main road. I noticed he was wearing old school driving turtles – brown leather palms and white knitted backs.

I sat for a few minutes, looking up and down the road. Then I sauntered over. Keys off the wheel, unlock the boot and drop in the gear: gun, plates, done. I popped the twirls back, made for the BMW and sat for a few more minutes. No one around, no one looking, no one caring. No eyes on the last little dance.

Three twenty-five. I was in a queue at Manchester Piccadilly train station with an overnight bag. I'd whipped home, packed and cabbed it up here in the last half hour. My train went at quarter to four and there were two huge backpacks in front of me, attached to a couple of Canadians. A big red maple leaf on each as ID. They're always terrified they'll be mistaken for Yanks.

Eventually the backpacks shifted and I bought a first-class return to Glasgow. I paid in cash and made a big fuss of counting the money out down to the last sovereign. Then I made the guy behind the counter check the next train out for me and give me a receipt. I wanted him to remember me.

I called Harry a few minutes later as we started to move. Yes, she'd got the three eleven. I rang off. I was alone in the carriage – just me and the complimentary magazines. I sank back into the seat and stared at the houses, bridges, trees and water flicking past. I thought of Strangeways. Normally I wouldn't piss on the place and here I was, setting myself up for a repeat visit. But if there was any other way of doing this, I couldn't think of it.

I tried to get some sleep but it was no good. Every time I closed my eyes I saw Noriko with her arms twisted behind her and eyes squeezed shut. And blood trickling down her neck.

7

Benny the dope dealer rang from the Moss while I was changing trains at Preston. He'd been keeping his ears open, just like I asked. 'Bit of knowledge about your man,' he wheezed as I picked up. 'Can you talk?' I had ten minutes before the Glasgow train came in. I stood in the quietest corner of the platform, by the night manager's office.

'Go ahead, Ben.'

'Aye, well. Lad who comes in here, he's got a mate who knows someone who knows someone. Anyway, your man in the Big House. The filth, Korda. He's tried for bail once and been knocked back, no word if he's trying again in the near future. Trial's set down for March and he's got . . . ' He was drowned out by a train crashing through the station, all twelve coaches of it.

'You'll have to say that again, Benny. Too much noise.'

'I said, he's got a load of shit piled up against him. Your man is charged with giving up the locale of some bloke on witness protection. A witness that ended up shot dead. There's plenty of pressure on the judge: no bail, longest possible sentence, all that style. He's looking at accessory to murder as well as the corruption.' He broke off for a second to hack up some phlegm. 'And just to juice it up a bit, your man was shagging some bird – also on witness protection, as it goes. So he's in grief for that and all. He was meant to be looking after her. Seems he took it a bit literal.'

Korda had obviously been a busy boy. 'There'll be a drink next time I see you, Ben.'

'Have a good trip, wherever you're going.'

We hung up as my train slid onto the platform. From the carriage I rang a cab firm in Glasgow and arranged to be met at the station in my own name. A few minutes after, Marcus called to say *that dog had a good race,* meaning he'd dropped the car off at Eddie Box's lock-up. Another piece slotted into place.

A smiling Polish girl brought me a free cup of tea. I kicked off my shoes and dozed for the rest of the journey.

Harry was waiting for me at the station, dressed as Jackie Onassis.

'Darling!' she cried, a little too theatrically, and kissed me on both cheeks.

'OK,' I said. 'I think we've all got the idea.' I took in the pillbox hat, the graphite grey suit and the ivory clutch bag. 'Very retro.'

'I like the look,' she said. 'Could have done you a Dusty Springfield or an Emma Peel, but I didn't think they were quite right.' She pointed over my shoulder. 'That little man is holding a card with your name on it. Has he come to arrest you?'

I followed her gloved finger and saw a grey-haired geezer standing just down from us holding a white square of card and revolving on his heels like a lighthouse, side to side.

'I think he's our ride.'

He was. He dropped us off at the hotel about forty minutes later. I gave the jock a very decent tip, asked him for a receipt and made a point of getting him to write it himself rather than giving me a blank one. We checked in and took the lift to the second floor. I gave the porter a score as he left. He thanked me like I'd donated him a kidney.

'This is nice,' said Harry, sliding back the floor-to-ceiling glass door. 'And we have a balcony.'

I gave the interior a quick coat. The room was Highland boutique: browns and tartans with designer vases of heather all over the shop. The bed was the size of a tennis court and the chocolate-brown sofa was wide, furry and looked comfortable to sleep on. I joined Harry on the balcony. It gave onto the loch about thirty feet below. A row of lights picked out a wooden jetty in the dark. The pale yellow beams fell onto a sea plane tied up beside it.

'Nice and peaceful,' said Harry. She had her arms laid along the railing and rested her head on them as she spoke. 'Have you been here before?'

'Once,' I said. 'A few years ago.'

'Work or play?'

'Holiday,' I said curtly, remembering the walks round the loch with my then wife Sara as we *talked things over*, dry bracken scratching our legs, the tiny leaves breaking off and blowing in the breeze like tea. Five years ago, to be precise. None of it made any difference.

'Do you want to change for dinner?' I said to Harry. 'Or are you happy as Jackie?'

'I think I'll put something else on.' She trotted into the room and started to unpack while I dialled Casey. It rang for a while, and I imagined him looking at my number, deciding whether or not to answer.

'Yeah?' Casey. Less than happy.

'How did it go today?'

A long, long beat. I could almost hear him weighing up if he wanted to speak to me.

'A lot of legal argument. One witness, theirs,' he said at last. 'Receptionist on duty at the hotel on the day. She said she saw me go in, that was that.'

'You're sounding a bit more upbeat.'

'Well, I suppose you get used to anything after a while,' he sighed loudly. 'What's going on, then?'

'Marcus will be back at work tomorrow. But I have to be away for a couple of days more. I'm sorry, Casey. I can't explain now but trust me: this is important. I'll tell you when we meet.'

'OK,' he sounded a bit happier knowing Marcus would be back in the public gallery the next day. 'Well, whatever it is that's taken you away, I hope it goes . . . to plan.'

'Thanks, Casey. One other thing. Need a favour. Your mate's flat in Benchill. The one in the high-rise. Is anyone using it at the moment?'

'Not so far as I know.'

'Could I use it for a couple of nights from Thursday?'

'I'll ask.'

'Thanks Casey.' I hung up. That was better than I'd expected. He seemed calmer.

'Are you coming?' I turned to see Harry at the window. She'd changed into an embroidered blue satin top and trousers and she'd put her hair up in a neat bun with a couple of black sticks poked through to secure it.

'Give me a minute,' I said. I splashed some water across my face, hung up my coat and glanced in the mirror to flatten my hair. A minute, indeed. Then we left for the dining room, nodding *good evening* at a smart-suited young lad who passed us in the corridor. Skinny black strides, thin black tie, shot cuffs. For a second I thought he looked familiar, but it went as quick as it came.

'Know him?' said Harry, reading my face.

'No,' I said. A gust of cold air caught me from somewhere. 'Just a shadow. But it's gone.'

She smiled and took my hand. 'Just while we walk into dinner,' she said. 'So everyone can see.'

The dining room was spacious and done out in green and brown. Thick, bottle-green drapes from floor to ceiling, a thirty-foot bar upholstered in tan leather and neat tables loaded with crystal and sharply folded linen. A short guy with an Italian look but a jock accent led us to our table by a window and flicked napkins out over our laps. Another waiter shimmered up with the menus.

'Well,' said Harry, looking round. 'This is some kind of alibi. Are you going to tell me what's so important for all this VIP treatment?'

'Let's order first.'

When the wine came and our glasses were filled, I told Harry about Noriko and why getting into Strangeways on the QT was my only option. Her face clouded over as I spoke, and she leant forward on one hand, shaking her head.

'I can't take all this in,' she said. 'Anyone else but you and I wouldn't believe it either.'

'I'm afraid it's true,' I said, and felt my face nod forward into my hands. The despair was sliding up over my back and shoulders in big thick waves. I felt her squeeze my arm. With a deep breath, I sat up again and took her in over the table. She looked anxious. I went on with the tale.

'Something's going down tomorrow, Harry,' I said. 'It'll be stuck on my toes and it'll mean a nailed-on pull from the filth for me. Which means at least one night's lie-down in the Big House.'

'Which will give you the chance to see this person,' she said, shaking her head again. 'Why couldn't you just ask him for a visiting order?'

I leant forward over the table, glancing round for lurking waiters.

'Getting a VO can take anything up to a week,' I said in a low voice. 'A week I don't have. And he might not want to see me anyway – getting matey with a face like me is hardly going to help his defence.' I drained my glass and poured another, then leant in again. 'In any case, I can't go official. It would put me right in the frame for what's coming up. All prison visitors get their snap taken these days. And if I'm the last one in to see Korda . . . well, I might as well ring up the filth and claim the credit. There's no link between this guy and me now. I don't want to make one.' I sat back.

'I see.' She took a sip of wine and the tip of her tongue appeared and ran along her upper lip. 'So all this is –'

'Evidence that I'm out of Manchester tonight. The receipts, the tickets, the cabbie, the hotel staff . . . it should all be enough to get me out again. I don't think it'll come to you being involved.'

'If it does, I don't mind,' she said gently. 'It's just the truth, after all.'

She broke off as my soup and her delicately sliced salad arrived. I took the opportunity to change the subject.

'Bob Devorty,' I said. 'You told me he headed up the crew who took over your place down in London.'

'Hardly noticed *that* gear change,' she said. 'But anyway. Pimps generally have a bad reputation, but his was worse than your average pimp.'

'In what way?'

'Well . . . apart from being a general sleazeball, he was supposed to be the go-to guy for people with more extreme wants.'

'Like?'

'It was all rumour, but there used to be a story about some film.'

'What sort of film?'

'An old porn film. No one you spoke to had ever seen it, they'd always heard about it from somebody else. And you couldn't buy it. The story was that you rang someone who rang someone else, and eventually some guy turned up with a can of film and an old projector and showed it to you. And then took the movie away. The story was the film showed someone being killed, but for real.'

I took a mouthful of wine and swallowed. 'Is any of that true?'

She shrugged. 'I don't know. But the story was that Devorty provided the girls for the movie. Or filmed it. Or hired it out. Whatever, it depended who you were speaking to. But all the stories connected him to the movie, for sure.'

'Do you believe he was connected?'

She swallowed a small mouthful of salad. 'I believe he was scum.' She chased a cherry tomato around her plate for a minute like she was thinking. 'Your Noriko, how old is she?'

'Early thirties. Why?'

'There was a Japanese girl at the parlour in West Hampstead. Wasn't there long, she wasn't really cut out for the game. Called herself Lucy. There aren't that many Japanese girls working. Was your Noriko ever –?'

'Not that I know. What did she look like, your Lucy?'

'Tall, long hair. Softly spoken. Nice girl – she was a student, I think.' She smiled. 'She wasn't very grown up for her age, though. She used to have this big pink Bagpuss rucksack full of kids' stuff. Notebooks with kittens all over them, pencils with big hairy gonks on the end. You know the kind of thing. She was always bringing in teddy bears. I think she collected them.'

I thought of the Beefeater teddy and the purple dragon in shades on the bed at Chalk Farm. If Noriko had been on the game, it was the first I'd heard.

'I don't think so,' I said. 'It doesn't sound like her.'

Later that night we sat on the balcony, wrapped in blankets and drinking brandy from room service. Harry talked about her art degree, then pumped me about Naples. I danced around the subject. We laughed, quite a lot, and I almost forgot why I was there. Almost.

About midnight, Harry reckoned it was time to turn in. 'I won't get much sleep tomorrow night,' she said. She stood, pulling the blanket further up round her ears.

'I'll be sleeping on the sofa,' I said, scooping up the brandy balloons and bottle. 'There's plenty of spare linen.'

'The bed is the size of Malta,' said Harry gently. 'We can both sleep in it.'

I took a long time in the bathroom. When I came out she was asleep, lying on her side and breathing quietly. I slid into my half of the bed and took in her smooth skin and shiny black hair spread out on the pillow in the warm low light. I switched the lamp off and turned away from her. Then I felt for the edge of the mattress and pulled myself a couple more inches towards it.

The next morning we were up early, strolling along by the loch. There was a mist, the peaty soil was damp underfoot and long grasses flicked little dark stripes across our strides. After breakfast, Harry went down to the hotel's health and beauty spa to do whatever it is women do in a hotel's health and beauty spa. I walked back to the loch to make a call.

I needed to sort a moody passport. If I got Korda out of Strangeways – a big *if*, but the only throw of the dice I could bet on at the moment – then the copper was going to need one. I had my own, of course, tucked away in my lock-up. It could stand the pull and still had six months to run. I called a guy I knew and we talked about greyhounds. *A really fast one* came in at five grand. All I needed was to get a smudge of the copper across to him and he'd do the rest.

The phone jumped as I hung up and it was Marcus, telling me he'd made the call to the Old Bill. Now there was no going back. I'd crossed the river and smashed the boat, good style. Marcus had rung Bootle Street police station anonymously and spun them a proper yarn: that he owed me money, that I had threatened to kill him, that I had a gun, that I was driving a silver Nissan and that I kept the motor up at Eddie Box's Gasworks Garages.

Mention a gun and the cops have got to take you seriously. A couple of uniformed boys would pay Eddie a visit. They'd find the car, call it in and hear it was stolen. Then they'd search it, find the Glock and the plates in the back, and it would be all hands on deck. Some plainclothes filth would come down and take charge, show Eddie my smudge and get told *yes, that's the man who came round yesterday evening*. With a story like that, they'd sit on my house and nick me as soon as I turned up. I should be in Strangeways by tomorrow morning, providing the filth didn't try for police custody.

I showered and sorted through my stuff on the bed. There were some things I didn't want to be nicked with, things I'd have to give Harry to take home with her. Both phones, all the spare cash I was carrying. I wrapped the bits up in a plastic bag from Asda, then went down to extend our booking in the room till four. There was a new girl on reception, a brunette with a bob and teardrop earrings. I paid her the extra dough in small notes, counting them out carefully, one by one.

Marcus rang again about three. 'That lad just called. The Old Bill have come and gone. Taken the motor with them.'

'Thanks, Marcus. I'll see you day after tomorrow. With any luck.'

'All right. Good luck, then.'

I punched in Devorty's number. Despite the time, he picked up sounding like he'd been in kip.

'I need to see you on Friday morning, Bob. First thing, at your flat.'

I felt him come awake the other end.

'That sounds interesting mate,' he said, suddenly all bright and cheerful. 'I'll be here.'

He must have smelt the money.

'Good,' I said, and hung up.

I was sticking the taxi and train receipts into an envelope when Harry showed, face red and shiny and waving freshly painted scarlet nails.

'Facial, pedicure and manicure,' she said. 'And a bunch of clingfilm and brown stuff.' She patted her stomach. 'Lost two inches.'

'It won't last and you didn't need it anyway,' I said briskly, sealing the envelope.

She took in the stuff spread out on the bed. 'Guess this means we're going,' she said.

I nodded. 'There's a train at four. We need to be on it.'

I scribbled an address on the envelope and laid it on the bed. I counted out a few hundred quid for now and shoved the rest of the cash into the Asda bag, along with the other odds and ends. Harry packed while I rang down for a cab. Now she was stood at the door in a plain black dress and leggings, tapping her watch.

'Here,' I said. 'Four hundred quid.' She took it and looked at me.

'This is more than we agreed.'

'I need you to hold something for me.' I handed her the Asda bag. 'Could you make space for that in your case? I'll pick it up in a couple of days.' She nodded, unzipped a side pocket and stowed it away.

We made the train with a couple of minutes to spare. The first class carriage was empty and stayed like that the whole way down. Harry slept peacefully for most of the journey, curled up on two seats across the aisle from me. Her chest rose and fell gently. I couldn't remember the last time I'd slept like that.

Half an hour from Manchester Piccadilly, I went into the bog. Taking a lump of dope out of my pocket, I broke it into three eighth-sized cubes. This would be my currency in the nick. Then I took a condom out of the pack of three I'd bought in Manchester, tore it open and thumbed the chunks of dope inside, right down to the teat. Twisting the rubber, I folded it over, tied it in a knot and held the parcel up to the light. No breaks or tears, good. I bit into the rubber above the knot and tore the spare latex off with my teeth.

I dropped my strides and kecks and squatted, bracing myself against the toilet door as the train took a sharp bend. I slid the little package up my backside, pushing as far as it would go. And then a bit more. Standing up, I could feel it. It wasn't comfortable, but it wasn't moving either. I washed and scrubbed my hands and dumped the rest of the condoms and scraps of latex in a bin.

The carriage was still empty as I gently prodded Harry awake. She uncurled and stretched like the inevitable cat.

'Are we there?' She yawned, and ran a set of shiny nails through her hair.

'Nearly. I need another a favour, Harry. Could you look after these for me?' I pushed my two phones across the table at her. The work phone and my other, the one Fat Blackmail had the number for. She looked at them blankly. 'I'm afraid my brain hasn't come online yet.'

'They're switched off. You won't have to answer them.' Fat Blackmail wasn't due to call. 'Then there's this.' I pulled out the envelope with the receipts. 'Could you drop this off to the address on the front tomorrow morning? It's my brief.'

'John Carlisle,' she read. 'Is this another bit of your alibi?'

'Yeah.'

'I'll be finished with my client about nine. I'll be down there by ten.'

'Thanks.'

'What if all this doesn't work? What if they keep you in?'

'If that happens, I'll think of something. Don't worry.'

'I'll worry if I want to,' she said.

It was nearly eight when I reached the end of my road. As I walked towards my flat I felt bodies in the shadows, understood the unmarked black van on the right was full of filth. I looked down at my feet as I moved, noticed how clean the pavement was, how wide the slabs, how free of grass and weeds. I felt the seam on the handle of my leather bag. There was the ridge, there were the stitches.

Movement around me, then shouts, the noise of van doors opening, boots slamming into the deck and echoing. A light went on in someone's house. They jumped me from behind, flipped me face down onto the deck and cuffed me. I didn't give them any trouble. I was just glad they weren't feeling trigger happy. Little snippets of grit cut into my cheek as I lay on the slabs, looking up at the dozen-odd filth gathering round me. They were well tooled-up. Radios cracked and boots crunched the gravel by my face. I was nicked.

8

They took me to Longsight nick on Stockport Road and asked me if I had a solicitor. I told them to ring John Carlisle. Then they slung me in a peter. It was flaking yellow and stank of unwashed bodies. They left me there for about an hour, then opened up, cuffed me, and trotted me upstairs for interview. John Carlisle was already there, legs stretching out from a bench in the corridor. There was a peach stone on the bench next to him. It didn't look too old – still some stringy flesh left on it.

They left us alone for a moment and I sat. John told me what I already knew: that a stolen motor had been found in a lock-up; that there was a gun and ammunition in the boot; and that I'd been identified as the driver who'd left it there last night. Fortunately, they weren't talking about an identity parade. Eddie Box must have stuck to the script.

'They're going to interview you about all this,' said John. 'Is there anything you want to tell me?'

'Not just now, John.'

They took us in for the interview. John and I sat opposite a couple of smug-looking plainclothes. I nodded at my name, address and DOB. I went *no comment* to all the rest of their questions. When they were done, and the younger of the two was stretching to turn the tape off, I told them I had a short statement to make. I leant into the tape machine:

'I had nothing to do with this car, garage or gun. I was not in Manchester last night, but at this stage I am not in a position to tell you where I was. That's it.'

Not for them, of course. A new tape went in lively and they started asking where I had been, if not Manchester. A few more *no comments* and they sacked it, leaving me and John together for a few minutes. He stood and slung his yellow legal pad into his briefcase.

'I hope you know what you're doing,' he said.

So did I. 'You'll be at the magistrates tomorrow?' I asked.

'Yes.'

'OK, we'll talk then.' He gave me a look and I shrugged. 'Thanks, John.'

They charged me with illegal possession of a firearm and ammunition. Then they took my dabs and a mug shot and walked me back to the cell.

I rolled onto the skinny mattress on the bed and lay on my back thinking. Harry would drop the receipts at John's office tomorrow. That and the statements off the jocks at the hotel should be enough to get me out of Strangeways, swiftnick. I hoped.

I turned my face to the wall and tried not to think of Noriko. Apart from Fat Blackmail, I was the only person in the world who knew she'd been taken. All her friends would just think she was away. I thought of the photo, the trickle of blood. Twenty minutes later, I slept.

They drove me to the magistrates under heavy escort first thing the next morning and stuck me in a holding cell. Ten minutes and the door was unlocked for John Carlisle, looking sour. He came and sat on the padded plastic next to me.

'There was a woman waiting for me outside the office when I got in this morning,' he said, in a low voice. 'Eight o'clock. She looked Japanese or Thai.

She gave me an envelope, from some hotel in Scotland. There's a receipt in there. Round trip train fare to Glasgow dated the day before yesterday. There's also a cab receipt for a trip from Glasgow Central to this same hotel. Also dated the day before yesterday. Is this anything to do with you?'

'I've got nothing to do with this gun and car caper, nothing at all.'

'Why didn't you tell me you had an alibi last night?'

'I was with a woman. She's married. You know how it is. I need her kept out of this.'

'Was that her, with the get out of jail free tokens?'

'She must have dropped round, spoken to a neighbour, sussed what went down. She knows what I am.' It sounded thin, but it was better than a premeditated stroke. I could see he wasn't buying it.

'Will she make a statement?'

'I need her kept out of this, John.'

John chewed his lower lip for a full minute. Then he shook his head and said, 'Tell me where you were. I'll do what I can to check it out. But you're still going away for now, you know that? And to Strangeways. They won't keep you here while you're going no comment, and there's no ID parade.'

'I understand. But please John, move as quickly as you can, yeah?'

I gave him all the details. I told him the names of the hotel staff I'd spoken to, right down to the porter. He would contact the hotel and the cab company, get someone local to take statements. It should be enough to show I wasn't anywhere near Manchester when the car and the gun got left at Eddie Box's lock-up. The brief made some notes and slid his pad back into his case as there was movement at the door. A couple of filth come to take me up.

'All right,' said John. 'Speak to you later, then.'

They took me along the corridor and up the steps into the dock.

The magistrate heard the word from the CPS, nodded, fiddled with his glasses and remanded me to Strangeways for seven days. A straight up-and-downer. I wasn't above the surface for more than two minutes and I was back in the holding cell within five.

I stretched out on the bench. I thought I'd have a long wait for the sweatbox to take me up to the nick, but they were back in ten minutes. A bit of a touch. They unlocked me again, took me upstairs cuffed up and stuck me in the back of a police car. Two twelve-year-olds in crew cuts and button boy gear loitered in the yard. They may have been kids but they were my escort. And – glancing at their belts – they were tooled up. One got in the back seat and cuffed my right wrist to his left, using bracelets on a chain about six inches long. My wrists were already cuffed together. I was beginning to feel like a bit of Swishrail. Then they turned on the siren and we made for Strangeways. Nothing like arriving in style.

It was drizzling by the time we hit the nick. The redbrick walls and tower jabbed out of the rain like a stone ship bearing down on a tug. I thought of all the men inside, buzzing around in reception, talking on the landings, maybe queuing for the phone. The lucky few would be at work or waiting to be taken down. And under all of this, the boredom. The constant struggle to find something to do to make the time pass quicker. *You do your time*, some guy once told me. *You do your time, or it will do you.*

Time at least was on my side that morning. I was on a roll, moving swiftly through the system like a rat in a drainpipe. The roll continued in Strangeways itself, once the coppers had handed me over. An old mate of mine called Jake Twinney – eighteen months for kiting – was number one on reception. I was sat in a cell off the main hall waiting to be processed when he tapped on the door, dropped the flap and asked how I was.

'I've seen better mornings,' I said, moving across to speak to him. 'Glad to see you, though.'

'Reckon you'll be here long?'

'Nope.' I moved closer to the flap and dropped my voice. 'Jake, you know that copper Korda. Is he on protection?'

Jake gave me a right look, but he also dropped his voice for the answer. 'No, he's never asked for the numbers. He's two-ed up on B wing with some face from Liverpool who's supposed to be keeping an eye on him.'

'And this Scouser is . . . ?'

'Off some firm. Word is, Korda dealt with this crew, now they're looking after him.'

'Can you get me onto B wing, Jake? I'll see you get a good drink.'

'Behave yourself.' He winked. 'I'll go and have a word.'

'Something else, Jake,' I said. 'Is there anyone around with a mobile phone? That can be trusted, I mean?'

'Every fucker's got a dog in here,' Jake hissed. 'More choice than the Carphone Warehouse. You know Sam Racster?'

I did, and that was about to make my life a whole lot easier. 'Yeah, he's OK,' I said. 'Is he holding?'

'Yeah, and he's a cleaner.' This meant he got about during lock-up and worked on the hotplate at mealtimes. That made him easy to talk to. 'Thanks, Jake,' I said. 'I'll speak to him.' I knew Sam well enough to know he'd allow the use of his phone if I asked him. Especially in return for one of the lumps of dope I had stuck up my backside.

An hour later, I was locked up on B wing with my dinner, three doors down from DCI Frank Korda. I didn't see him. The wing had been dubbed up for food half an hour earlier, my screw told me. They'd unlock us for association at two. For most of the cons, association meant the chance to socialise or make a phone call. For me, it would mean the chance to get into the copper.

My peter was empty, which was another touch. They'd put a new arrival in later for sure, but for now I was on my tod. I scratched at the prison nosebag. It was the normal shite – two sausage rolls and an apple turnover slightly heated up – but I was hungry so I forced them down.

About half one, I went and had a good listen at the door. No movement. I went behind the khazi screen at the back of the cell, dropped my strides and squatted. I felt around and slid the joey out, then washed it and my hands at the sink. I emptied the the gear into a screw of paper out of the bin, stuck it in my back pocket and lay down on the bed to wait for the unlock. It came just after two: keys rattling in dozens of locks and the sounds of cons spilling out onto the landings.

Some screw twisted a key in my door, pushed it open a few inches and moved on. I stayed put for a while, then sauntered out. My cell was on the threes – the third floor – and most of the cons were grouping on the landing below where the pool and card tables dwelt. There'd be a couple of free hours before we were locked up again, and the lads were making the most of it.

I turned left and paced slowly along to Korda's cell. The door was half open and I glanced inside. One guy lying on a bed reading *The Mystery of Edwin Drood*. I couldn't see his face, but he was tall – his trainers stuck out over the end rail. A second geezer was sitting at a small Formica-topped table, making skinny roll-ups. I pushed the heavy metal door open further. Roll-up guy raised his head at me.

'Can I help you, mate?' Pure Scouse, and not that friendly. I glanced over at the bed. Korda lowered the book slowly and looked across at me. He was wearing rimless glasses and he'd lost a bit of weight since Monty's photo, but it was him all right.

'I think it's you I'm after,' I said to Korda. 'I've got toothache.'

A beat. The Scouse looked confused. The copper flicked his eyes over me for a couple of seconds, then hooked the specs off his nose and sat up, swinging his feet onto the deck in a big, powerful movement.

'It's all right, Ronnie,' he said, still looking at me. 'Do us a favour, eh? Pop out onto the balcony. See no one barges in.'

Still looking like he was wrestling with String Theory, the Scouse split, pushing past me in the doorframe as he went. Korda put his book down on the bed and tucked his glasses into a breast pocket. He stared at me with intelligent green eyes. His rolled-up sleeves showed powerful forearms. He looked like a man who had slept well.

'As I say, I've got toothache,' I repeated.

He nodded, stood, and blocked out the light from the high barred window. 'Then you better not fight today,' he said.

'All right.' I took a step into the corridor and glanced along the landing. Scouse Ron was leaning on the rail a few yards down, looking through the suicide net at a game of pool on the floor below. I dipped back into the cell. 'I should have a bit of postcard with me,' I said.

'I don't have mine,' he said. 'But you didn't expect that, did you?' He nodded at the table and chair. 'Why don't you sit down?'

'I'm fine.' I pushed the door to and leant against the wall. Korda crossed his arms and rested his chin on a set of knuckles. I saw he had a scar on his right temple, about half an inch long. It was deep, like someone had done him with a chisel.

'I heard about Monty,' he said, gruffly. 'He was a good man.'

'He was.'

'We knew he'd appointed you his successor, for the cancer. Heart attack took him though, is that right?'

'It did,' I said. 'And I am. Shame you didn't think about a successor yourself, before you got nicked.'

'What do you want?' he said, curtly.

'Monty asked me to take care of his corner. Which means I'm here to look after yours.'

'Are you indeed?' Korda's eyes swept over me. 'How do I know I can trust you?'

'You don't,' I said briskly. 'And I don't know I can trust you, either. But I've gone to a lot of trouble to get in here, Korda. At least you know I'm resourceful. That should be enough reference for now.'

Korda said nothing. His eyes hooded as he stared at me. No matter how many gold stars I got from Monty, I could feel his brain working out all the angles, just to be safe.

After about a year, he tipped his head back and spoke. 'So why *are* you here?'

I gave him the spiel I'd prepared. Firstly, Noriko needed her dough urgently. Secondly, he, Korda, was looking at being away for a long time. In helping her, I could help him. I was here to get him out, collect the dough owing to Noriko and leave him to get on with the rest of his life.

'I know what the Crown's got on you,' I finished. 'You're going down, and you know it. You won't be able to rely on a Scouse minder for the next five or ten years.'

Still no trust in those eyes. 'Who said he was a minder?'

The guy was starting to piss me off. 'I'm sure you can take care of yourself, Korda. But think about it. All the faces you put away over the years, they'll all have a grudge, something to work out on you. Or maybe you want to stay looking over your shoulder for the next ten years.'

If anything I'd said was worrying the filth, he wasn't letting on. 'Just for the sake of argument,' he said, 'what if I'm interested?'

I looked round the cell and saw a couple of tubes of toothpaste on the sink. I picked one up and dropped it on the bed next to the rozzer's book.

'You'll be needing that if all goes according to plan,' I said. 'You'll be needing to eat it.'

He flicked the tube a glance. 'And?'

'Someone called Sam Racster will come to your door tomorrow evening at seven. If he says the dog is running, you're to eat that. All of it. If he says the meeting's off, do nothing and wait till Friday at the same time when he'll have another message for you. If it's on, down that lot at seven. You'll start to feel –'

'Nauseous. My heart will race. My skin will go grey and my lips will go blue. I know.'

'You'll certainly look like shit. Ring the cell bell at eight and tell the screws you think you're having a heart attack. They'll take you down to the doctor, who will be very nervous about an unconvicted copper stiffing out on his watch. So he'll send you out to Crumpsall Infirmary and be quick about it. We'll lift you at the hospital and you're away.'

'And then?'

'Schlep you down to the Smoke to join postcards with your lovely pal Bob, stick you in a safe house while we wait for a moody passport, then we all split for Switzerland to cut up the goods.'

It sounded very simple. Too simple.

'It sounds very simple,' he said. 'Too simple.'

'You got any better offers?'

A pause. His eyes held mine. 'And how do I know you can pull this off?'

I don't like rozzers at the best of times, and the best of times this was not. Korda was beginning to piss me off good style. But I needed him. No Korda, no dough, no Noriko.

'You knew Monty and you trusted him. Would he put a mug up as his successor?' I waited a beat but he didn't answer, only looked at me. Prick on a stick. 'Let's look at the facts: I got myself in this pisshole this morning, specifically to talk to you. I'll get myself out first thing tomorrow. So don't you think I can spring you tomorrow night? The moves to put this kind of caper together don't come out of any beginners' manual I know of.' I scooped up one of the Scouse's skinny rollies and lit up. Blew smoke and waited a moment. 'What do you say, Korda? Do you stick or twist?'

He drummed his fingers on his arm for a good few minutes, then shifted and seemed to relax a bit. 'All right,' he said. 'See you tomorrow. At the hospital.' He unhooked his arms and we shook, briefly.

'Unless there's a change of plan, we don't need to talk again,' I said. 'Till tomorrow. Be seeing you.'

'And you.'

I walked out of the cell and down the landing. That had been a pissing contest, pure and simple. And I wasn't sure who'd broken it.

The Mickey Mouse was still in situ, leaning on the railing.

'Thanks Ronnie, I'm off. Anyone take any interest in my visit?'

'Just the two geezers across the landing. But they're a pair of divvies. They don't know what day it is.'

I nodded thanks and went looking for Sam Racster.

9

It was half ten the next morning when I heard I was getting out of Strangeways. A screw came to my cell and told me there was someone downstairs with a bail warrant. Uncurling myself from the bunk, I stood up and followed him off the wing to reception where I signed for my stuff and they turfed me out the gate. John Carlisle was waiting for me in his blue Vauxhall estate. I jumped in.

'Thanks for the lift, John.'

I expected him to start up the motor. He didn't. 'I got on the phone to the Cameron House Hotel first thing yesterday,' he said, staring forward and not making eye contact. 'They remembered you very well. Especially with all that money you were flashing around. Twenty quid tip to room service for bringing up a bottle of brandy? Nice. The Glasgow solicitor I retained to get the statements said everyone in the hotel had something positive to say about you. What an impact you made.'

He shot me a swift angry glance.

'Those receipts were particularly handy. Worked a treat on the judge this morning. All in all, he was more than happy to buy the idea someone meant you mischief and dismissed the car and gun business as an attempt to stick you in it. So here we are.'

'Thanks, John.'

'Don't mention it.' He turned the key in the ignition, savagely. 'And don't pull a stroke like that again.' He twisted round at me. 'I'm not a fucking idiot. I've known you long enough. I know what the game is. But don't use me like that again. If you do, you'll be looking for another solicitor. I've got my limits.'

I sat with my bag between my legs, staring out front. 'Thanks for your help, John. There'll be a decent drink for you next week.'

'Let's hope that's all there'll be.' He sighed deeply. 'I'm going back to the office. I suppose you want to be dropped somewhere?'

'Please. I think it's on your way.'

John dropped me at the taxi rank in Piccadilly. I took a run up to Harry's pad to pick up the phones and cash, then had the cab take me to Victoria Station for Marcus's shop. I made the gaff by half eleven. He was due at court after lunch.

'Eddie Box did all right,' I said, taking off my coat and standing in the office doorway where I could catch some colder air from the main shop. The place was an inferno, as usual.

'Yeah. I went and dropped him the rest of his dough this morning,' said Marcus. 'I was in the area anyway. He told me forensics went right over the garage, they were there till late Saturday. Said the jam butties and blue filth lines on site scared a couple of punters off. I gave him another couple of hundred to make up for it.'

'Thanks Marcus. I'll settle up with you later.'

'All right. How was the nick? You get what you wanted?'

'I think so.'

'You want some tea?' I nodded and he went to the corner to brew up. I flapped my shirt to circulate some cool air. I had another favour to ask. When we were sat with the tea I said, 'I need a bit of help tonight, Marcus.'

'Still to do with this business? Noriko?' he asked. 'Go on.'

'Could you sit on Strangeways this evening? I need to know when a car – or it could be an ambulance – leaves.'

Marcus sighed. 'From when?'

'Eight. Should be done by ten at the latest.'

'All right. You're calling Casey at lunch?'

'Yes.' I realised I'd not asked about the trial. 'How did the lads do last night –' I stopped. Strangeways had fucked with time, as usual. Today was Thursday. 'Sorry – night before last?'

'One waited but his juror didn't show. Must've had a lift home instead. The other lad followed his man onto the bus but lost him a couple of stops up. Looked round and he'd gone from his seat. They'll be trying again tonight.'

'Keep me posted, yeah?'

'I will. Another thing. There's a woman I think we should be looking at. Young girl, looks like a student. Starting to look sympathetic, makes a lot of notes when his brief's cross-examining, that sort of thing. Could be worth a third follower.'

'Women don't take bungs, Marcus. Men are more corrupt.'

'That's a bit Sid the Sexist, mate.'

'It's also true. Honestly, not worth the effort, mate.'

Marcus tugged off his beanie and scratched his nut. 'Well, you're the expert.' I could tell he thought I was off the mark.

'Keep me posted,' I said. 'About the rest.'

It was half twelve when I split. I grabbed another cab home to Chorlton and took a long shower, scrubbing harder than usual and washing my hair twice. Even after that, the cheap disinfectant stink of the jug was still hanging around so I brewed up some proper coffee and stood over the pot in the kitchen, breathing deep. It takes a while to get Strangeways off your skin.

The clothes I'd been wearing went into the rubbish bin. With a towel round my waist I lay on the sofa in the front room and sipped at the coffee. Three spoons of sugar. Now to business.

I'd hardly taken breath since Fat Blackmail took Noriko. I'd slapped the last few days together on the hoof. Now I was planning to bust a corrupt cop out of jail and go on the run with him. And then smuggle him out of the country, lay hands on Monty's money and buy Noriko back from Fat Blackmail.

I'd have to stay away from home after today. I'd been in the 'Ways, and might have been seen going in and out of Korda's cell. Assuming I got Korda out, the cops and the prison would be over his moves in the last few days with a microscope. The fact I'd been in and out so swift was a nap for a good look, and I could be in for a pull. I'd been lucky so far, but there'd be a full scream out for Korda and the stakes would be a lot higher. Too high for my liking, particularly as I'd be nursemaiding an ex-cop I didn't trust. Fuck this.

The scratch of paranoia started to pick at me. I wasn't thinking straight. I was gambling more than I could afford to lose. My brain flicked over to a casino where I used to play chemmy. It was a middle market joint, like a Holiday Inn with slot machines. By three in the morning, there were two types of punter left: the serious players and the seriously deluded losers. I used to watch the losers drift round the tables, fiddling with the few chips they had left, hoping for the lucky chance that might put them back on top. They all looked the same. Now I was worried I looked like them. Was I in too deep here?

I closed my eyes for a couple of minutes, tried to refocus. Now was not the time for self-doubt. I stood and moved to the desk. It was one fifteen, lunchtime at court. I buzzed Casey. The background told me he was in the street.

'What the fuck is going on?' he said. 'I heard you were inside. You still there?'

'Walked first thing. All a load of bollocks. What about you?'

'Two coppers in the box this morning. We landed a few blows, as it happens,' he said. 'My brief got the original transcript of the alleged trade in the hotel room admitted as evidence. The fucking original, you hear that? Turns out the filth made a second transcription, the one they submitted for the trial. Just as well we fucking queried it. There's a few interesting differences.'

'Go on.'

'Remember Dicky Eden?'

'The guy who stuck you in.'

'You got it. Well, Mr Eden mentioned a guy called Roy Donovan while we were talking. Apparently he's a face Eden did a lot of business with. In the first transcript we've got Eden saying "And then Donovan came round," but in the filth's it's, "Oh, a man came round." Looks like the cops are trying to keep some villain out of the picture for their own purposes. My brief managed to make quite a lot of it. Played the tape, pointed out the differences to the jury. I think at least one more of them is coming onside. Young girl, looks like a student.'

'That's good, Casey.'

'It's starting to look like a police fit-up and the good Judge Chipchase isn't happy.'

'Glad to hear it.' Time to change the subject. 'Is it still OK to use the Benchill flat from tonight for a few days?'

'Yeah. Still there. You want to come round and get the keys tonight? After six, yeah?'

'I'll give you a call when I'm on the way.'

We rang off and I poured some more coffee. Time to get on. I perched on the arm of the easy chair by the window and looked along the road, sipping the brew. It was a cul-de-sac. Nice and quiet. Good and safe for a thief, which is why I'd bought it when me and Sara split up. Very difficult for someone to put eyes on you if they can't use moving wheels or watchers walking through. Anyone cruising past my building would have to cruise back the other way a few minutes later, which is always a bit of a give-away.

As I said, time to get on.

I picked up the dog again and dialled a cab driver I knew, a guy we called Kaluki Ken. I woke him from a quick kip in his motor down Back Piccadilly in the city centre.

'Don't you ever sleep in your bed, Ken?'

'Depends how it's been going at the tables. And whether the cab belongs to me or not.' Ken would sometimes sell his cab to pay a gambling debt, then lease it until he had the money to buy it back again.

'What about now?'

'Cab's mine, but I'm a bit short otherwise. What can I do for you?'

'Do you fancy a fare tonight?'

I felt him sit up straight. He could smell the earner. 'Go on.'

'Can you be on site in Yew Tree Lane this evening? Halfway down on the right-hand side. Eight o'clock onwards? It'll be me and a special parcel.'

'How special?'

'Very. It could be pretty hairy, Ken.'

'I'm just picking you up. I don't get paid to ask questions, just drive people about, that's all.'

'Thanks. Dwell till half ten, then piss off if there's no show, all right? You'll be paid anyway.'

'No worries. See you this evening, mate.'

I hung up and went into the bedroom to get dressed. I pulled on black jeans, boots, dark top and jacket, and packed a leather holdall with a couple of days' clothes, shaving gear and a few other odds and ends. Then I went round the flat checking for moodies. There was nothing dodgy lying around, of course, but it doesn't hurt to double-check. Tonight's caper might go very wrong, in which case the next boots through my front door could belong to the Old Bill. Last, I emptied the bathroom and kitchen bins into a bin liner. I'd dump it in a skip somewhere, later on.

I left at two. I didn't know when I'd be back again.

I called Georgie Manning when I was on the road and asked if I could drop round. He said yes, and I made his front door in the Moss by half two. He led me into the kitchen. As we passed the front room, I saw the light blue carpet was rolled back into the corner and there was wood and a workbench stood on the floorboards.

'Didn't know you were a DIY enthusiast, George.'

'Shelves. I've been here six years and I've still got a ton of shit in boxes upstairs.'

He switched on the kettle and I leant against the worktop trying to find the words. I had a very big ask and it would be well within George's rights to say no, particularly at such short notice. I looked up and saw him watching me.

'Whatever it is, friend, probably just easiest to come out with it.'

I nodded, and filled him in on some background. Noriko, kidnap, Fat Blackmail, money, most of the rest. And the copper, Frank Korda. The kettle boiled ignored, and he cupped his chin in a big meaty palm.

'Sounds like it's been a busy few days,' he said. 'How much time did you say before you had to get the money for the exchange?'

'Today's Thursday. I've got till Wednesday next. Six days left.' He raised an eyebrow. 'I need to get the copper out, Georgie. If he gets the office from me, he's all set to fake a medical emergency. That'll mean they have to take him out to casualty this evening. That's when I need to lift him. And I need some help.'

There was a very long beat. Georgie turned his back, boiled the kettle again, made two coffees and passed me one, all in silence. He took a sip.

'If I say yes to this,' he said, 'will that mean we're even now?' I hadn't thought of it that way. I opened my mouth but he got in first. 'Including Newcastle? All square, including Newcastle?'

If that's what it takes, I'll go along with it, I thought. What I said was, 'Yes, George. Including Newcastle.'

'We'll need a shotgun,' said George, all businesslike now. 'If it's a handgun, the screws might not take it seriously. I can get hold of one. But you carry it, right?'

Fair enough. 'OK.'

'I'll carry a baseball bat or similar. Can you pick up a couple pairs of overalls, workers' style? And what about wheels?'

'In hand.'

'All right then. When do we go?'

'Half seven. I'll pick you up.'

George gave me an address. 'Just by the empty shop,' he said. 'You know where I mean?'

'I do. Seven thirty, then.'

I drove across to Laurie's car shop in Cheetham Hill. His assistant, Hattie, was sat in reception so he nodded me out onto the tarmac. 'Something over here you might like,' he said loudly, for her benefit.

He loped across to a silver Jag. I followed.

'The renter is the red Saab over my shoulder,' he said. I glanced across – it was a late convertible. Two doors, black roof and hood. 'Where do you want the other motors?'

'The first in the car park of the Lloyds pub just down from my gaff,' I said. 'The second I need on the corner of Harpurhey Road and Waterloo Street, close as he can get it, anyway.'

'And the Saab?'

'Northenden Golf Course. In the car park.'

'OK. I'll give you a bell in an hour and tell you what you're looking for.'

'Another favour, Laurie. Can of petrol in both the nicked motors. And a couple of sticks of wood and some rags. Can you do that?'

'Ahhhh. Aha,' he said. He had the look of a man who knew the value of torching the odd car. 'Easy enough. Now: the motors won't be properly rung, mind. But they will have new plates, and new barrels on the ignition. Keys on the driver's wheel arch, OK?'

'Thanks.' I pulled his fifteen hundred quid out of my pocket and pushed it into his hand, keeping my back to Hattie and the office. 'Speak to you later, Laurie.'

Half four. I drove down to the Arndale in the city centre and did some shopping. A long overcoat in Korda's size, some loose-fitting sweatpants, a T-shirt and trainers. Then I nipped into a chemist and bought hair clippers, razor and toiletries. There was a hardware store on the ground floor where I picked up a pair of bolt cutters. The army surplus at the end of the row gave me the balaclavas and the overalls. And that was it. I slung the lot in the boot and drove across to Casey's for six.

'You fucking put it on a person, don't you?'

Casey was sat at his dining table, jingling the keys to the Benchill flat. I'd just told him who was going into it tonight.

'I'm on fucking trial and you want to bring extra grief to my door?' He was deeply pissed off, but he was trying to control himself. 'What happens if it comes on top? No one will be able to use the Benchill flat again. That's going to cost me. Never mind the aggravation. You'll have the full scream out for that prick.'

'We'll be away first thing tomorrow morning.'

He gritted his teeth and skidded the keys the length of the table. They dropped off the end and fell in my lap. I scooped them up. 'Thanks, Casey.' He shook his head at me. 'How did it go this afternoon?' I said.

'Marcus was in,' he said. 'Lot of chat over the transcript with the jury sent out. Chipchase wanted the copper who'd made it called in.'

'And?'

'He's on holiday, apparently. But the chat wasted a bit of time.' He shook his head at me. 'Good luck with tonight.'

'I'll be in touch.'

I'd used the Benchill flat before. Nothing much had changed. I unloaded the gear, checked the bed linen and stuck the food in the kitchen. Then I washed and scrubbed up in the bathroom, had a piss and left. As I was pulling out of the car park, Laurie rang. Motor one in the Lloyds car park was a dark blue BMW. Motor two up by Crumpsall was a silver Volvo. I thanked him and drove to my street to drop off my own wheels.

A quick glance up and down the road, then I opened up the boot and fished out two carrier bags: overalls, balaclavas, bolt cutters.

Shut the back, ping it locked, then pull on the turtles and up to the Lloyds to find my new set of wheels, the BMW. It was about five minutes away. Every step I took, I felt more and more detached from the world around me. The pavements felt spongy, the street-lights looked too bright, everything was weird.

10

I seemed to have been walking on autopilot. When I came to, I found myself staring at a dark blue BMW. I ferreted under the driver's wheel arch. Nothing. Where are the fucking keys, Laurie? Hang on, there's another blue BMW over there. No one around, move across, have a feel, bingo. I bleeped the doors open and tucked the bags out of sight in the back. Then I checked for the petrol, rags and sticks in the boot. All there.

When I slid behind the wheel, I found I'd forgotten how to drive. It took a minute to get the ignition key in, then I sat trying to remember which pedal was the clutch. Far left, sure it was far left, clutch, yes. On the left.

The work phone rang and I snapped out of it. It was Sam Racster from his cell in Strangeways.

'Hello?'

I dragged the phone to my ear. The words wouldn't come.

'Hello?'

It's on or it isn't. You decide now. You choose. Tell him or hang up. Tell him or hang up. I snatched in a breath. It felt harsh across the back of my throat.

'Tell him the dog's running.'

'The dog's running,' said Sam. 'Yes.' The line went dead. Sam was reliable, a mate, and he owed me one. The blow I'd stuck on him had helped as well. He was well pleased to help out. And as a cleaner, even if association was over, he could get to Korda's door and hiss through the crack at him.

I looked at my watch: seven ten. A few minutes and Korda would start to swallow that tube of toothpaste. Another hour or so and he'd be ringing the cell bell, feeling sick and looking grey. I'd fired the starting pistol. No turning back now. I twisted the ignition and pulled out of the car park, heading for the Moss and the meet with Georgie Manning.

Seven thirty. Georgie was wearing gloves and carrying a black bin-liner wrapped around something about two foot long as he came out of the gaff. The shotgun. He laid it on the deck behind the driver's seat.

'Did you get me some overalls, friend?'

'Bag in the back.'

He leant across and pulled a pair out, then slid the passenger seat back and reclined it as far as it would go. Keeping out of sight. Two men in a motor are more likely to get a pull than one. He wriggled into the overalls and zipped them up the front. 'Brown,' he said, looking down. 'How did you know this was my colour?' A thin joke, but better than none. Maybe.

I fired the motor and we drove for the hospital. On the way, I took a turn down Waterloo Street to check for the Volvo. There it was. Pulling up for a few seconds, I shot across the road, grabbed the keys off the wheel arch and checked they worked. The lights flashed and there was an encouraging *thunk* from the locks. I locked it again and jumped back into the Beamer, dropping the keys in Georgie's lap. Then I drove for North Manchester General Hospital, locally known as Crumpsall. We parked a few streets away.

It was eight o'clock exactly. I cranked my seat back till I was lying at the same angle as Georgie and pulled on my own overalls. Then I outlined the plan to him and we went over a few details. It didn't take long and we fell silent about quarter past. The car was getting cold so I turned on the heater. Georgie cracked his knuckles. With gloves on, his hands looked massive in the yellow streetlight.

My phone jumped. It was Marcus, saying he was pulled up on the corner of the car park across from Strangeways with a good view of the main gate.

Half eight. My phone buzzed with a text from Ken, just saying 'OK'. He'd be parked up at Yew Tree Lane, then.

I thought about what should be happening in Strangeways right now. Any minute, Korda would be ringing his cell bell, screaming for a doctor. A screw would trot along and take a look. The copper would look sick and grey, so the screw should buy the story. They'd take him along to the duty medic. The sawbones would give him the once-over and, assuming the chemicals in the toothpaste had done the business, order a swift visit to the local casualty at Crumpsall. They might not do it for an ordinary con, but Korda was hot property.

Eight forty-five. Were they getting Korda cuffed up for the trip? Had they dialled three nines for an ambulance to blue-light him? We could do without it. Paramedics can get a bit lively sometimes.

Noriko, I thought.

Nine fifteen. Nothing from Marcus. I turned off the heater. There should have been some action by now. I resisted the urge to call him back. I lit a cigarette, cracked the window. Georgie had his eyes closed, looking Zen.

Nine twenty-five. Maybe Korda had turned me in, for the brownie points. Just as well Marcus was on the gate to give me the office if there was more than one car.

Nine forty-five. It was cold. I'd been watching the clouds of our breath for the last ten minutes. Five more minutes and I'd –

My phone rang. 'They're in a taxi, a white Audi,' said Marcus. 'Uniform in the front passenger, another in the back with matey boy. They turned right at the bottom of Southall Street.'

Heading our way. 'Thanks,' I said. 'Drive carefully.' I hung up. 'OK, George?' I asked.

'Ready,' he said. I could feel his spine straighten and crack with tension. My chest was tightening. I wiped my mouth. The hospital was about three minutes away. The prison taxi would take about fifteen minutes to get there, tops. I texted Ken and told him to stay put.

It was like someone edited the tape. I twisted the ignition, and then we were sat in the hospital car park about a dozen yards away from the A&E entrance, pulled up in some handy shadow from an overhanging tree. There were two unmanned ambulances parked up by the doors on yellow-crossed tarmac. The taxi would have to stop a few yards away. Good. Nearer to us and further away from potential problem-causers. Hospitals are bad places in terms of wannabe heroes. Coppers spend a lot of time in them, for one thing. And paramedics seem to think they're the law half the time. Must be the uniform.

We'd be coming from behind the taxi, which would help. I stretched into the back seat. Across came George's bin liner: a sawn-off shotgun inside, and a baseball bat. I put them both on the deck between my feet. I gave George a balaclava. Still on his back, he laid it on his chest.

'They shouldn't be too far behind us, George. You OK?'

'Yeah, man.' His voice was level. George was weaned on pavement work and he had the powerful confidence that comes with it. He had one hand on his chest, the other was across his stomach. I saw him flex it in the half-light. It moved with a slow, supple ripple. I imagined him crushing stone and letting the grains run out of his palm.

Headlights, and a white saloon with a yellow cab logo on the driver's door flicked past. George sat up and I reached down for the sawn-off and the baseball bat. I passed the wood across to him as he pulled his bally down over his face.

Someone hissed, 'Let's go!' From a mile away, I saw it was me.

We opened our doors together, stepped out and walked fast for the cab, tools held down. There was a man and woman leaning in the light by the entrance, smoking. Two figures crossing the car park. Too late to worry about that now.

The cab's passenger door was opening. I grabbed the handle and tore it wide. At the same time I heard George rip open the back. I showed the shotgun to the screw in the front, then swung it to point at his crotch.

'Keys now, or you'll lose your bollocks.' I leant in, felt the metal rest in his lap. He was young, about twenty, premature receding hairline, mouth open, terrified.

'Keys,' I repeated.

He nodded down at a green canvas bag at his feet. I gestured *give it here*. Not taking his eyes off my face, he reached and handed it over. I caught a movement as the taxi driver shifted towards the door and swung the shooter up level with his head.

'You wanna die? Head between your knees. Slow.' The driver folded over in three jerky movements. I took a step back, clamped the bag under my elbow and unzipped. Familiar bunch of keys inside. George had the baseball bat under the second screw's chin. The man was fat and triple-chinned, and his belly flopped out over his belt. I rang the keys at George, he grabbed them and Korda knew to jerk his arm over the screw's gut for George to unlock him.

I snapped a look at the entrance. The smokers were a few feet away, watching. One man, in a green porter's coat. One woman, a nurse in a short blue tunic. Mouths gaping in comic symmetry. They'd both frozen. The ash on the nurse's fag had grown and curled. Just as I looked, it broke off and fell to the deck.

I swung back as George slung the cuffs on the tarmac. Korda made to climb over the fat screw, looked at the gut and opened his own door.

Another figure stepped into the light from inside, clocked the scene and stopped. I didn't see if it was a man or woman. I arced the sawn-off at the screws and driver as George waved Korda round.

'Mobiles,' I snapped. I gestured at the young screw's balls with the gun. 'All three in his lap. Now.' I pointed at the driver. 'And you – keys. In his lap.' Two silver phones and one black dropped onto the lad's crotch. Then the keys. I scooped the lot up and slung them way off into some bushes as George took Korda by the elbow and jogged him to the car. Then I reached in and ripped off the radio handset.

'Any of you fuckers move or give it the heroics and I'll shoot this fucking taxi up,' I hissed. 'Now bow down your heads.' The trio dipped their nuts in time, I kicked both doors shut and swung round. The nurse saw the sawn-off and gasped. Her fag had burnt down to the stub. I jogged for our motor. Behind me, I heard a man shout, 'Get a phone!' I didn't look back. A couple of seconds and I was . . .

Something cut again. George had gunned the motor and slid into the passenger seat. Korda was crouching down in the back. I was behind the wheel, slamming it into gear, shouts and screams from the ambulance bay . . . I twisted back and saw two or three more, one in uniform, filth, yes filth, he'd be getting the number, plates were dirty, but still – assume they'll be on the police radio any minute now – just go. *Go*.

I took the one-way exit system and kept my speed respectable till we were off hospital tarmac. Then I did the left and gunned it to sixty up Delauneys Road. The lights at the end were red. I jumped them, swung left. *Fuck, fuck, fuck*. Down Crumpsall Road, it's broad and sweeping, a tidy gradient, look in the mirror, nothing up our arse, glance down, Georgie's seat flat, he's staring ahead, doesn't want to distract me, push it to seventy, get to the end and swing into the council estate on the left, rundown and crapped out, no one's going to give it three nines here.

I braked hard. Korda bashed into the back of my seat as we stopped dead. George had his door open, tearing into his boiler suit as he half fell out. He rolled it off, ran round the back, wrenched the door open, pulled Korda out, slung his boiler suit in, kicked the door shut, gripped the copper's elbow and crossed the road, walking him swift to the next motor, two turns from where we were.

I pulled the BMW round and drove further into the estate, wrenched left at the top of a cul-de-sac and rolled into a small parking area. The lights picked out a white goalpost painted onto the wall at the back. All the windows overlooking were back rooms: bedrooms, bathrooms. All of them dark.

I pulled up, skipped out and, keeping my turtles on – no prints, no prints – tore out of my overalls and lobbed them on the front seat. Round and beep open the boot: a can of petrol, two sticks with rags tied at one end. *Thank you, Laurie.*

Drop the gun on the deck, splash petrol over the seats, overalls, seats again. Almost done. I grabbed the stick, splashed juice, slung the empty can in the back. Rack down the window, kick the door shut. Now. Step back: one, two, three, four feet, clutching the wand. Time to party. Lighter sparks, stick goes up and I toss it into the motor in one swift movement.

Despite all the motors I've torched (and there have been a few) I was still surprised at the speed and force of the blast. With one big *voosh* – and that's the exact sound – it was off, taking all the evidence with it. No time to stick around and watch the fireworks, though. I scooped up the bin liner with the gun and walked briskly out of the playing area and down an alley. Popping out the end between the houses, I crossed a tidy little green, did a left and then a right to where the Volvo was neatly parked. George was stretched back in the passenger seat. Korda, I couldn't see.

'Where's –'

'In the boot,' said George. 'His choice. He just opened up and jumped in. Never said a word. Looks like shit, though.'

I got in and twisted the keys. 'Let's just hope he doesn't spew up in the back.' I pulled out and headed for Rochdale Road. I felt George move in the dark.

'Four and a half minutes since we left the plot,' he said. 'So far so good.'

We heard the sirens as we hit the junction. Screaming and screaming, louder by the tick. *They're looking for three men in a BMW, two in boiler suits, heading away from the hospital. I'm dressed smart and unless they actually pull me, I'm alone in a Volvo.*

The filth skeetered through as my lights went green. Two cop cars on full blast. I did what any responsible driver would do: ignored the change and stayed put. One of them swung towards us, shot a glance our way, saw the one body and screamed on the way we'd come. I watched their lights shrink in the mirror.

'Two jam butties, was it?' said George.

'You got it.' I slipped off the handbrake and pulled away. Feeling a little safer, I did the left down Queens Road, past Phillips Park Cemetery and into the 24-hour supermarket opposite the City of Manchester Stadium. George stretched and opened the door.

'All that excitement's made me hungry. I'll pick up something for dinner and get a cab home,' he said. 'Good luck with the rest, friend.' I watched his broad back bob away towards the brightly lit plate-glass windows. He seemed to be counting his change as he went.

The Volvo was in shadow, there was no one around and no cameras. I got out and walked round to the boot. Korda's big frame was folded into the space, head resting on the bump of the wheel arch. He looked up at me without speaking.

'Just you and me now and we're a long way from the action,' I said. 'Why don't you upgrade to the front?'

Without a word, he swung out his long legs, stood up and trotted to the front, stretching as he went. I joined him and we drove east, then south, keeping under the limit and with my minces firmly on the mirror all the way. By the time we made Yew Tree Lane I felt pretty safe. Ken's cab was parked up halfway down the road. I flashed the lights and pulled up.

'We're almost done,' I said to Korda. 'Just go and sit in the back of that cab. Don't talk to the driver. I'll be with you in a few minutes.' He undid his belt and hopped out, making for Ken's motor. I pulled away slowly and turned down a dead-end track. It was about two-hundred yards long with houses, then it veered off left. I went straight ahead on a track, narrow and thickly lined with trees. I opened up and had a quick gander round. No dog walkers or doggers, not at this time of the year. And a good way from the nearest house or traffic. I splashed petrol all over the shop and did the thing with the stick. The flames jumped across the seats in sheets and the Volvo went up in thick stinking clouds of smoke. Picking up the shooter, I jogged for Ken's cab.

'Benchill,' I said to Ken, slipping back the divider. 'The estate. Tell you where when we're on site.' I closed up and sat back. We drove in silence, Korda staring out of the window at his side of the road. Lights, cars, street signs, couples and groups slipped past. A couple of Christmas trees in windows, an offie on the corner with lads larking around in the light from the shop as it spilled out onto the deck. Short cuts of other people's lives.

We swung onto the estate and Ken slowed down. I pulled the divider back again and hissed my directions – *left, right, left, pull up here.* I tapped Korda on the shoulder and we piled out, leaving Ken to wait. I'd be back in few minutes.

Up to the ninth floor. I unlocked and nodded Korda inside.

'OK,' I said, leading the way to the front room. 'Strip off and stick your gear in here.' I tore another bin liner off the roll on the sofa and shook it open. 'There's soap and towels in the bathroom. Have a shower and there'll be clean clobber for you after.' I took him in properly for the first time. Like Georgie said, he looked like shit. Face gunmetal grey, lips dull blue.

Korda chucked his glasses case on the sofa, then stripped in front of me. His back was ripped like a rower's, his calves bulged like a cyclist's. He had a powerful body and he was in pretty good shape. He filled the liner, dropped it on the floor and walked from the room, feet slapping on the deck. Didn't say a word. A few seconds later I heard the shower start up.

I got gloved-up again and gave the shooter a good wipe down. I'd drop it off for George to collect later. He hadn't fancied wandering round Asda with a sawn-off in his basket. Korda emerged just as I finished, dripping and twisting a red towel round his waist.

'Bedroom up the corridor,' I said. 'First left. Clobber for you there. Bed linen in the cupboard. Food in the kitchen. Help yourself.' He nodded, turned smartly and left the room.

I stripped off and showered quickly, then dressed in fresh gear. A few minutes later I stuck my head round the copper's door to find him staring out the window. He was still wearing the towel.

'I'm heading out now,' I said. 'Need to dump the schmutter. I'll have to lock the front door, there's no latch. I'll be about forty minutes, OK?'

He turned his face to me. His skin was shiny and somewhere between grey and green – like the bloom you get on bacon, only angrier. His lips looked even bluer after the shower. He nodded, but said nothing. For a second, I wondered what he was feeling. Then I decided I didn't care much. I left the flat, locking it shut behind me.

Ken was calmly reading the *Manchester Evening News* and listening to the radio when I made the cab. I gave him the venue.

'Alrighty.' A couple of minutes' peaceful driving with some laid-back jazz on the speaker and my breathing slowed a little. Ken cleared his throat.

'That bloke,' he said thoughtfully. 'Didn't say a word while we were waiting for you.'

'No easy chitchat, then? No celebrity gossip?'

'No. Felt his eyes on me, though.' He jabbed the air with V-spread fingers. 'Just like that. Back of my neck.'

'That's his game, Ken. Just here, please.' He pulled up by a skip and I nipped out to sling in the bin liners. My gear and Korda's. I slid back in. 'Northenden golf course, please.'

Ken chuckled. 'Would have brought my clubs if I'd known.'

We pulled up a few minutes later. I could see the Saab. It wasn't alone – plenty of golfers left their smokers behind overnight when they'd had one too many at the nineteenth. Grabbing the shooter, I slid out and stood at Ken's window.

'Money will be dropped off for you at the club sometime in the next few days, Ken.'

'When you can.'

'Next couple of days. Thanks for the lift.'

'Be seeing you.'

'And you.'

The gun went in the bushes by the pro-shop, still wrapped in black plastic. George would be down to collect it early doors, before any staff showed up. I crunched across gravel for the Saab, felt for the keys, and opened up. Bit cramped. I slid my seat back thinking Laurie must be using jockeys for drivers these days. I made for the Benchill flop feeling knackered.

Fifteen minutes later I walked into what felt like an empty flat. Anxiety flickered up, but when I put my head round his door I saw Korda in bed and akip. The clothes I'd bought were folded over a chair. Didn't look like he'd even tried them on.

I crept into the kitchen and made tea in the dark, then walked the cup into the liver. I kept the lights off and lit up, staring out of the window at distant car headlights. This was one crazy fucking caper, and it had only just started.

I necked the tea and went to make up my own bed. A few minutes later I was lying back, noticing the pillow smelt of fag smoke. In fact, it had lit up and started to talk. It told me it was looking forward to Christmas.

Someone else was thinking my thoughts. I realised I was already asleep.

11

I woke before the alarm. A couple of seconds on my back and I remembered where I was. Then I heard noises from the kitchen, and the television was on. I swung out of bed, pulled on some strides and a T-shirt and walked to the living room. Korda was stood by the window, wearing the track pants and top I'd bought him. He was eating toast and watching himself on TV.

'We made the overnight news,' he said, glancing at me. 'I'm surprised. Thought we'd be safe till the morning bulletins.'

I watched for a moment as his mug was splashed across the screen, then looked back at the real-life version. The green bacon sheen had gone, and he'd shaved off the moustache and taken the clippers to his hair. Now it was short and neat and a little bit darker. Didn't look much like the smudge on the box. He tore another bite and gulped it down.

'I could be an item for the rest of the day.' He turned to look at me. 'But you were expecting that, weren't you?'

I nodded at the telly. 'Was that local or national?'

'Local. But it might make the nationals. Depends what else is going on.'

I looked at my watch: four forty-five. 'We need to get on the road by half five.'

'Bob Devorty?'

'Yeah. And we've got some arrangements to make.'

'Are we coming back here?'

'Depends on the scream. We'll stay in London if we have to.' I thought of Monty's empty flat in Chalk Farm. 'I've got a place.'

'All right. What arrangements?'

'I need to get you a moody passport.'

'I've got one.'

I must have looked surprised.

'You don't spend thirty-odd years in the force without making a few contacts. Off the book, I mean. He laid his plate on the sill. 'The prison dialled three nines last night.' He flicked a tiny little grin. 'As you'd expect.'

I nodded. *Obviously*. We'd seen the cars.

'After that, the police intelligence unit will have put the word out,' he said. 'But the patrol cars won't have my mugshot until six when the morning shift comes on. Same goes for the nicks around Manchester. Did you fill the car up yet?'

He was beginning to piss me off again. 'It's full,' I said abruptly.

He looked amused. 'They might have sent my snap through to the petrol companies. Which means my face could be stuck up next to the till in the service stations.' A beat. 'But you knew that, didn't you?'

I didn't, as it goes. I looked at him. 'They're always camera-ed up, anyway,' I said. 'We need to stay away from them.'

He picked up his plate and stared back at me. Breathed in sharply and his shoulders rose. 'I'll be ready in ten minutes,' he said. 'I don't think I have much to pack.'

Under the shower jets I tried to focus on the game in hand. I still had a huge fucking mountain to climb, and I didn't know if Korda and Devorty would help or hinder my plans.

None of this felt real. It was like I was living in someone else's dream. Maybe I hadn't woken up yet. I was about to drive a copper that I'd just bust out of jail halfway across the country to take control of a stash of stolen money, so I could pay ransom to a bunch of kidnappers that my old mate Monty had apparently ripped off. No, I'd be waking up any minute now. I dressed and went into the kitchen. Korda was making tea.

'You want one?'

'I'll do it myself.'

'As you wish.'

He went and I made toast, thinking I had no idea how to relate to this man. He was filth, but he'd jumped the fence. So that made him what, exactly? A villain? Or a free transfer? And what was he to Monty that Monty had trusted him like he did? This line of thought was freaking me out.

I looked at my watch: six minutes past five. I padded into the liver. Korda had his arse parked on the windowsill, drinking his tea and looking at the telly with the sound low. I stood and ate my toast in silence, staring out of the window. Still dark. A light came on in the block opposite and a twirl of neon in the window started to flash *Merry Christmas* at me.

'I should say thank you,' he said, after a year. 'For getting me out.'

'Don't mention it.'

He killed the sound. 'How much do you get? For your corner.'

I took another bite of the toast.

'I'm assuming it mostly goes to Noriko,' he said. 'But I'm sure Monty would have made you all right. That was his style.'

I didn't like the way Korda talked about Monty, as though he knew the old boy better than I did. Then I thought about Noriko, wrapped up and terrified. 'It's not about the money,' I said angrily.

Korda gave me that flick of a grin. 'Then what is it about?'

Time to give it up. 'Someone's kidnapped Noriko.' I looked at him right in the eye. 'I need Monty's money to get her back. Otherwise you'd still be in Strangeways.'

His face changed in a blink. The amusement went, the jaw hardened. 'What do you mean, kidnapped? Who kidnapped her?'

'If I knew that, we wouldn't be here.'

Korda leant on the ledge, staring out over the estate, his hand splayed on the sill, middle finger tapping on the woodwork for what seemed like an hour. Then he straightened and turned back. 'You should have told me that inside.'

'I couldn't take the risk,' I said. 'That you wouldn't come.'

He started to snap his thumb and middle finger. Slow and loud, snap snap snap. 'You should have thought about that,' snap snap snap. 'I've known Monty a lot longer than you.' And stop. He picked up his mug. 'We can talk about this in the car.' He made for the door, then turned in the frame.

'The trainers you bought me,' he said. 'They're size ten. I take a nine. We'll have to get another pair when we get out of Manchester.'

We'd been driving for a while before Korda spoke again. As we left, he adjusted the seat and reclined it as far as it would go, without being told. Then he seemed to go to sleep. I had the radio on, to see what – if anything – the Old Bill were giving out on his escape. BBC local and Piccadilly Radio both had him on the six o'clock news, but well down the list. We lost the signal not long after. We were way down the M6 by then and it had started to rain. I drove with nothing but the sound of the wipers for company.

Korda woke around seven, pumped his chair back up and stretched. 'Well this is better than B wing,' he said. 'Just about.' I glanced over to catch him looking at me intently. 'How we doing?'

'All right.'

He swept a hand over his window to wipe away the mist, then looked back at me. A beat. 'Now tell me about Noriko,' he said.

I ran through the script. Parcel, photo, phone call, recording. *Monty owed us money, we have his woman.* The ten-day deadline.

'Do you have the photograph?'

'Not with me.'

'And the mobile number they gave you?'

'Went dead immediately after.'

'Have you tried it since?'

'No.'

'What's the number?'

Fuck this. 'I don't have it with me,' I snapped.

'Any idea what Fat Blackmail means?'

And again. 'How the fuck should I know?'

'I knew Monty ripped some people off for money,' he said. 'That wasn't like him. He wasn't himself since the cancer.'

'I wouldn't know.' *He'd been blanking me for months before he died.*

'He was on a lot of pills. And methadone, topped up with charlie. Helped dull the pain, he said.' A beat. I felt totally cut out. I didn't know about any of this. 'What did this Fat Blackmail sound like on the phone?'

I shrugged. 'The voice was distorted, I don't know.'

'English, foreign?'

'British, probably. Why?'

'Kidnapping is what's called a signature crime. All ethnic groups have them. The Turks are into heroin. Chinese do extortion. Black villains shoot up a lot of nightclubs. Kidnapping is a signature crime for East Europeans. Did Monty ever have it with any East –'

'Not that I know of,' I cut in. 'And that little list sounds racist to me.'

'Not racist. Culturally aware. Kidnapping virtually died out in Britain until the Russians went soft on the revolution and the wall came down.' He splayed his paw on the dashboard and tapped his middle finger. Fuck, that was annoying. 'The Met has a kidnap unit. It's very secret and very busy. And all down to former citizens of the old Iron Curtain countries.' He rapped his finger in time to the last few words.

'If you say so.'

'I do.' He pulled out the little metal case, stuck his glasses on his nose and squinted out the window. 'Services two miles ahead. I could do with the bathroom.'

'Your lot tend to dwell at service stations.'

Korda shook his head. 'The Manchester motorway patrols might have my description, but it's probably Brum round here. They won't have a picture yet.' He snapped his fingers under his chin. 'And I've changed enough, anyway. Bathroom and a cup of coffee. Please.'

I looked at the dash clock. Seven twenty-five. 'All right.'

I swung the Saab into the car park a few minutes later. Korda was wearing the long coat I'd bought him over the tracksuit pants and top. He didn't stand out. Collars up against the drizzle, we made for the caff. It was full of steam and truckers.

'I don't seem to have any cash on me,' said Korda as we made for the counter. 'Do you mind picking up the tab for this?'

I almost cracked a smile. 'All right.'

The joint was selling breakfast fat in various combinations, and there was a self-service fry-up. We bought coffees and sat. Korda was staring into his cup. He seemed to have zoned out, despite the telly blaring in the corner.

'Monty,' I said. 'How did you meet, then?'

Nothing.

'Monty,' I repeated. 'How did you meet?'

Korda snapped up like he'd been asleep.

'Sorry, I . . . ' He tapped his finger on the Formica for a moment. He seemed to be gathering his thoughts. 'Monty. Great man. We grew up in the same corner of the world. The Wishwood estate, in Islington. Very upmarket these days. The sixties, it was pretty rough.' His finger danced on the table. 'Couple of big firms grew up round there. You've heard of the Quarley family?'

I nodded. Three main brothers and a handful of other kids. One of the biggest crime families in the Smoke until a few years ago. Largely retired now.

'Well, the Quarleys came from the Wishwood. Their mum lived there until she died. And that's where Monty and I come from. Stop me if I'm telling you something you know.'

'I knew that's where Monty lived when he was younger, till he married –'

'Elspeth, his first wife.'

'Thing is, Monty's never mentioned you. And I've known him, and known him *well*, more than fifteen years.'

A mum dragged her kid past our table on the way to the bogs. Korda leaned forward. 'In the early days,' he said, 'Monty wouldn't have admitted he knew a copper. The later days, it still made sense to keep each other quiet. Wouldn't have looked too impressive on my CV. And some of your lot would scream "grass" if they got a whisper, wouldn't they?'

'Some of them would.'

'It was when I was eight or nine. My mum was dead, my dad worked long hours. I was a latchkey kid. Monty was in his early twenties. His mum lived three doors down. We all knew he was a bit of a villain, but it didn't make any great difference on the Wishwood.' A pause. 'We knew what mattered then. Family and friends, that's what came first.'

'So what were you to Monty?'

'Little brother I guess. You know he had a brother called Ted? Who went missing, presumed dead, a long time ago?'

'He mentioned him occasionally.'

'Monty wasn't a great one for *all our yesterdays,* was he?'

'No.'

'Anyway, most of the kids on the estate lived their lives outside school on the street. And Monty was always around. He was a real snappy dresser in those days. Bit of a mod.'

'A mod?'

'Not the music, the clothes. Smart suit, made to measure from a tailor down City Road called Kolsky's. Narrow cut, straight strides, little square tie, real polished shoes.'

I remembered the dance hall in Monty's story. The smart lads bouncing and spinning. Then my mind flicked back to the funeral, the lad talking to Noriko, the one she raised her veil for. The dark suit, the shot cuffs. A shadow danced, then darted just out of sight like something I'd forgotten; something I could understand if only I had it explained to me.

'Hello?' Korda.

'Sorry, I was somewhere else. You were saying. Monty.'

'I was. Well, he used to play football with us when he was around. He even organised a team one winter. I was tall, gangly. Not much good at games. But he was a good man – he looked out for me. And he got on well with my dad, which helped.'

He took a mouthful of coffee, set it down and rang the lip of the cup. 'Time went on and my dad died. I was fourteen and social services were sniffing around. Wanted me in a kids' home. I didn't want to go. Monty sorted me for money and the rest, and we managed to bat off the DSS until I turned sixteen.' He drummed his fingers. 'Then I signed up for the army, did a few tours. When I came back, Monty was a serious face. But we were still OK. And then I went into the job.'

The job: this is how most Old Bill refer to the police force. Like it's the only job in the world.

'That must have freaked Monty out.'

'At first, yes. It did. But friends are friends, in the end. That's what me and Monty reckoned.'

Some of this was making me very uncomfortable. Monty friends with an Old Bill and saying nothing. The idea of the old guy giving up bodies to the man opposite me. Monty as a grass. I tried to force the thought down, but it kept sliding back.

I pushed my cup away. 'Let's go,' I said. 'Starting to fill up in here.'

Korda stood up. 'I'm going to use the facilities. And – could I get a sandwich or something? Used to a decent breakfast.' I gave him a handful of change.

Ten minutes later we were back on the motorway. We drove in silence for a while. Korda was chewing through his sandwich and I was lost in thought. He finished eating, wiped his fingers on a napkin and drummed them on the dash for a minute.

'Something you ought to know,' he said. 'I can hear a question in your head. The answer is, *no*. Monty never gave me any names. No clues, nothing. We never traded like that. Is that what you wanted to hear, Joker?'

'What do you mean, Joker?' I said, feeling the anger come up.

Korda ran his finger along the dash like he was checking for dust. 'Monty did tell me about some of his mates.' My spine cracked. He saw the shift. 'I didn't want to know names. So he used nicknames. Didn't know who he was talking about half the time. I didn't know who Joker was until last year.'

I felt cold and sick, like I'd not slept for days. All this was busting my view of Monty. I was trying to keep hold of the man I knew. 'Why was I Joker?'

'Some card games, like chemmy, it's the card you can use for anything,' said Korda. 'Monty called you Joker because he said you were like that. You could do anything.' He twisted his head towards me. 'True, isn't it? Who else could have got me out of nick like that?'

'Monty thought I could do anything?'

'Anything. That's why you were the Joker.'

I took this in. 'What else did he tell you about me?' I said.

I felt a shutter come down. For a while Korda said nothing. Then he shifted in his seat and spoke. 'You had a bit of grief last year. Something to do with a detective in the Manchester police. Man called Hamilton Jacks?'

'Maybe.'

'Well, Monty came to me asking for some knowledge about that situation. I found out and passed the knowledge back to him. Seem to remember it all worked out for you. In the end.'

Now I wanted to change the subject. That had been a bad time. 'Did you ever help anyone else? Apart from Monty?'

Korda said nothing. We covered another few miles in silence. Then he pulled the topcoat tighter around him and started to speak.

'It started when I'd been in the job a couple of years,' he said. 'I'd seen a few things by then. Minor enough. You might nick a burglar, find his tools a few feet away. In a bush, whatever. Of course, he dumped them when he heard you coming. But your statement said you *saw him dump his tools*. Tidies it up for the jury. Not a problem. Used to call it goodwill corruption. Got the job done. So I knew how it worked.'

He was staring out the window. Fucking bent copper. The bent copper was talking again.

'I was the custody officer in Charing Cross nick one morning. Came on duty at eight. Looked through the book and found out Monty was in the cells. Nicked overnight for going equipped. Tools on him, game set and match.

'When the last shift went off duty, they did what they always do. Sure you've seen it, Joker. Statement gets stuck on a clipboard, along with his custody record and the evidence bag. With Monty's tools in it. All hung up behind my desk, for the next shift to process when they come on. And it's the only statement. No copies.

'So there I was, all alone. Sweating. Thinking about Monty, who'd looked out for me and kept me out of a kids' home, been my brother, almost my dad. After a bit, I made up my mind.

'They didn't have cameras around the stations in those days. I took the statement down and burnt it in the toilets. The tools I hid in my bag. When the next shift came on, there was no statement, no record and no tools to charge Monty with. If they'd interviewed him again, the defence would have torn them to shreds.

'And there was no evidence. Some idiot had lost it. We had nothing on him. So we had to let him go. The officer who booked him in got the blame. And that was how it started.'

Korda fell silent. We hit the Smoke not long after. I tried to concentrate on driving through the rush hour and the meet with Devorty, but I kept seeing Noriko's face in front of me through the rain.

12

We parked up on a side street off Albion Road about twenty minutes later. Korda stretched and thumbed behind us. 'Little park down there. Got its own herd of deer. You wouldn't expect that in the middle of a city, would you?'

'I've never thought about it.'

I wanted this bit of the day over. I was here for Noriko, no other reason; I didn't like Devorty, and Korda made me uncomfortable. And I was looking at ten years minimum for my antics last night, if it all came on top. All this shit was putting me on edge.

'Come on,' I said. 'Devorty's waiting.'

A minute later and we were pressing the bell for 132a. No reply. I tried the pimp's landline. Nothing. His mobile went straight to voicemail.

'Fuck this,' I said. 'The prick is expecting me.'

'Is he expecting *me*?' said Korda.

'No, he's expecting news,' I said. 'Told him I'd be seeing him this morning. Nothing else.' I looked up and down the road. The parade of shops opposite was busy. Despite Korda's changed appearance, I didn't fancy lingering here for any length of time.

'Fuck him,' I said, angry. 'We'd better find somewhere to dwell for a bit.'

Korda laid his hand gently on the door. It gave immediately and swung open on its hinges. 'Always worth a try,' he said. 'Shall we?'

I shrugged and followed him in. He led the way to the first floor and 132a. There was noise inside, a radio. Korda rapped on the woodwork. 'Maybe he couldn't hear the bell,' he said. No movement from inside. He bent down and peered through the letterbox. Straightening up, he pulled his sleeves down over his mitts and put his weight on the woodwork.

'Korda —'

He whapped his shoulder against the door and the wood round the lock gave way like balsa.

'Korda, what did you see —'

He was already inside. I snapped my sleeves down over my hands and followed him in. The flat was dark and smelt of sulphur. I bumped the front door closed and followed the copper down the corridor. His bulk blocked my view until he made the lounge. Then I saw the rest.

Devorty was sat upright in a chair in the middle of the room. His arms were twisted and tied behind him and there was a thick silver stripe of duct tape across his mouth. His legs had been taped to the chair, three or four thick bands of silver from knee to ankle. He was wearing a white shirt that had been torn open, letting his belly flood out over his belt. His chest and stomach were white and hairy and slashed in several places. There were thick trickles of dried blood running down his flesh. Old blood stained his green trousers black. He stank.

Korda switched off the radio and leant on the wall. 'We've got a problem,' he said.

Forty minutes later we were sitting in Monty's flat in Chalk Farm drinking black coffee. The milk in the fridge had long gone off.

Despite the smell of corpse, I'd given Devorty's flat a careful spin before we split. I couldn't find his bit of postcard anywhere, nor his numbers. Korda had also been busy. He'd checked the other rooms, then spent some time examining the living room, Devorty's body and the silver tapes strapping him to the chair. Filth can be useful sometimes.

Now Korda took a mouthful, did the drumming thing on his cup and looked at me. 'What do you say, Joker?'

'What do *you* say? You're the fucking detective.'

'There was no sign of forced entry,' he snapped. 'So either he knew the people who came to the door, or they bluffed their way in.'

'They?'

'Almost certainly. Devorty was a fat bastard. One person couldn't wrap him up alone. And there was no sign of violence on his body, apart from those slashes from the Stanley knife. No bruises. So he didn't get the chance to put up a fight. That means two or more people. Experienced, too.' I shrugged *if you say so*. 'They knew what they were doing,' he went on. 'Except they didn't know him well.'

'What do you mean?'

'The bathroom was full of heart and blood pressure pills. Coversyl, beta blockers, all the rest. I think he died of a heart attack. Fright, probably. It certainly wasn't those Stanley cuts they were giving him – they were just flesh wounds to liven him up.' He stroked his upper lip for a moment. 'Question is, did they get what they wanted?'

Korda didn't seem too bothered by Devorty's death. 'Shouldn't the question be *who the fuck did it*?' I said.

Korda bit his knuckles. 'I pulled Devorty's file, back when Monty approached me in January. He'd lived in that flat for a decade. And he'd been more or less retired for years. He was easy to find. If anyone was after him for something in his past, they'd had found him long ago. No. This is more recent. And I've seen it before.'

I felt the tension twist tighter up my spine. 'When?'

'Trial I sat on once. Not my collar, I came in later. Bunch of Serb gangsters trafficking women into the Smoke. Anyone bounce onto their patch and they used to wrap them up like Bob. Then they went to work with a Stanley knife.' A beat. 'Then we have Noriko, kidnapped. And kidnap is an East European signature crime.'

There was something else going on here. 'What about Heathrow?'

'What indeed.' He stood and went to the fireplace. It was full of Noriko's stuffed toys and brightly dressed dolls. They used to piss Monty off. *Look at that, it's like having a fucking baby round the place.* For a second, I thought he was back in the room.

'Did you notice Wednesday's *Daily Mail* on the side?' said Korda. 'And the pint of milk next to it? I think he went out to the shops on Wednesday morning and they followed him in. Been dead two days.'

'This must be down to Heathrow, Korda. You're away, Monty's dead. So they go for Devorty.'

'Korda rolled the idea in his brain for a moment. 'No one knew about Devorty,' he said. 'He didn't do any of the organising. He just brought the knowledge. No . . . if anyone fancied a bit more than they got, they'd have come looking for me. I paid them all off. Not big Bob.'

I went to Monty's window and looked out. 'Are you sure you didn't tell anyone else about Heathrow, Korda?' I said quietly.

He carefully set his cup down on the mantle. 'Why do you ask that?'

'Or maybe you set your crew onto Devorty when you knew you were getting out of Strangeways. To get his numbers. Now you've got two sets.'

'Or maybe you did, Joker. To get his numbers. And now *you've* got two sets.'

We stared at each other. I tried to read his expression but there was nothing there. 'For the moment,' I said levelly, 'I have to think about Noriko.'

'So do I. Monty was my friend. And then there's the money. My plane ticket out of here. So we're on the same game. What do you say, Joker?'

'I say, stop calling me Joker.'

He looked at me, a smile at the corner of his lips. I bit back my fury – and suddenly had a thought. 'Who's Devorty's successor?'

'I don't know if he even had one.'

'All that fucking heart medication in his cupboard, he must have had one.'

'Yes . . .'

'If he has a successor, his successor will know about me,' I said. 'And when they find out about Devorty, they'll come looking. For me.'

'Except no one knows Devorty's dead,' said Korda.

'Let's find a phone box,' I said.

We found a telephone well away from CCTV. Korda stood a few feet away while I muffled my voice and called it in to the Old Bill. With any luck, Bob's last dance would hit the local news. Then there was the bush telegraph once he was found. Maybe his successor would hear and get in touch with me. If he had one. And if he knew about me.

I realised I'd hardly registered a man had died. But then Bob Devorty was nothing to me. I hung up and stared at Korda's back. I felt the dead end closing in.

We walked back to the Saab. I couldn't let Korda out of my sight. And he wouldn't want to let me out of his sight either. If I was following the money – or Noriko – then so was he.

I was as depressed and despairing as I'd ever been. All I had to show for the last five days was a copper round my neck; a man I didn't trust as far as I could spit him. I didn't want the prick anywhere near me, but near me was the only safe place for him to be.

We made the car. I had five days to find a million quid or find Noriko. This was fucked up. I found myself behind the wheel. Korda was speaking.

'I need a proper set of clothes, Joker. And some trainers that fit. Can we do that?'

'What about the scream?'

'I may be Top of the Pops in Manchester, but down here I'm in line behind half a dozen Al-Qaeda terrorists, a serial killer and a couple of big-time Charlie bank robbers. The Met don't give a fuck if it comes from north of Watford. They won't be looking for me. An anonymous department store will be quite safe.' He nodded at the dash. 'We can check the midday news, if you like. See if I'm on it.'

He wasn't. We drove for the centre.

Half one and we were walking into Soho. The sun was out, thin and wintry. We'd parked up round the back of Oxford Street and I'd bought Korda a cheap suit and some other gear. Now he was hungry.

We made the bottom of Frith Street, a gaff called Jimmy's, squeezed between an Italian coffee shop and a barber's. Monty had taken me here a few times. There was a blue canopy up front with the name picked out in white. It looked like the sixties.

There was a tall geezer by the door, puffing on a Sherlock Holmes pipe. He nodded at us as we went in and downstairs. The place was crowded with lunchtime punters. A waiter in black and whites showed us a table in the corner, and we ordered. I thought about Devorty. The cops would be all over his pad now, scene-of-crime guys dusting and taking photographs.

'So what's the game, Joker?'

I leant in. 'Why don't you tell me what you think?'

'Start with what we know. Monty's dead, Noriko's kidnapped. You run after the money to get her back, get me out, and then we find Bob Devorty's been killed. We know Monty ripped some people off. Fat Blackmail is one of them. Kidnap is an East European stroke. If Monty was having it with some Serbs, Albanians or whatever, then we have a suspect. Or two.'

'For Fat Blackmail or for Devorty?'

'Maybe it's the same crew.'

'That doesn't make sense. Fat Blackmail's waiting for me to get the money. Why kill Devorty?'

'I know. There's something missing here, Joker. Thank you.'

We sat back as the waiter brought our food. When he'd gone I said, 'You told me you'd seen those cuts before.'

Something dropped down behind Korda's eyes. 'They were Serbs,' he said. 'Nasty crew. But they're all inside. And for a while.' He cut into the kleftico on his plate. 'This looks good.'

'Monty always liked it.' I grunted and scooped up a fork of moussaka. 'Apart from the three of you, who else knew about Heathrow?'

'Why?'

'Maybe someone spewed.'

'Maybe Bob spewed,' said Korda. 'I never trusted him.'

'He never trusted you,' I said. 'He told me that's why the chop-up was so complicated, with the numbers and all.'

Korda laid down his fork. 'I stipulated the chop-up because I didn't trust Devorty,' he said. 'Bob was an idiot. And he was an idiot in debt. I told you, I pulled his file.'

'Tell me about Heathrow,' I said. 'Maybe I'll see a connection.'

Korda shrugged and started to talk.

Devorty had gone to Monty with knowledge on a shipment of cash, he said. Devorty could deliver the day and the flight but he didn't know anyone in Heathrow who could get him inside. So Monty came to Korda asking for knowledge, nothing more. He reckoned – rightly – that even if Korda didn't know the arrangements at the airport, he could find them out easily enough.

'I decided I wanted in on the coup,' said Korda, chewing on his food. 'I wanted out of the job. It had fucked me over. Thirty-five years of my life and it had fucked me over for lots of reasons.' He shook his head. 'None of which you need to know.

'And Monty needed money, he was desperate. He was on his arse with the private doctors and the cancer, and he was in a rush to get the job done while he was still well enough to do it. So he was in a hurry.'

Korda had bankrolled the entire operation, plus he knew someone at the airport who could deliver up the stand the plane would go to. According to Korda, this was only decided an hour or so before the plane actually touched down, so you needed someone right there on the day.

Korda paid off the inside guy out of his pension fund and also sorted a baggage handler to steal airside passes the night before the coup went off.

'They're not Fat Blackmail,' said Korda, reading my mind. 'No imagination. And they never knew the whole, anyway.'

On the day of the coup, Korda got word on the stand, then Monty and Devorty schlepped to the plane dressed as security. They wrapped the handlers up and had the prize off the plot before anyone noticed what had happened. They cut through the perimeter fence and trans-ferred the cash to a van with Korda at the wheel. And that was it.

I figured they'd had a lot more inside help than Korda was letting on. 'And then?'

'The money turned out to be in big notes. Monty's launderer said it would take a while to clean up. We handed it over and he flew it off.'

'Devorty told me.'

'The little charmer. Anyway. Come October, we got word the money was ready. And then they nicked me the next day. So here we are.'

The waiter took our plates and brought coffee. Then, for the sake of it, I asked, 'What were you going to do when you got the money?'

'Monty and I both had reasons to go abroad. Monty wanted to go to Japan with Noriko. And he had some thing about visiting Gibraltar. Apparently that's where Ted was the last time he heard from him. And I was going abroad, too.' He looked at me. 'There was a woman.'

'Was?'

The shutters came down. 'We were going away.'

I was about to push him when my phone jumped. It was Harry. I couldn't hear a word. 'I'm going to take this upstairs.' Korda nodded.

Up to the street. Harry was still talking. 'Harry, I didn't hear a word of that.' I dipped past a waiter from the cafe next door. 'What did you say?'

'I said, did your Noriko marry a guy called Monty?'

It was like someone slapped me in the mouth. 'Yes. How did you –'

'Your Noriko is my Lucy. The Japanese girl from the parlour in West Hampstead, for sure. I called up someone I used to know. She remembered her. Listen, she was a lovely girl. I want to help.'

I twisted round and buried my chin into my chest, trying to rack up the volume against the traffic. 'Harry, no. You've done enough.'

'Chickenshit. I still know people in London. I can help. Why do you think you're the only one who can do anything?'

'Harry,' I hissed. 'Bob Devorty's dead. Someone cut him up.'

The line went silent.

'Oh Jesus. Who did it?'

'I don't know. I'm working on it.'

'He was an arsehole, but . . . *oh my God.*'

'Stay out of this, Harry. It's too fucking dangerous.'

There was a long silence. A rickshaw whipped by, bell jingling wildly. Then something struck me. 'Harry, was this Lucy at the parlour when Bob Devorty took it over?'

'I don't remember. I don't think so.'

Or maybe she was. 'Harry, I'll call you later. I've got to go.'

'Don't hang up. Look, I'm going down to London tonight anyway, to see my friend . . . '

Was that friend, or boyfriend?

'I know people who know – knew – Bob,' she said. 'Girls who used to work. I'll ask around. Lucy, or Noriko, was a nice girl.'

A nice girl. She had a face like a watercolour and a laugh like a handful of bells. Harry was right. I needed all the help I could get.

'OK Harry, but be careful, all right?'

I hung up and went to get Korda.

We were driving in silence. The copper had been withdrawn when we left the restaurant; now he was dozing, seat racked back. I was deep in thought, turning over my options. Monty's money was fucked. Even if Devorty's successor wised up and made contact, I only had five days left. As for the rest, it was a total fucking fuck-up. Links and connections formed in my head, ran down blind alleys and crashed into the wall.

I thought of Devorty's corpse, wrapped up like a Sunday joint.

I glanced over at Korda. What was he keeping to himself? He stirred and opened his eyes. Maybe I spoke aloud.

'Joker.' He stretched and clacked his seat up straight. 'Where are we?'

'Couple of hours out.'

He rubbed his eyes and slotted his bins on his nose. 'Any ideas yet? About Noriko?'

I thought of the bank in King Street. 'I'm working on it.'

He leant on his window and stared out. 'It's all a game, Joker. You know that. I nick you, you wriggle out of it. Then I nick you again.'

'And now?'

'You're playing Fat Blackmail and he's got all the cards.'

'Has he?' Silence. A few more miles and I said, 'Did you do it?'

'Do what?'

'Give that guy's name out? The one on witness protection who got killed.'

He splayed his paw on the dash like before. Middle finger, tap, tap, tap.

'I wasn't bent,' he said. 'I just helped an old friend out. That's all.'

Yeah right, I thought. What I said was: 'So how come they nicked you?'

'I couldn't account for a lot of my movements because of Heathrow. I was dead in the water. And there were other elements.'

'The witness you were shagging, you mean?'

Korda said nothing.

'Those cuts on Bob. You recognised them, you said. Where from?'

'A trial. A crew of Serbians.'

I took a punt. 'The trial where the witness got killed?'

'It was. But they're all in jail.'

'You think there's some connection?'

He sighed impatiently. 'I think Bob Devorty talked too much. I think he had some nasty friends. He blabbed about Heathrow, some gangsters paid him a visit. And the fat man died.'

Anger shot up me like an electric shock. 'For fuck's sake Korda, I've had enough of this shit. Tell me what you know.'

'I've told you.'

'Have you? Tell me the rest.'

'I've told you.'

'Tell me what you fucking know!' I was screaming now. And my foot was pressing down on the gas. I pulled out and shot past an HGV. I glanced at the filth and leant on the juice a bit more. Then I realised what I was doing and let the needle drop.

'Monty never told me you were like this.'

'Monty's dead.'

'Yes. Yes, he is.' Korda cleared his throat and shifted in his seat. 'Ever seen a movie called *Bad Day at Black Rock*?'

I sighed deeply. What the fuck was he talking about now? 'Spencer Tracy,' I said. 'Yes, I have.'

'He turns up in town, someone's been murdered, and everyone's in on it. I know how he feels.' He leant his head back on the rest and closed his eyes.

'Bad day at Black Rock,' he said.

13

It was four in the morning and I was standing naked in the living room of the Benchill flat. Anxiety was clawing at my gut, tugging and clutching. I couldn't catch my breath. My windpipe had seized up. I tried to gasp in air but all I felt was my throat closing, I saw it in my head, shrinking, tighter and tighter. I couldn't breathe. How long did I have – three or four minutes? – lungs empty, tight now, dizzy, spinning . . . I glanced down at my hand on the window ledge, nails bitten to the quick, nails, shouldn't bite them like that, was this the last thing I was going to see before I choked to death? A tingle spreading up from my thighs, up and along the arms to the fingers, it's all shutting down . . . *stop it, just stop* . . . I stumbled back a couple of paces, half-tripped to the couch, *close your mouth, that's it, close your mouth, through the nose, it feels wrong but it's the only way, very slow,* snatch some air in but it's not enough, *no it's OK, going to be OK* . . . chest is loosening again, *you can breathe through your mouth now, yes you can breathe,* throat's relaxing, drop the jaw open and breathe it in, *yes that's it, it's OK again, just breathe slowly* . . .

I sat slumped on the couch. Breathing deep and feeling the air in my lungs. Trembling, approaching OK.

I'd never had a panic attack before, but my daughter Lou had suffered from them once. The first is the worst because you have no memory of coming through it. So you panic even more.

I heard Lou's voice in my head. The know-all tone she reserved for her dad. *A cup of tea would be a good idea here.*

I went into the kitchen and put the kettle on. Then in the bedroom I pulled on strides and shirt. I saw the phone lying on the bed where I'd dropped it. I scooped it up and rolled it in my palm. Then I made tea and sat on the sofa in the dark.

I had to look at it again.

The phone had woken me about ten minutes ago. My old phone, the one Fat Blackmail was calling. It was lit up and buzzing in the dark. Groping across for it I saw the screen, an envelope, spinning. *You've got a message.* I clicked to open. A video clip.

It started with a close-up of a newspaper, the front page of yesterday's London *Evening Standard,* Friday. The camera pulled back and I saw Noriko wearing a short yellow dress, sitting in front of a dirty, green-painted wall. She was terrified. Even on this tiny screen I could see her shaking. A man's grunt, indistinct from off right – her head turned in his direction, bewildered eyes looked up at him then back down to the sheet of paper in her lap. She picked it up. Her ring finger was tightly bandaged. The paper wavered in her hands.

'Today is Friday,' she read. Her voice faint, metallic. *An echo; an empty room with no carpets.* 'Your ten days are up on Wednesday. They want the money. The exchange will take place in London. They will contact you on Wednesday morning at ten.'

She looked up, straight into the camera. 'They want me to show you this.' A beat. 'To encourage you.'

The camera moved in as she dropped the paper and pulled at the bandage on her finger. It unrolled white, then rust, then red. It zoomed in on a finger, bloodied and shaking. And the nail had been torn out.

The screen went black.

I'd rolled off the bed and stumbled into the living room, the image of her torn finger branded into my brain. I saw the knife jammed under it, sawing back and forth in the flesh, side to side and cutting deep, her screaming and begging and being held down so they could do it, swapping to the pliers and the final grunting tug as it was torn out of the nail-bed. Her carefully black-painted nail.

Then it all overwhelmed me and I couldn't breathe.

I held the phone in my hand, the pain in my chest was threatening again. *Do it.* I punched buttons to replay the clip. And again. I watched for clues. Where was she being held? I found none. I watched again. Again.

I let the mobile drop onto the sofa and buried my head in my hands. What the fuck was I going to do? I had no leads, no ideas, no hope. I had a copper on his toes in the bedroom and a dead man in a miserable pimped-up flat in London. I thought suddenly of Casey on trial in the Crown Court. It was too much, all of it. I was playing the big man, but I was no big man. I couldn't do it. Time to cut and bail out. Get out of here and keep going.

Casey could look after himself, Korda could turn himself in or leg it and Devorty . . . Devorty was dead. I had money at Amy's, enough to get me out of the country, down to Italy, start again there . . . with her. I'd keep in touch with the kids, they'd come and visit me, I'd stay there till this had all blown over. Plenty of people had done it before.

But I kept slamming up against Noriko. Noriko and Monty. I couldn't go. *I'm a straight face. I don't let people down. I have to find a way. Monty trusted me. In his last seconds, he trusted me.* This was a different sort of insanity. *Just stop all of this. Just think. Think.*

I had never intended to let Fat Blackmail get away with kidnapping Noriko, but how I would do it – a jump at the handover or tracking them down beforehand – had taken second place to getting the dough together for the fallback. Now I didn't even have sight of a fallback and there were five days left.

My mind went to the bank in King Street. It was researched, all the work was done. Truck, uniforms; all the rest was pretty much in place. I hadn't finished manning the team yet but that wouldn't be impossible, even in the time left.

The problem was the likely prize. I had knowledge that pointed to about half a million quid. There were safe deposit boxes on top of that, true; they could yield any amount of tom – rings, necklaces, all the rest. Then there was cash or other valuables. On the other hand, they could be empty. We wouldn't know until we prised them open. But looking at Fat Blackmail with a villain's eyes, I was pretty sure he and his chums would rather have a few hundred grand than a murder charge on their backs.

And the exchange had to go down, because Fat Blackmail wanted it to. I had no say in how it would happen. All I could do for my part was show up with as much real cash as I could get my hands on. Which meant doing the King Street work as soon as possible. Today was Saturday. I'd give myself today and tomorrow to prepare. And I'd go Monday morning.

I went back to bed and surprised myself by drifting off almost immediately.

*

Korda knocked on my door at half eight shouting there was breakfast in ten minutes if I wanted it. I lay in bed for a second, thinking
about my situation. Detective Chief Inspector Korda was cooking me
breakfast. Had I woken in an alternative sitcom universe? One where a
professional criminal finds himself shacked up with a bent copper *with
hilarious consequences!*

Jesus H. Christ.

Korda had made scrambled eggs on toast. I had a forkful. They were
OK.

'I heard you up and about early this morning, Joker,' he said. 'Guilty
dreams?'

'Message from Fat Blackmail.'

'Saying what?'

I pushed the phone across the table. 'Video message. Take a look.'

He watched the clip without expression. When he was done, he laid
the handset in front of him. 'They make her talk,' he said levelly, 'so you
can't hear their voices.'

'Gold star, Korda.'

'Did Monty ever have it with any Serbian gangsters?'

'Why are you so obsessed with this Eastern European connection?'

'Because I'm a detective. I make connections and I detect crime.
Did he?'

'Not that I know of. I thought he told you everything. He was your
friend.' The inflection was a sneer.

'Not everything, Joker.' He pushed away his plate and dropped his
face into his hands. Then he seemed to make his mind up about something and straightened up. 'The witness protection business,' he said,
'the man I'm supposed to have betrayed, the guy who got killed.'

'I remember.'

'The trial it all related to – it was about people-trafficking. Women brought from overseas and forced to work as prostitutes, mainly in London. Some of them conned, some of them kidnapped. All of them forced to have sex with men against their will. That's rape. Hour after hour, week after week.'

He stopped and gathered himself for a minute.

'It wasn't my collar. I was seconded down to London to mind one of the witnesses. I used to work in Clubs and Vice, Joker. I knew the game. This witness was a woman. She'd been a maid in one of the flats the Serbians ran as a brothel. Took the phone calls, sorted the money, you know what a maid does.

'She got to know the girls in her flat, heard their stories. She was a good woman, kind. So she went to the Met. Clubs and Vice put the flat under surveillance, then the rest of the crew and eventually nicked them. There was a trial, they went down. I minded her before and during. It took about a year to come to court.' He stopped talking and stirred his coffee, absently. 'We got close,' he said, at last.

I thought of how he reacted to Bob Devorty's death. 'Didn't know you had any emotion, Korda.'

He held my gaze. 'You don't know anything about me, Joker.'

'And these Serbs. It was them that cut the competition up with a Stanley?'

'Yes. It was.'

'But I thought you got the whole crew.'

'Honestly? You never get the whole crew. There's always someone who gets away.'

He stood and went to the kitchen. I heard the kettle go on. Five minutes and he was back with two fresh coffees. He laid one in front of me.

'And you think there's a connection there?' I said. 'That doesn't seem very likely to me.' In fact it seemed more likely to me that Korda was up to no good. I just couldn't work out how.

'Maybe Monty – '

'Shut the fuck up, Korda.' I was angry, suddenly. 'Maybe Monty nothing. The man's not here to defend himself.'

'His mind wasn't right, Joker. The doctors put him on methadone. It suppresses the cough if you've got lung cancer. Helps with the pain as well, so Monty got himself some more. Off the books this time. The amount he was taking gives you side effects. Paranoia, hallucinations. And he was topping it up with charlie, to keep himself going. He was fucked, Joker. Schizoid, paranoid and fucked.'

I shook my head.

'Last time I saw him, he could hardly remember his own name,' said Korda. 'He was going on about Ted, how he'd let him down, how he should have looked out for him better. For God's sake, Ted's been dead thirty years but Monty was acting like he was still alive. His mind was going. Trust me.'

'The only person who can tell us if Monty was into this crew for dough is Monty,' I snapped. 'And he's dead.'

'So here we are.'

Korda drummed fingers on the table and took a swig of coffee. 'Fat Blackmail is relying on the fact that you're a villain and won't go to the police,' he said. 'That's why he took Noriko. If you'd been straight, if Monty had been straight, this would never have happened.'

He stood up and moved to the window. It was drizzling and the estate looked grey. The only flash of colour was the twist of neon, still flashing *Merry Christmas* from the block opposite.

'People-trafficking's pretty rare, Joker,' he said, quietly. 'Whatever you read in the papers, there's not many crews that do it. And they know about kidnapping. Safe houses, laying people down, moving them quietly. They know what drugs to use to knock them out and what it takes to wake them up.'

He turned and leant against the sill.

'Am I a prisoner here?'

'No.'

'Can you get me a phone, then?'

'Who are you going to ring?'

'I still have friends, Joker. Friends who could help us. We need to know if they've found Devorty, if they're getting anywhere with it. Maybe something about that Serb crew.' He snapped his fingers irritably. 'I still know coppers down in the Smoke. They'll know I'm out by now, they'll be expecting a call, one or two of them anyway.'

I thought for a minute. If he wanted to turn me in, he could walk out the front door, then go and dial three nines from a box. But there was no evidence to link me to the jail caper except him, and he wouldn't want to stick around for the return trip to Strangeways. And he might dig something up – it was his job, after all. He'd delivered for Monty in the past. Maybe he really did care what happened to Noriko. Maybe I had some of the old guy's credit.

'All right, I said.'

'What about you?'

The bank in King Street. 'I'm going to try and raise some money, for Noriko.'

He nodded. I stood to clear the plates. 'Your woman,' I said. 'The one on witness protection. Was she why you did the Heathrow job? So you could go away together?'

He nodded. 'And start again.'

'Where is she now?'

'Still on witness protection.'

I picked up the plates and made for the kitchen. Then I stopped in the doorway. Might as well ask.

'What's her name?' I said.

Korda was leaning his big frame on the sill and staring out of the window again. He answered with his back towards me.

'Carmen,' he said softly. 'Her name is Carmen.'

14

I went out and bought Korda a prepay phone along with a voucher for twenty quid. Back at Benchill I found he was in the bath, so I dumped it on his bed and split for Marcus's shop. As I drove, my brain ran over the possible candidates for driver for the King Street job on Monday. A couple of names came up. They'd need a call, pronto.

John Cooper Clarke was selling a bookcase to an elderly couple out front when I made the shop ten minutes later. I followed the slipstream of hot air to the office and found Marcus on site, brewing up. There was news about the trial.

'The judge, Chipchase, stood it down on Friday afternoon till Tuesday,' he said. 'The prosecution looked like death warmed up all morning and Chipchase was probably feeling guilty he'd given him his germs. He didn't look too smart himself.' The kettled snicked off and he made tea. 'So. How did your caper go?'

'Not great,' I said.

'No news on Noriko?'

'Yes, but it's not good. I've got some shit to sort out,' I told him. 'But I'll drop round and see Casey this afternoon.'

'He's gone off to see Stella and the kids.'

'You shouldn't be —'

'He rang me from a callbox on Friday afternoon,' snapped Marcus. 'He sounded like a bag of shit. He's right on the edge. I told him to get out of town, take a break. Now then.'

He whapped a mug down in front of me and some of the brew slopped onto the desk.

'OK, sorry Marcus. Fair enough.'

'All right, mate. Remember, some people take it harder than you, eh?' He tore off a strip of kitchen paper and mopped up the tea. 'Now. You want to hear about Eddie Box?'

'Eddie? Has he had any more visits?'

'A very suspicious plainclothes on his own with a bunch of photos, wanting him to pick the geezer who dropped the motor off.'

'And did he?'

'Yeah, fortunately. But the copper was very suss. All the smudges looked very like you. Eddie wants some more folding, for the inconvenience.'

'All right.' I peeled a couple of hundred off my roll. 'Can you give him that next time you see him?'

Marcus nodded and stashed the dough in his back pocket. 'Is there a problem?'

'Just tell him the only person who can bring him trouble is him. But if they call again, he should get vague about the guy who drove the motor. Time passing, old age, that sort of thing. All right?'

'What do you reckon's going on? Why the renewed interest?'

'Maybe someone saw me speak to Korda, maybe the minder blabbed. They can't prove anything. I've not been back to my pad. If they've gone round asking questions, the Wessons will just say I'm away on business – which I am, far as they're concerned. I don't think the filth can prove anything.' I drained my mug, stood and put a mitt on his shoulder. 'Marcus, thanks for everything. Be in touch, yeah?'

'All right, mate. Be seeing you.'

I split. As I walked to the motor, I took out my phone and dialled Tom, a retired kiter who was helping out on the bank work. Yes, he could make a meet – up in Cheadle. He gave me the address.

I went into full work alert on the drive up. I took plenty of back doubles going through the city and spent an hour coming on and off the motorway till I was sure I was alone. No one ever got nicked for being too careful.

By one o'clock I was satisfied and headed out to Cheadle and a coffee shop off the high street. The waitresses wore black with starched white aprons. Tom had said it reminded him of Joe Lyons, whatever that meant. I stepped inside and looked around. Lunchtime on a Saturday and the gaff was packed. Noisy kids, ill-tempered dads, tired mums clutching bags and boxes and the warm smell of a short-order chef behind on his omelettes.

Tom was sitting in a booth in the corner. Light cream suit, a regimental tie, white hair and a long, strong face. He looked like a retired diplomat just back from the tropics. A wiry arm stretched and flicked an imperial wave my way. I wove through the tables and we shook.

'All right, Tom.'

'All right, chief. You hungry?'

'Just some tea, I think.'

He beckoned a waitress across and ordered another pot and fresh cups. Then he reached inside his jacket and slid a bulky envelope across the cloth.

'Unit six,' he said. 'It's on the industrial estate in Plymouth Grove, on the right past Devonshire Street. Heading south.'

'Any trouble?'

'None. I'll ring the agents today and say I'm taking it, get them to have the lease ready for . . . ?'

'Wednesday. I'll be finished with it by then.'

'Fine,' he said. 'Wednesday. They think I'm properly kosher. You'll have the place to yourselves. Gaff's got a mortice, a Yale and a brass padlock. I gave them two hundred holding deposit.' He gestured at the envelope. 'Your twirls, chief.'

Tom had used an old trick to get the keys. He'd rung a few estate agents and got shown round some warehouses and light industrial units around town. When he'd seen a good place, he'd asked to take another look and made the right noises. The third time he asked for a gander, they trusted him enough to give him the keys for a solo shufti. At which point he'd trotted off and had a duplicate set cut for me.

Tom was smiling. 'All about looking the part, chief. All about looking the part.'

The tea showed up. Once the waitress had split, I pushed an envelope over to him. 'As agreed, Tom. Two hundred for the deposit. And a monkey for you. Honours if it goes well.'

He stowed the cash and flicked the teapot. 'Shall I be mother?'

On the way to the motor, I called Georgie Manning to call the work on. I asked him if Monday was OK for a trip to the flicks.

'Fine with me. No plans otherwise.'

'OK, George. Are you around tomorrow?'

'Any time. Just ring, friend.'

I got behind the wheel and headed for Amy's in Ladybarn. The old girl had been doing a bit of needlework for me over the last month. Three plain blue tunics with scrambled egg on the shoulders and chest.

Security guard uniforms from the dressing up box, but they'd work for the short time they'd be in the public eye. One for me, an XXXL for Georgie and a spare. Which might be a problem if the man behind the wheel now was a big fella.

Amy didn't ask any questions, as usual. I whisked the dog's bed up and grabbed some more money while she clattered around in the kitchen. As I dropped the carpet back, she forced a massive bacon sandwich on me without the option.

I dwelt for a while as United was at home and there was no point fighting through the pre-match traffic. A second cup of tea and I split.

I had to see a man about a van.

It was gone three by the time I was on the road for Dud and his body shop at Stretford. Parking up round the corner, I rang the bell about half past. Dud opened up looking grimy. He was expecting me.

'All right, mate? Come on in.' He was on his tod, but he dubbed up the front before leading me through to the spray booth. The van was there, covered with a mucky grey dustsheet. He whipped it off to show his handiwork.

'What do you reckon?'

I reckoned it looked good. It had been a long white transit when I'd bought it at auction last month. It was now a dark blue with TSTS Security and a moody telephone number and web address stripped along both sides. He led me around the back. The cashbox chute looked convincing. It was only for show – the money would go into the front with us.

Dud showed me the *let's pretend* security guard helmets, which he'd also sorted. They looked OK. Dark blue metal with chunky black chinstraps, they had big heavy visors to cover our mugs and hide us from CCTV, inside the bank and out on the street. I tried one on.

'How do I look?'

'Wouldn't recognise you, mate.'

'Thanks, Dud.' I pulled the helmet off, gave him a grand in twenties and told him the van would be picked up Monday, early. He offered me tea but I had to keep moving. I wanted to get to Tom's warehouse before the final whistle blew at Old Trafford and the roads thickened up again. On the way up I stopped at a small garage I knew had no CCTV, juiced up the Saab and bought a can of unleaded. Dud's handiwork wasn't going to stay around too long after the work on Monday morning.

Next, a locksmith, about half a mile down the road. Old pal. I dropped in and got a second set of the warehouse keys cut, then drove on for Tom's slaughter up in Longsight. The gaff was dubbed up of course. I slipped the twirl into the big brass padlock on the gates. Opened smooth as you like. Stepping in, I slid a chunky iron bolt across behind me, and made for unit six. The keys let me in.

The slaughter was around forty foot long and needed a good coat of paint. I walked to the far wall, drew the bolts on the small back door and twisted the Yale. There was a yard bordered by a chain-link fence out the back. That would have a hole cut in it tomorrow night for a swift exit after the van was torched. Good.

Outside again, I paused for a moment, looking at an ugly grey building squatting over on the left. Longsight nick. A bit too close for comfort in an ideal world, but the unit was the best available on the getaway route and people – including Old Bill – often missed action under their own noses. That was the theory, anyway.

I made Benchill about half seven with fish and chips for two. Korda was edgy and distant. He said he'd made a couple of calls but found no one home.

'I didn't leave a message, for obvious reasons. I'll try again tomorrow, Joker.'

He cleared the plates, washed up and then made his excuses. 'Didn't sleep too well last night,' he said. 'Think I'll turn in early.'

I spent some time watching the TV, trying to relax. I dropped off on the sofa around ten. When I woke, Audrey Hepburn was on the box. Her and Cary Grant running around Paris with Walther Matthau looking sinister in the background. I'd seen the flick before so I went to bed. It was just after midnight.

Harry never worked on Sundays but she was an early riser. When I rang her at half ten I could hear city traffic.

'I was just about to call you,' she said. 'Hang on, it's too noisy here. Let me just . . . ' The sound dipped. I imagined her in a neat green suit I'd seen her in before, hair tied up and weaving through knots of Christmas shoppers to get off the main drag. She was speaking again.

'Bob Devorty's death is all over the WG bush telegraph,' she said.

'WG?'

'Working Girl. It means prostitute?'

'Got you. The line's bad.'

'OK, well. I've got a couple of friends, female friends. They're in the business. One of them helps run a big co-op in Stamford Hill. A co-op is where the girls take on a place as a collective and run it together. Anyway, a lot of women pass through the place, my friend gets to know what's going on. I called her. She didn't want to say much over the phone. I'm going to see her tonight.'

'What about your man?'

'He's working.' On a Saturday? A thought struck me again, about Harry's one-time boyfriend. The copper Dave Craze. Maybe she was . . .

'Harry. Are you seeing Dave Craze again?'

Street noise ran in from the other end to fill her silence. Must have been nearly a minute. Then, 'Just don't go there, all right?'

'I'm sorry . . . '

'Just don't. Now look, I'll see what my friend knows about Bob. If I get anything for you, I'll give you a call, OK?'

'Harry, we don't know for sure his death's connected to Noriko –'

'I'll see what I can find out.' Her tone had changed completely. 'I've got to go now.'

I rolled my phone in my palm for a minute. Monty, Noriko, Fat Blackmail, Korda, Devorty, Heathrow, Serbian gangsters, now Harry. None of it made any sense.

I needed the money. I needed to get on.

I was parked up just round from the Arndale in the city centre. Business started at eleven on Sundays. I schlepped in, looked for a sports shop and bought four big holdalls for the next day. I was back in the motor half an hour later.

I still needed a driver. I rang a couple of numbers: Paulie MacNee was in prison, Jimmy Davenport was out and he didn't have a mobile phone. I left a message for him to call me back as soon as. Under normal circumstances, without a full crew so late in the day, I'd be thinking about sacking the coup. At this rate I'd have to get Korda behind the wheel tomorrow morning.

Hmm.

I twisted the ignition and drove. There was a guy called Ray Sergeant who lived up in Hattersley. He was game and a decent wheelman. And he was always in on a Sunday. I'd go up and see him.

As I reached for my phone, I realised I only had one on me. I'd left the other one at the flat, shit. After the Friday night video, I didn't want to miss a call from Fat Blackmail. I'd whip up to Benchill first and schlep across to Ray's after.

The flat felt empty. I walked in calling Korda's name. No reply. Bobbing my head round his door I saw all his clothes had gone. *Fuck it.* What had he done, gone to the laundrette or something, the prick? I strode into the living room, then the kitchen. There was a note stuck to the fridge. Snatching it off, I read: *Thanks for everything Joker, but something's come up. It won't wait. Good luck.*

I went to the sink and burnt the note on automatic, letting the ash drop onto the aluminium and wash down the plughole. *Fuck it.* I didn't need the idea of Frank Korda running around town today. My mind was screaming this was all wrong. I didn't want to think what it meant – Korda splitting. And why now? What had *come up* for fuck's sake? I'd bought him that phone – who had he fucking called?

Bastard. Fucking cozzer bastard.

Then there was the flat. What if he got nicked and gave me up? Fuck it. I'd have to shift, and shift now. Prick.

I stormed into the bedroom and tore the sheets off the bed, laying one flat on the deck and dumping my clobber onto it. I knotted the ends into a bundle and shot into the kitchen, slung all the dirty dishes into the sink and ran some water. While the sink filled up I piled back into the lounge with a damp cloth and started wiping any surfaces we might have touched, where was the fucking remote, that would have both our dabs all over the –

Wait a minute. A noise in the hall. Key in the lock. Someone was letting themselves into the flat.

I walked lightly to the lounge door, snapped it shut to within an inch of the frame and stuck my eye up to the gap. The front door half opened, then came the sound of the key being slid out of the lock. A jingle as the bunch went into a pocket. Now it swung wide and someone stepped through, closing up behind him.

The light was off and his back was towards me. I only got his outline. Stocky. Bullet-head, shaved. Then he felt for the switch, clicked it on and turned towards me in one swift movement, face full on. I pulled the lounge door wide open but I didn't move. I couldn't. I just stood, cemented into the frame. The guy in the hall half-shrugged and smiled at me.

'Hello mate,' said Monty.

15

The clocks had stopped in the dark. I stared at Monty for hours.

'I said, hello mate.'

He held out a hand and took a step towards me. The smile faltered. Somewhere, a window shattered and I stumbled, back into the lounge. I couldn't speak. No words. He followed me.

'I saw you in your coffin,' I gasped. 'Noriko showed me. I watched her put a little purse of sovereigns in your hand. Something Japanese, she said –'

His voice was husky. 'Mate, mate, please. Let me explain –'

'Explain? You fucking explain. Why aren't you dead?'

'You got to hear me out –'

'You're dead! What's it all about, Monty? What the *fuck's* going on?'

'Listen, I need your help –'

I stepped up to him, grabbed his coat. It was real. He smelt of fags, sixty a day. This was no ghost. I jumped back and shouted at him.

'Sit down! Sit the fuck down, where I can see you.' He trotted to the sofa and sat, sinking into the cushions. Then he winced and rattled a box of pills out of his pocket, dropped a couple into his palm and necked them.

I watched all this breathing shallow, heart thumping.

A splash of running water from the kitchen. I'd left the tap on.

'Stay here,' I said, 'Jesus Christ,' and went and turned it off. I stood a moment over the sink, trying to get a grip. *Monty* . . .

Back into the lounge, expecting him to be gone like a ghost. Still there, staring dumbly at the carpet. His face looked older and thinner. And he'd shrunk some, under the coat. I dragged a chair across from the table and sat a few feet from him, legs either side and leaning on the back.

'Mate –'

I held up a hand for silence, then collected my thoughts as best I could. And as I did, I felt the anger boiling up. 'You're dead. Noriko's kidnapped. Devorty's been cut up and frightened to death. I bust Korda out of jail to get at your fucking money for Noriko's ransom. I'm looking at ten years for that, Monty. Ten years minimum.' I could hardly believe my own story. I stared at him, listening to the breath rasp through my pipes. 'Do you want to tell me what the fuck's going on?'

'I'm so sorry.' He wasn't looking at me. He was staring at the floor. The silence stretched out endlessly. And then I felt something go *click*.

'The kidnap,' I said, quietly. 'It was a scam.'

Nothing.

'Monty?' I said, my voice even softer.

He looked up at me. A watery set of eyes. And I got my answer. 'I needed you to get Korda out for me.'

Rage. One-hundred per cent proof. I was across the room, standing over him, shaking him by the coat like a dog. 'You cunt,' I shouted. 'You lousy fucking cunt. The funeral, the letter – you faked it all? And Noriko.' I wanted to kill him. 'Do you know what I thought? Do you know what I've done? Ten years of my life, all my life –' I had him by the collar now '– how could you fucking do that? How *could* you?'

'You got to hear me out, you got to,' he rasped. 'It's Noriko. Just hear me out, please, mate . . . '

'Mate? I'm not your fucking mate!' I wanted to give the old bastard a slap, a right fucking slap. Instead I grabbed him, shook him. I shook him again.

He wasn't going to fight back. His hands flopped by his sides. He was a sack in my fists. I let go like he was covered in boils, faced the wall and punched it, hard. The blood was pumping through my nut. I rested my forehead against the wall, trying to get myself under control. 'You tore her fingernail out,' I said, too softly for him to hear. Then I turned round and looked at him. I stared for a long time.

Monty shifted on the couch but held my gaze. His eyes were pale, his skin was sallow. He seemed diminished. Not the powerful villain I had known.

'Is the cancer real, out of interest?'

'Yes,' he whispered. 'That's real.'

'And Noriko?'

Now he was trembling. 'She's gone, mate,' he whispered.

Suddenly I felt very calm. Something had happened to this man in the last ten months. He was broken. Totally fucked. I stood, went to the kitchen and got him a glass of water.

'Thanks,' he said.

I sat down across from him. I could hardly bear to look at the old guy. 'So, what's your story?' I said.

He cleared his throat and began to talk. It was a long tale, stretching back more than forty years. This is what he told me.

*

Bradford, 1962.

Monty had a brother called Ted. Though the pair of them looked almost identical, he was younger than Monty and didn't have Monty's confidence or his animal cunning. Monty was the villain and Ted played catch up. The foot soldier to his brother's general.

Ted hung out with a little crew from Bradford. They were mods, and he spent a lot of time up there. This crew didn't do much, except maybe turn the odd chemist over for the pills, but they fancied themselves. Then one night there was some trouble over money. So they hopped onto their little mod scooters and went to shake down some Indian guy. But it all went wrong, and the Indian got killed. Mr Desai, that was his name.

I remembered the story in the envelope from Jenna Pleasing.

They all went down for it, Ted for being an accessory after the fact. He hadn't been in the room when Mr Desai got stabbed. He got four years.

'It was my fault,' said Monty. 'I should have been a better brother for him. I should have seen he wasn't cut out for the game, kept him away from those pricks in Bradford, but I didn't. The guilt fucked me up, good style.'

Ted did his time badly. He was pretty much broken when he got out, said Monty. After a while, he left London and went abroad. Monty had a letter about a year later, from Gibraltar. Then nothing. Years after, there was a letter from a Chinese bird in Hong Kong. She said she was Ted's wife and that he'd disappeared. She thought he might have gone back to England. There was a child, apparently.

'That was the last I heard,' said Monty. 'I didn't think Ted would leave a kid. I assumed he'd died or got himself killed. So that was it. But I had the guilt on my back. I blamed myself for how he'd turned out. He was my little brother. I should have looked out for him.'

Eleven months ago.

In January, Monty was diagnosed with cancer. He let the National Health Service do its bit for a while, but when the pain got really bad he looked elsewhere. He tried everything, anything, spending all of his long stocking in the process. Then there was the clinic in America.

Monty paused, looked me straight in the eye. 'I couldn't sleep, mate. I couldn't eat. And I had the fear. About my death. You drown, you know. Your lungs fill up with fluid and you drown in your hospital bed.'

America took the rest of his money, so he started borrowing. Then he fucked a couple of people for dough. He went on the methadone, organised his own supply, for the pain. The amount he was taking made him paranoid all round, though he didn't realise it. And then there was the charlie. To keep him going. It kept him awake at night, which didn't help his head. In time, he stopped being himself. His personality was getting scrambled. He was blanking me by now, and a lot of others. Then the cancer spread to his neck.

'Noriko was going crazy. She left me for a while, said she couldn't watch what I was doing to myself.' He broke off in a fit of coughing which lasted for five minutes. I watched his face turned red, then grey. I went to the kitchen and got him more water. He went on.

Bob Devorty then popped up with his coup. Monty knew him, but not well. Devorty had the Heathrow knowledge, but they needed an inside man. That's when Monty went to Korda. Normally he wouldn't have dreamt of it, but he was desperate. To his surprise the copper came in, equal partners. Somehow the caper went down all right. The money went abroad, but they had to wait while it got cleaned.

I nodded. 'I know, Monty.'

Then came the bit that should have been hardest to believe. But with Monty's cancer, and the drugs, and the madness, and his paranoia, and his fear of losing Noriko, and his fear of death and knowing how he was going to die, I saw how it had happened. How it had all unravelled.

July.

It was a Saturday morning and Monty was on his way to a Chinese doctor on the Fulham Road. He had been standing on a corner checking the house numbers when Ted walked up to him.

'I believed it and I didn't believe it,' said Monty. 'It was him, though. Apart from anything else, he still looked just like me.'

Ted had been searching for his brother for a couple of years. 'He'd had a lousy life,' said Monty. 'Never made much money, left a couple of kids with their mothers. He just scraped by most of the time, ran up some debts and moved on. I looked at him and saw a man who'd made no impact on the world.' Monty shut his eyes and was still. I thought of the body I saw lying in the coffin. Here it came.

'He was on the sick, stuck in a pissy little council flat. Did nothing with his life. Get up, shuffle out, buy a bit of grub. Watch TV, go to bed at four in the morning. It was like he was dead but he hadn't fallen over yet. Fucking sad sight.' He coughed, reached for his water.

Monty couldn't do much for Ted until he'd collected on Heathrow. 'After that, me, Ted and Noriko would find ourselves somewhere to dwell. I wanted to live in the sun for the time I had left. Go to Japan with the girl. And I could give Ted a few decent years, look after him. Balance the books.'

October.

Monty was getting heat for the money he owed. Serious heat.

Then he got the final word from the last doctor. They gave him six months. A few days after, word came through the money was ready, tucked up in a strongbox in Switzerland. Enough money to keep Noriko and Ted safe. Enough to sort Monty out with his pain-killer of choice.

But then Korda got nicked and what was left of Monty's world fell apart. He sent someone in to see the copper in Strangeways and the message came back: *Get me out.*

But he couldn't do it. He was out of dough. He owed everyone money and he'd fucked everyone off. He had a drug habit to deal with and needed all his energy just to stay alive. He was paranoid and scared and dying and he didn't trust anyone. Not even me.

Three weeks ago.

Monty went to see Ted in his Fulham flat. He let himself in and found his brother dead on the floor. Heart attack.

Monty paused in his story. It was easy enough to fill in the blanks. I went into Ted's flat, saw Monty sitting there staring at his brother's body. And then I understood.

'So that's when you decided, Monty,' I said. 'To have Noriko bury Ted, instead of you? To get away from all those people you'd fucked?'

He nodded, miserably. 'That was the start. I was out of my mind. And I just looked at Ted and I thought, how can someone die and leave nothing behind after more than sixty years on this fucking planet? But I was going the same way. I'd be dead in a few months and there'd be no one to look after the girl. It was the fucking waste, the horror, just the nothing of it all. The nothing.'

He bent slowly forward, his head fell into his hands. A few minutes and he straightened. His face was grey and pinched but his eyes were dry.

Monty called Noriko and talked her into it. Then he went to see Devorty. That wasn't too difficult – Bob was desperate for money. And he trusted the old guy.

They moved Ted's body. Noriko did her bit, dialled three nines and played the grieving widow. Said she'd found him on the floor. Monty was known to be dying, so there was no post mortem. If Noriko said the man on the slab was her husband, then he was her husband. So that was it. Ted was now Monty, and Monty was dead.

The old guy fell silent again. I could feel something swelling in my throat. I stood up and walked to the window. The sky was clouding over again. Looked like rain.

'Then what?' I asked. No reply. 'You wrote me that letter, Monty. Your last request.' Still no sound. I had to go on. I didn't want to, but I had to. 'And you took a Polaroid of Noriko, and sent it to me. You told me she was going to die unless I got your money. And then you sat back and waited for me to get Korda out.' I felt sick. 'Go on,' I said in a dull voice. 'Finish it off.'

'Devorty helped,' said Monty at last. 'He staged the kidnap. Went round to Chalk Farm, knocked some stuff around. Walked Noriko to the car. We knew Rose would be looking, that time of day. He brought Noriko to me in Ted's flat. That's where we stayed.'

I was still at the window. 'Rose was for my benefit,' I said. 'To make it convincing. You knew I'd go down and ask questions.'

'I don't know what to say, mate . . . ' He stopped. Coughed again. 'I thought you'd never do it. I didn't trust anybody. I thought . . . ' He fell silent again. I stared out the window. 'I couldn't ask you to do it. I couldn't find the words.'

I turned and saw the shame on his face. He hunched over, buried it in his hands. He stayed like that for a while. 'You have to understand,' he said, eventually. 'I was a mess. I was a fucking disgrace. I'd broken all the rules. I'm sorry, mate. I'm so sorry.'

My stomach was churning. Anger spiked through me. I tried to keep my head together and think. Where did this leave everything? I chased shadows again and gave up.

'Fuck this, Monty,' I said. 'Korda's gone and Devorty's dead. So no numbers, and no money. It's all been for nothing. Why are you here? To apologise? Well it's too fucking late. Go home to Noriko. Send her my love.' The anger was coming up again. I moved to the table, reached for my fags and sparked up. I wanted him to leave.

'I've not finished, mate.'

'Yes you have. Go fuck yourself. And fuck your wife, too.'

'I don't have Noriko any more. Someone's taken her.'

Then Monty began the final part of his story.

On Wednesday, he'd gone round to see Devorty and found him dead. He shot back to Ted's. The place was turned over, and Noriko was gone. Almost losing his mind, he left the flat and spent the night driving around in his car, looking for her. He had no idea what was going on: Devorty dead and Noriko gone – it fucked with his head. It took a while to get himself together. In the end, he made a decision. He'd come and find me. Soon enough, he remembered the Benchill flat. I'd forgotten he'd used the gaff last year. The old bastard still had a set of keys.

'Bullshit, Monty,' I said. Was I meant to believe him now, after all this? And if someone else had snatched Noriko, they knew that Monty was still alive and he was running a scam. Why would they have sent their demands to me? *Yes*, I thought. *The video text*. This might be one of the cruellest things I ever did, but it would show me if he was telling the truth now. I brought it up and gave him the phone.

'Press that,' I said. He did, and he watched. His face fell in on itself, and he started to cry. I could tell it was real. It was the truth, now.

While I listened to all this, night fell.

If it wasn't for his cancer, I'd have given Monty a leathering already. He told me to do it if it would make it right between us again. At one point, he got a knife out of the kitchen and striped his forearm a couple of times, showed me the blood. Like he'd run out of words. Run out of apologies.

And then there was Noriko. Someone had her. Someone who was expecting me, and a million quid, on Wednesday. Three days.

We talked on. There were a lot of questions, very few answers. It was hard to come to terms with this new Monty. I'd had the old villain on a pedestal and couldn't believe what he'd done. He fucked me – fucked with my head, and fucked with my future. If I'd gone down for springing Korda, I'd never have seen my kids again. Sara would have made sure of that.

But now, I started to see him again. Monty always had credit with me, right from the day I met him. I'd always been able to drop my problems on his toes, he'd always come onside. Even with all the lies and the deceit of the last week, I couldn't forget that.

And Noriko. How much could I blame her? She'd done what Monty wanted. I couldn't know how unwilling she'd been, how much he'd forced her.

In the end it came down to me wanting to believe him. Because if Monty had always been the fuck-goat he was today, then my life was worth the same lousy sack of shit that his was. All I had was the memory of when he was good. A straight face.

*

I told Monty about the bank in King Street and that he'd be driving. Then I called George and we made a meet by the Water Park. Monty took a bit of explaining, but in the end Georgie calmed down and we went over the details for the work tomorrow. Then I drove Monty up to the unit in Longsight and we cut a hole in the chain link fence round the back. Back at the flat, I spread a map of Manchester out on the floor and we went over the getaway. Then I told him to make up Korda's bed and go to sleep.

It was about half nine. I lay on the sofa with the lights off and tried to make the whole day a dream. I opened and closed my eyes, let my mind wander, hoping it would somehow refocus the afternoon and wake me up in a different place with a different future.

It didn't work. I went to bed and lay thinking of Noriko, frightened and bleeding. Was Monty asleep next door, or was he staring into the dark, or crunching more painkillers? I found I didn't care. My emotions had closed down completely and I was running on fumes.

I heard the old guy creeping along the corridor to the bathroom, then the sound of him pissing into the toilet. A pause, then more water splashing. I heard him grunt and he pissed again, just for a second.

My mentor was a sick old man and his body was closing down. In the end, he'd die screaming for his mother, just like the rest of us. I turned on my side and went to sleep.

16

I was standing in Dud's garage with Monty. Under the cold work light the old guy still looked rough, but better than he had yesterday. His outfit was OK. He'd do.

'All right,' I said, handing him a helmet. 'There's your ride.' I gestured to the moody security van. He nodded. There was a scratch of gravel on concrete as George stepped out from behind the motor, tucking in his tunic.

'All right, George,' I said.

George smiled briefly, then glanced at Monty and looked away. 'I'm fine, friend,' he said softly.

I turned and checked the gear laid out on the deck. Four grey security boxes, looking like small suitcases stood on their end, handles moulded into the top. A big sports bag folded inside each. A canvas bag by the boxes, zip open and about to spill its guts: bolt croppers, tape, drill, cuffs, all the rest. And resting gently on the top, the two handguns Georgie had brought that morning. They glinted at me dully.

I looked at my watch: five o'clock, Monday morning. Slotting my helmet on my nut, I dropped the visor. 'OK,' I said. 'Let's go.'

Monty drove with George and me in the cab. It was still dark and the traffic was thin. We flicked through Stretford and Hulme: closed-up shops and chemists with windows barred against the local smackheads.

Then the tape cut and we were pulling up at the bank in King Street, visors down for the cameras in the street.

I felt the chill as I jumped out and gave the road a quick coat. No one walking. A van pulled away a few hundred yards down, then turned the corner. Its light blinked out of sight. I went to open the street door as George and Monty shifted the gear out of the van. Twenty seconds and we were in the darkened foyer. Monty raised his hand in salute and stepped outside. Five more seconds and I heard our van fire up and drive. He'd be back later.

I stepped up to the bank door and slotted my key in the lock. I knew there was no alarm here because of the cleaners, but I still held my breath. And felt the levers move, click and slot into place. I pushed the door open and waved George through. Two quick trips for the gear. We were in.

Visors still down for the cameras inside, we locked up and headed across the carpet. Yellow streetlight picked out desks, seats and ads for low-rate mortgages. We let ourselves through the door by the counters and made for the lift. George pressed the call button.

Another cut. Now we were in the basement. We slid the gear out by the scrap of light filtering down the stairwell. No cameras here, good for us. Lucky lucky privacy law. I knocked up my visor and pulled out a skinny torch. Flicking my beam around, I took a couple of steps along the corridor to the vault doors. A quick flash on the locks and gates said nothing had changed.

'Is this it?' said George softly. His light flicked at the cleaner's cupboard we were going to spend the next few hours in.

'You got it.'

It was six by four – half the size of a prison cell. Opening up, our lights picked out mops, buckets, shelves of cleaning stuff. It was going to be an uncomfortable few hours.

'OK,' I said, reaching for the drill, an old-fashioned crank-handle type. I set to work to make a spyhole, to clock any action in the corridor. The wood was thick and it took a few minutes. I knelt and brushed away the sawdust. Time: ten past six.

'Think that's it, Georgie.'

'In we go, then.'

The gear went first, among the cleaning stuff. Guns on a shelf. Then George stepped in and folded himself into a scrap of space. I was going to have to stand. I shuffled in and pulled the doors closed behind us. We waited.

The waiting is always the worst part, particularly on heavy work and the work we were waiting on was very heavy indeed. Some say you shouldn't think of the price you'll pay if you're nicked. Me, I reckon it concentrates the mind. We were looking at fifteen apiece for starters if all this went tits up. The state frowns on armed robbery.

It wasn't meant to be this way. When I'd got the knowledge for this jug, my first thought was a screwer. So I'd brought in a bell man to deal with the alarms on the vault. He was the best I knew, and he'd never let a bell get the better of him yet.

The idea, he told me, was to read it with an oscilloscope, replicate it, then put his version on the bank's cable. It's known in the trade as fitting a loop. It meant the bells wouldn't go off when we started to cut and blow into the vault. But the guy had thrown in the towel. He said he could probably do it if he put in some time at home on his own gear, but time wasn't on our side. The original knowledge was a few months old and things could change.

I lifted my right leg and stretched it.

'Careful, friend.'

'Sorry George, was that you?'

'Uh huh.'

I went back through the plan in my nut. Every second Monday of the month, a security van delivered half a million pounds in what's called 'fit' money. Fit, that is, to go into the two busy cash machines outside the jug. It arrived just after half nine and was brought down here to the vault in the lift we'd just used.

There would be two people waiting. They would process the money into the smaller packets needed for the cassettes that fed the cash machines outside. Then they'd lock up and schlep upstairs to carry on their usury. It took around forty minutes. They could be male, female, or one of each. I was hoping for two men. On a blag, you always prefer to deal with men. Women are more likely to scream. They wouldn't be heard down here, but you could do without it.

I looked at my watch. Six fifty. George shifted and pushed against something. I heard one of our fake security boxes scrape across the concrete a couple of inches.

'OK down there George?'

'I could do with a stretch.'

'All right.'

We opened up and made like we'd got out of bed. And back inside, door shut.

We waited.

Seven thirty. George needed another stretch. I let him go first, then took my turn. One at a time, otherwise the two of us might get tangled piling into the cupboard together. I closed up and stuck my mince right up to the hole. Kept my eye fixed on the lift door.

Eight. A vibration from my phone, now switched to silent. Text from Monty. He was in position, ready to move in for the last act. Text back, stow the handset.

Ten past. When the work was done, we'd walk out, visors down. Not up in the lift to the bank, but out through a fire door. Opening the door would set off the alarm. This would give us cover as we split; there would be customers from the bank and workers from the offices milling around wondering if it was a drill or kosher.

Eight forty-five. Through the spyhole, I saw the lift fire up, ascending to the floors above. All quiet down here. I felt George reach for his helmet and hold it in his lap.

My back was starting to hurt. I hadn't drilled the spyhole quite high enough and had to bend slightly to look through. Mild ache at first, but now shooting pains were searing across both shoulders and up my spine. Fuck it.

Nine twenty. A whirr from the lift. And it was coming our way.

'We're on, George.'

He slid his helmet on. I did the same, visor up, then put my eye back on the hole in the woodwork. The lift doors opened. Two men – thank fuck for that. One a big lump, the other short and skinny. Both in their thirties. They walked past and opened the strong room using a key each, one tagged red, one tagged blue.

They were chattering about the weekend's football. Sounded like the big guy was a Red, the other a City supporter. The gate swung open and the big guy moved out of sight. Skinny stood just inside the gate checking a ledger. Then Big moved into view carrying a lidless trunk, heading for the lift. I heard Skinny on the phone inside the vault saying the floats were coming up.

Sound of the lift doors closing, whirr of the car going up. Quick glance at my watch. Nine twenty-five. Security van due any minute now. I counted seconds in my head, eye to the hole. Little and Large were banging on about football, backs towards us. Good.

The time came, as it always does. The phone in the vault jangled, Sid Little went to answer. I heard: 'Yeah? Cheers, Roger.' Clunk as the blower went down. Then the lift thudded and hummed and started to descend.

George was at my ear. He'd unrolled and stood silently over the last few minutes. He'd have his gun ready. Mine was on a shelf. I reached in the dark and curled my fingers round the butt. Time for the last move. I squeezed George's arm behind me. We swapped places, quiet, slow. He was now taking up the front, eye at the hole. I was behind his broad back, blind to the action now. The next bit was George's call.

Sound of the doors opening. Something dragged along the deck. A beat, then two. I was hardly breathing. I lowered my visor, felt the metal hinges rotate.

Sudden light and a crash of movement as Georgie slammed through the doors. I moved in his slipstream, darted left to come round in front of the panic button by the lift. What I saw was good. Big George had the two men by the scruff of their necks, pinned against the corridor wall. Two security boxes, one on its side, the other a foot further down towards the vault.

I grabbed Skinny, sliding my gun out and resting it on his temple. George did the same to Eddie Large. They were waxworks: faces rigid, eyes flicking up towards the steel pressed on their foreheads. I pulled up a fake Scouse accent and spoke.

'It is not in our interests to hurt you. We're here for the money. Do as you're told and everything will be fine. Do you both understand?'

Little and Large looked terrified. And blank. Little shook his nut. 'What?'

The buggers hadn't understood me. I moderated the tones and tried again.

'It is not in our interests to hurt you,' I said softly and firmly. 'We are here for the money. Do as you're told, and everything's going to be fine. Do you both understand?'

They nodded, slowly and in time.

'Good,' I said.

George stepped away. I turned to Skinny. 'What's your name?'

'Michael. It's Michael. Please, don't —'

'And what about your friend?'

'*What?*' Skinny went blank again.

The big man spoke up. 'Darren,' he gasped. 'I've got a wife and two kids. Please don't shoot.'

'No problem, Darren.'

George moved in with the tapes, cut to size and stuck on a small sheet of wood in our kit bag. He peeled them off and smoothed a strip across Darren's mouth and then Michael's.

'Darren and Michael: faces to the wall, hands behind your backs, lads,' I said.

They moved and Georgie snapped the ties on their wrists. We prodded them into the vault and roped them into chairs, faces to the wall. Stage one complete.

We could get to work.

Here was the vault: squatting in the middle, a Chatwood Milner safe, door wide open. A rack of steel shelving up to the ceiling. Metal step ladder folded up against the rack. The shelves were crowded with bags and boxes and a couple of cases. All the containers were tagged and all the boxes had padlocks. A table in the centre of the room for counting and sorting.

I motioned to George to help me shift this table across to the vault door. My job was to pack the boxes and watch the lift. George was to empty the Chatwood of its folding and bring the notes across for packing.

We got weaving.

The readies were split into 5K bundles and there were plenty of them. The trays from the safe were full of euros and bundles of fifties. I didn't count them – that would have been bad mazzle.

Nine thirty-five. I heard George get to work on the boxes with the bolt cutters: three big bundles of dollars and two gold Rolexes, cardboard tubes of Krugerrands, shiny and new.

Then the vault phone jangled, cutting the silence like a slap in the face.

George moved fast, swinging Big Darren off his chair, propelling him to the phone and stripping off the tape across his mouth. I jammed my shooter under the guy's chin and rasped, 'Here's your chance to prove you want to go home, Darren. If they want something, stall them. One word out of place and you're dead. Do you understand?'

He snapped a quick frightened nod *yes*.

'Good.' I picked up on the fourth ring and put the receiver at his ear.

'Hello?' Darren was looking straight into my eyes, though he couldn't see them through the visor. Yammering from the other end.

'No problem, but can it wait ten minutes? We're in the middle of some figures. Don't want to lose the thread.'

Yammer yammer.

'Fine. See you in ten.'

I replaced the receiver. 'What did they want?'

'Euros. Big withdrawal on the foreign counter. They're nearly out.'

He wasn't lying, I could tell.

'Well done, Darren.' George slapped the tape across his mouth again and walked him back to his seat. Then he nodded at a shelf of unopened boxes.

'No,' I said. 'Let's go.'

We packed the tools and shifted the boxes and bag to the foot of the stairs. Georgie darted back into the vault and was back with the two keys – one blue, one red. He closed the gates up, locking Darren and Michael inside. Meantime I flipped my mobile and sent the text to Monty to tell him we were on our way.

Georgie was back at my shoulder. I nodded.

The knowledge was that the fire alarm would not sound when we opened the door at the bottom of the stairs here, but it would when we came out at ground level. I twisted the handle and pushed it open. Not a sound. I slung the bag over my shoulder and picked up my boxes, one in each hand. Georgie had his. We started up, two steps at a time. At the landing on the ground floor, we stood and listened.

No glass pane to look through. Nothing to tell us what to expect on the other side. Too late to worry now. I dropped my boxes, grasped the bar, shoved it up and pushed.

The alarm screamed. I felt it drill into my nut, flooding the stairwell with noise. George stepped out first, the bigger man to meet any trouble head on. I stooped for my boxes and followed him out.

Only a few people. A couple stopped and dithered, wondering whether to leave or stay put. I looked at the bank doors. If there was going to be trouble, it would come from there.

We moved. Four paces and we were at the street doors. George held them open for me with his body. I glimpsed bank staff milling around on the other side of the glass, their faces saying, *Is this real or is it a drill?* They were too busy worrying about their customers to notice the two security guards walking across the shared lobby.

Two security guards carrying boxes and heading towards a security van. An everyday sight in every city in the country.

We walked swiftly for the van a couple of yards down from the door and piled in. Monty slipped into gear and pulled away. I watched the side mirror as we moved. Cashiers and customers on the pavement. They looked confused but not worried. No one had done a headcount yet. No one had noticed Darren and Michael were missing.

The lights were on our side as we swung out into Cross Street. Red as we hit Albert Square, but we were front of the pack. Monty pulled the van left and we were heading south. OK.

Georgie had gone over the seats into the back; he was at the rear window, looking for trouble.

'Anything, George?'

'All clear.'

We were still visors down, for cameras. Bit suss to anyone who looked, but no one did, of course. The world was too busy with its own life.

Traffic thinned as we pulled away from the centre. I began to relax a notch. Nearly done. Christ, we'd swum the Channel on this one. Slapped together, short notice, dead man on the firm. I wondered if my luck would hold for Fat Blackmail and the rest.

Then it all shattered.

'Fuck, fuck.'

Monty saw it first, I was a split second behind him. A few yards down, a Toyota swung out of the cark park by the big Chinese, misjudged the distance, hit a Transit van and skidded into the path of a bus on the other side of the road. The bus swerved into an HGV and that was it. Horns and shouting all over the shop and all four lanes ahead blocked. We were tucked up behind a Mini. A glance in the side mirror told me there was no way back. We were going nowhere. We were fucked.

Fuck fuck fuck.

Wait a minute.

One chance: stick the prize and the helmets in the holdalls and split on foot. 'George,' I hissed. 'Open the boxes, get the dough in the hold-alls, quick –'

'No.' It was Monty, his voice cracking but calm. He took charge. 'If we move that Mini in front, there's a gap. I can just about do a U-turn.'

The film cut and we were on the street, visors down. The uniforms worked, they always do. Monty ordered the driver of the Mini out, we each grabbed a wheel arch and bumped the motor about three feet left. Sirens in the distance – filth for the smash-up. Better fucking move. All back in the van. Monty did the turn and trimmed the mirror off a 4x4. Fuck that. Left and left and we were on Oxford Road. Monty gunned the engine for Longsight and the slaughter. I wiped the sweat off my palms on the front of my shirt, leaving a dark blue stripe down each side.

17

Half ten that night and I was back in London, walking fast down Edgware Road. It was noisy and thick with traffic.

I saw young lads chatting on flash mobiles, a mile-long pink limo with a hen party hanging out the windows, late-night shops for unlocking mobile phones, two men tooting hookahs, burger bars and a fruit shop, a tired-looking woman closing up for the night.

I was thinking about Korda. A bent copper who played straight. Had me believing he cared about Noriko then fucked off. Why? Where had he gone? How did he fit in to this crazy fucking Fat Blackmail caper? I chased shadows, lost them again. Gave up. Monty had an idea about finding Korda. Leave it till then.

I'd driven down with the old guy that evening. The day in Manchester had gone swiftly after the work. We'd dumped the van at the Longsight slaughter and left George to torch it, he used the hole in the fence to skip out. Monty and me had driven the Saab to the Britannia Hotel, taken a room. Georgie joined us for the chop-up soon after. He took the Krugerrands, tom and dollars and agreed to let us have the cash for Noriko.

And then we split. After the exes for Roman the cleaner, who'd sorted the keys, Dud the garage guy and old Tom, there was half a million quid in the back of the car.

Monty slept most of the way down. We hit town about nine and checked into the Metropole, a bed factory on the Edgware Road. I got us a twin room.

'They'll think we're a pair of gingers,' said the old guy as we made our door on the sixth floor.

'I don't give a fuck what they think,' I said, and left him alone while I went to hide the dough.

I took the two holdalls with the cash and walked a few hundred yards up the road, looking back to see that Monty wasn't following. I made for another bed factory where I checked in for a couple of nights. There, I whipped the side off the bath and stashed the dough behind the panel. Right now, I didn't know what the fuck was going on and I sure as fuck wasn't going to give Monty the chance to leg it with the folding. That's why the prize had to go well away from his eyes.

I finished putting the side back on the bath, stood and stashed the screwdriver in my jacket.

'What's the deal with this gaff on the Wishwood estate, Monty? Tell me again.'

It was now almost eleven on the Tuesday evening. We were sat in our room at the Metropole, eating the sandwiches I'd picked up on the way back. The old guy was sitting hunched over, chewing slowly and not meeting my eye. He sighed and looked up.

'It's Korda's bolt-hole,' he said huskily, cleared his throat. 'His dad's place. He held onto it when he died, kept the rent up when he was in the army. And after. No one knows about it. The filth didn't raid it when he was lifted, so not even they know. It's where he'll have gone.'

'Unless he had secrets from you.' I tore a corner off my roll and chucked it down. First time I'd eaten all day. Monty hunched over and took another bite. His hands trembled.

'Why did you do it, Monty?' I said.

He looked up.

'Why?' I repeated. 'All those lies. Why didn't you just come to me and ask?'

'How old are you, mate?' he said quietly. 'How old? I've forgotten.'

'Thirty-nine.'

He grunted, played with his food. 'I'm seventy-one and I've got cancer.'

'And?'

'You don't know what it's like to be my age and this sick. Remember how fit I was? Well, it's like this: first of all you can't run so fast. Then you can only jog on a good day. Then the day comes you know there's no point. Your lungs, your legs, they're just going to get worse.'

He took another bite. I noticed crumbs and bits of food down his front. Like someone who didn't care.

'And then you notice all the closed doors. All the chances you had you never took. When I was a kid the summer lasted forever. Last summer went before I noticed it start.'

He looked down at his half-eaten food and shook his head. Screwing up the paper, he dropped it in the bin.

'Did Frank tell you I used to take him and the other kids for football?'

'He told me.'

'There was a place down in Brighton I used to take them, for a kickabout, a bit of a walk. Devil's Dyke. Big fields and a fucking great slope, drops right away really sharp. I think I took you there once.'

'I remember.'

He coughed. I waited while he sorted himself out. 'You know when you walk across the Downs from the hotel, that little fort you get to?'

'Some kind of Victorian folly. Half ruined.'

'That's it. We'd drop a couple of coats for goalposts. Five a side, you know the style.'

I looked at my watch. It was getting on. 'If you say so, Monty.'

'Well, this day, the kids were playing, I was watching. Then Frankie Korda gives the ball a fucking great whack and it flies right up over their heads and starts bouncing for the slope. We all jogged to the edge. Ball had gone too far already. Steep. We just stood and watched it bounce. Bang, bang, bang, hitting the ground, speeding up. Then another spin and it was gone. And that was it. Had to go home.' He gave a little wheeze of a laugh. 'Rest of the kids were well pissed off at Frankie.'

I stared at him. Why was he telling me this bollocks? 'Get to the point, Monty. If there is one.'

He looked at me, gave an embarrassed smile. 'Sometimes you get ideas in your head. Things that happen – they just stick there. Won't go away.'

He rattled out his pills and necked a couple.

'Strange thing. After that, whenever a bit of work went wrong, or I ended up in the jug, all my life, I always thought about that football getting away from me. But I changed the end. In my head, I climbed down the slope, poked around, found it. I always imagined finding it.' He paused then gave me a sudden smile. It was so like the old Monty, it took me by surprise. 'Wherever I was, I just imagined having that football back. I imagined that the kids got to carry on playing football, just the way they should have done. It was like whatever was bad, whatever I was facing, I could get through it. And I always did.'

I shrugged. 'Go on.'

'This is going to sound like bollocks,' he said. 'But it changed with the cancer. When they told me in January I tried to go after the ball. I mean in my mind, mate. Like I used to.' Now his face fell. 'But I couldn't get off the edge and down the slope. I was just stood there, watching it bounce away.'

'Why are you telling me this, Monty?'

He coughed, raised his head and met my eyes.

'I don't expect you to forgive me,' he said quietly. 'I just want you to know why I did it. I couldn't see an end to the story any more, mate.' His breath rasped in his chest. 'Do you know how it feels to be completely and utterly helpless?' I looked away. 'I just hoped that if I set it up right, you could write the end for me.'

Then suddenly he dropped his head in his hands and started crying, shoulders heaving with sobs, wheezing as he gasped breath in. After a few minutes, he looked up at me, eyes running and cheeks wet.

'What have I done? What are they doing to her, mate?' he whispered. 'What are they doing?'

There was a long silence. 'We need to get going,' I said.

Korda's secret gaff was on the second floor, along a concrete balcony. No lights. I paused at the door for a second. I had no idea what the cozzer's game was and I was right on edge. I loided the lock gently, leant on the woodwork. We stepped inside. The gaff felt empty. I switched on the light.

The place had been turned over, and turned over savagely. Chairs slashed, cupboards emptied, carpets torn up. In the bedroom, someone had skinned the mattress down to the springs; pillows were torn apart and feathers lay everywhere. The floor was rubble. Even the bath panel had been smashed. I climbed across the piles of broken furniture in the lounge and drew the curtains.

'Any ideas, Monty?'

He shook his head. 'None.'

'Are you sure?' I didn't have the strength to be angry. 'Sure this wasn't you? Or Korda, laying another trail of lies for me on your behalf? More mischief?'

'No, mate.'

'No, mate.' I didn't believe him. But I didn't think he was lying either. I didn't know what was true anymore. I had absolutely no touchstone left.

'You know,' I said. 'I can't even be bothered to talk about this. I don't care who did it. I don't care if it was Fat Blackmail or you or Korda or Noriko or Bob Devorty come back to life.'

'There's a way we can find out,' said Monty.

'I'm not interested in a séance, if that's what you're about to suggest. I'm already dealing with one dead man, and that's quite enough trouble for one day.'

The tiniest smile flickered across Monty's face. 'You don't have to trust me,' he said. 'Frank's got a stash. Come here.'

He stepped out into the hall. I followed as he got down on all fours and started pushing at the skirting board with his palms. It started to shift. With a grunt, he slid it up and out. There was a gap behind it.

'Goes right back into the wall,' he hissed. He slid his hand in and groped around, found something and pulled. Out came a slim silver flight case. 'Creature of habit, our Frankie,' he muttered to himself.

Back in the lounge with the light on I sat on the torn-up sofa and clicked the case open. Inside: five grand in thousand-quid wraps; false passport and driving licence with Korda's mugshot on both. Another passport: I flipped it open. For a woman, name of Jane Ballantine. Olive skin, bobbed black hair, big eyes and a nice smile. There were a couple of grey files in the case too. A few sheets of paper in each: photocopies, lists of names, lists of bank accounts. A couple of charge sheets.

'This is stuff Korda's copied from police files,' I said. 'And there's something else, a smudge.' It was a geezer, thickset with a couple of days' stubble on a very square jaw. He had thick black hair, little tails flicking out from behind his neck; it almost touched his collar. And I'd seen him before, I knew it. Where the fuck? I flipped the snap, a name printed on the back: Predrac Bassam.

I held the picture up. 'Do you know him?'

Monty had been sitting back, resting. His face was tired and his eyes opened very slowly. 'Never seen him before.'

I thought back to Highgate and the tall guy I saw at the end. The long hair, the jaw like a paving stone. *He took long strides through the gates and nodded at me as he passed, as if we knew each other.*

'Well, he knows you,' I said. 'He turned up to your funeral.'

'Really?' Monty sat forward, took the snap and studied it. 'Swear I've never seen him, mate.' I was sure he wasn't lying.

There was another snap under the files. Korda, with his arm thrown over a woman's shoulder. The same woman, Jane Ballantine. Same nice smile. Stood next to them was another guy with a moustache. Police issue.

'How about this?' I handed it across. Monty glanced at it.

'That's Frank, of course. The bird . . . I met her a couple of times. She's called Carmen. Carmen Pinto. She was Frankie's girl. Other guy, no idea.'

'Any idea where Carmen Pinto is?'

He shook his head. 'But she was the reason he did Heathrow. So they could go away –'

'And start again. How touching,' I said.

'He loved her, mate.'

'Did he.' I didn't believe anything about Korda. And maybe Monty didn't know him as well as he thought.

'You sure about the bird?' I asked. Monty nodded. 'Because here,' I dropped the passport in his lap, 'she's called Jane Ballantine.'

'I'm pretty sure,' he said. 'But my memory's not what it was.' He shrugged and handed the gear back. I dropped it in the case with the rest.

'Well, at least we know Frank's not been back here since . . . well, all this,' said Monty. 'Not with his stash still in place.'

'And he fucked off from Manchester yesterday,' I said. 'I wonder where he is? Maybe he's crashed on a chum.' I looked up. 'Maybe he's staying round your pad in Chalk Farm, Monty. Maybe you gave him the keys. Maybe he's waiting outside for us now, or maybe he's down the hotel having it away with the half mill, then you and him and Noriko are going to Disneyland for a couple of weeks. Maybe he's going to spend his cut on a sex-change operation and call himself Francesca.'

Monty took all this without reaction. Dead man walking. I stood up. 'OK, let's leave Frankie-boy a message.' I tore a corner off one of the files, wrote my phone number and JOKER on it. I gave it to Monty. 'Stick that behind the skirting and cover it up. Go on.'

I watched him do it. He slid the wood back in place and we left, taking the case with us. Back at the hotel, he was in the bathroom when my phone rang. Harry.

'Thought you'd still be up.'

I looked at my watch: ten past one. 'Didn't realise it was so late. Are you back in Manchester, Harry?'

'Still in London.' The dull acoustic told me she was inside. 'I've got something for you. It's a name: Adrian. He had something to do with Bob Devorty's death.'

I sat up straight. 'Says who?'

'Bush telegraph. My friend who runs that co-op. Couple of other girls too.'

I was breathing light. Maybe a scrap of hope.

'Who is this Adrian?'

'Some Serbian thug. A pimp.'

My brain raced. *Kidnap, it's an East European crime, Korda said.* 'Where is he?'

'Don't know. He's got lots of fingers in lots of pies, but he's very careful.'

'So how do I find him?'

'Talk to some whores. That's what I'm going to do.'

'Harry, no. You've done enough.'

'I'll decide that.'

'No you fucking won't! Just leave it . . . please.'

'I knew her. She was a nice girl.' She was so quiet I could hardly hear her.

'Harry –'

I heard the jingle of doorkeys. 'It's OK. I'm just going to make a few calls,' she said. 'See a couple of people, that's all. Adrian's mainly north London. Why don't you start there? Talk to some girls.'

I sighed. Truth was, I needed all the help I could get.

'All right, but you be careful. And thank you.'

I hung up as Monty came out of the bathroom.

'Ever heard of a Serb pimp called Adrian?' I said.

'No,' he said. He doubled up coughing for a minute, then straightened up and wiped his mouth. Red spots on each cheek.

'Did you ever fuck any Serbs for dough?'

He looked embarrassed. 'Done business with a couple,' he said. 'But we're OK.'

I was too tired to know if I believed him or not. I went into the bathroom, taking Frank Korda's case with me. Korda knew a lot about Serb gangsters. What the fuck was going on? Where was he?

Monty was asleep when I came out. I padded over to the bed, stuck the flight case under my mattress and climbed in. I was exhausted. I felt the case push up through the springs and make a little bump under me. It was the only thing that felt real, just then.

18

Tuesday morning, eight o'clock.

I should have known it was a lie.

We were sat on a bench in Russell Square eating bacon rolls from the cab drivers' hut on the corner. The same bench we sat on before we went into the Imperial for that business with Jimmy G. I remembered the lines from Monty's letter, the one Noriko had given me after the funeral. *I can see the gaff clearly from here, I can even see the window of the room we met Jimmy in.*

I looked up. There it was. Only he shouldn't have been able to see it; not back then, when he said he was writing. There would have been too many leaves on the trees in August. They'd have blocked the view.

'Enjoying your food, Monty?' I bit into my roll. He nodded but looked wary. Maybe he caught my tone. I bunched the wrapper, slung it in a bin and waited for him to finish.

'OK,' I said. 'Maybe Korda will call me, maybe he won't. As far as I see it we have two options: we can wait around for ten tomorrow and the call from Fat Blackmail mark two, or we can follow up any ideas we've got and look for Noriko. We might get lucky.'

Monty started coughing. It went on for a while. 'I want to try, mate,' he said at last. His face was the colour of old newspaper. 'We might turn something up.'

'It's either that or the London Eye,' I said, and sat forward. 'That call I got last night. Word is that Bob Devorty's death was down to a Serbian gangster called Adrian. Let's look at what we actually know. You go round to Devorty's and he's dead. You go back to Ted's flat and Noriko's gone. The two are almost certainly connected. Or it's a fucking big coincidence.'

Then I told him what Korda had said: kidnap, signature crime, Stanley cuts, the trial, Carmen Pinto.

'And now your little Frankie fucks off,' I said. 'So what's his fucking game, Monty? Any ideas?'

Monty blanked my tone on Korda. 'Whoever did for Bob has Noriko,' he said.

'Maybe,' I said. 'But this Serb connection is all we've got. Adrian's a big-time pimp, he must be known. You said you had it with some Serbs.'

'Did a couple of deals with them. Some brown I ripped off from a firm in Leeds. Don't know them well, though.'

'Can you raise them? Find out if they know this Adrian?'

'One of them has a few bricks in a caff in Green Lanes. I can go up.'

I looked at my watch. 'All right, let's move. We've got a little over twenty-four hours before Fat Blackmail makes contact. We need to get weaving.' I brushed crumbs off my front and made to stand. Monty stayed put.

His head nodded forwards into his hands. 'What are they doing to her, mate?'

'She's merchandise. They'll be looking after her.'

'Apart from tearing her fucking fingernail out, you mean?'

It was the first time he'd showed any anger since he'd risen from the dead. 'Just try and focus, eh?' I said.

He wiped the back of his hand across his mouth and pulled out a pack of fags. 'You want one?'

I thought about his cancer but said nothing. 'All right.' We lit up. I gave him a minute to calm down.

'While you're calling on your Serb chums, I'm going to buzz round a few knocking shops. See if this Adrian is as famous as he's cut up to be.'

He tugged on his smoke and nodded. Then he coughed for a full minute. Hawked and spat on the deck.

'You done?' He nodded. I stamped out my half-smoked fag, thinking of Korda and the Serb trial, the witness he was nicked for giving up.

'Was Korda ever bent for anyone else?' I said. 'Apart from you?'

'No.'

'You sure?'

'He never did it for money. It was friends with Frank; not dough.'

I thought of how the young Korda had got Monty out of Charing Cross nick. Nothing happens in isolation.

'All right,' I said, 'let's go. Call me if you get anything. And be careful.'

'All right.' He stood. 'Be seeing you, mate.'

'Yeah. Be seeing you.'

I waited for him to cross the square and bob out of sight, then I fished out the photos from Korda's stash. I'd whipped up to the other hotel and stuck the case under the bath this morning, but I'd kept back the snaps and some of his money, for exes. He owed me, anyway.

I looked at the picture of Predrac Bassam. Who was he? It worried me: the man was at Monty's funeral. Now his smudge turned up connected to Korda somehow. And where the fuck had Korda gone anyway? Some very nasty connections started to take shape in my nut, but none of them fitted together.

Then I looked at the snap of Korda, Carmen Pinto, and the geezer with the moustache. I knew the guy with the moustache, though I'd not let on to Monty last night. Pulling out my phone, I punched in a number. The switch at Bootle Street nick in Manchester answered. I asked to be put through to Sergeant Dave Craze.

'He's not here any more,' said a bright voice.

'Do you know where he is now?'

'I'm afraid I can't tell you,' she said.

I hung up and dialled another number. Three rings, and Harry answered.

'Harry, you all right?'

'Hi, yeah I'm fine.' The background told me she was outdoors, somewhere with plenty of traffic. 'Got nothing for you yet.'

'Harry, are you seeing Dave Craze again?'

There was a long beat. I heard a bus rumble past.

'I told you not to go there,' she said. I could hear the anger.

'Harry, I need his number. It's important.'

Silence.

'Is it about Noriko?'

'Yes.'

She sighed and I thought I caught the start of a sob. 'I'll see if he'll let me,' she said. 'I'll call back.'

She hung up. I tapped the photo against my knee. If she didn't give up his number, I could probably track him down but it would take time. Five minutes later and the phone rang. It was her.

'I gave him your number. He says he'll call you.' Her tone was sharp. 'Sometimes you really push it, you know that?' She hung up.

Last time Harry got into Dave Craze for me, she paid quite a price. Feeling bad, I walked out of the square and hailed a cab.

Midday. I was walking past Pentonville nick and it had started to rain. As I passed the grim cream-coloured walls, I wondered if anyone I knew was in there. I'd never done time in the 'Ville myself, but it had a reputation as a right screws' nick a few years back – one of the places the prison service sent you if you didn't toe the line.

After I'd spoken to Harry, I'd spent an hour in an internet café near King's Cross. I turned up a few message boards where men who used prostitutes reviewed their experiences. The posts gave all the details, addresses of flats and brothels, the lot. I scribbled down a list for north London and got weaving.

I'd called on a few likely flats as a punter. Then I'd flashed some of Korda's cash and asked a few questions. Nish. If any of the woman I met had heard of Adrian, they weren't talking.

I was heading for my fifth gaff now. The message boards gave it plenty of good reviews. Can't say I was looking forward to the visit, though.

I passed a dry cleaners and realised I'd overshot. Turning on my heel, I counted the shops back up the road. Here it was. A blue-fronted gaff with big windows of opaque glass. It called itself City Lights Spa and claimed to be a health and sauna club. I pushed at the door. It didn't give. I saw a white bell with 'Press' scribbled in red biro on a scrap of card jammed behind it. I pressed. Movement from inside and then the door buzzed. I was in a tiny lobby, with a Perspex window on the right and an empty chair behind it. A woman appeared. She looked like Denis Norden in drag.

'Are you open?'

'Always open here,' said Denis in a light Irish accent. 'Twenty for the half hour, thirty for an hour. Prices in the room start at forty.'

'I'll take a half hour, thank you.' I pushed three tens through the gap under the Perspex. She picked up a folded white towel with one hand and scrabbled about under the counter with the other. There was another buzz and the shabby white door in front of me clicked open.

It was a big room, crowded with women dressed like they were off to a nightclub. A jumble of cocktail dresses, spangly tops, straw Stetsons; a pair of denim shorts with a big buckled belt stamped BOY TOY; red high heels, black high heels, tiny black dresses and calf-length patent-leather boots. Some women were sitting on a bench along the wall, a couple played a pokey machine pushed in the corner, one was eating rice out of a Tupperware box. All of them carried small white clutch bags. And they all looked up at me. Two or three smiled.

Denis Norden appeared at my shoulder and handed me the thin white towel. 'Who would you like?' she said.

Roll the dice. 'Who's the newest?'

She pointed to a woman in her twenties hitting the pokey machine. 'Holly's not been here long.'

Holly: tall; tiny white shorts; skimpy white shirt; high white heels. Her own heels were red with the drying skin from an old blister. She smiled at me and her teeth were grey.

I told her my name was Paul and she led me downstairs, past a sad-looking Christmas tree. The air got warmer and damper. We were in a wide, white-tiled corridor, wood-panelled doors left and right. I glimpsed a line of showers as we moved, a door open onto a Jacuzzi, a room with a massage table. Holly stopped at a door and knocked. No answer. She pushed it open and waved me in.

The small room was panelled with dark wood from floor to ceiling. There was a red floor-light and a wooden bench built into the wall with a thick brown plastic mattress laid on it. A folding metal chair on a hook. It felt like a ship's cabin and it smelt of baby oil and wet wipes. Holly clicked the door shut and slid a tiny gold bolt across.

'Now we are private,' she said. An accent I couldn't identify. I sat on the bench. The plastic squeaked and I pulled my coat round me, chastely.

'Where are you from, Holly?' I asked.

'From Croatia.'

'You like it, here?'

'In London, yes.' She held her clutch bag in front of her, snapped it open and closed. 'Would you like a massage?'

'Your English is pretty good,' I said.

'Thank you.' Click open, click closed.

'How much is the full service, Holly?'

She looked relieved. 'One fifty.'

I took out three hundred quid in fifties, handed them across. 'You want to talk for a bit?' I said. She took the cash, stuffed it into her bag, snapped open the metal chair and sat.

'Are you a journalist or police?'

'Neither.'

She reached into her bag and pulled out a pack of long thin cigarettes. She lit up and leant back, blowing the smoke at a vent in the wall.

'The journalists bore me shitless. They never have money and they want me to tell them about celebrities who come here. The police let you see their warrant card and expect you to fuck them for nothing.'

Her English really was very good. I told her so.

'I'm a university graduate, Paul.' *Bingo*, I thought. 'Do you want counselling? Some of the guys who come here just want to talk. I call it counselling: they talk and look and don't feel bad when they go home to their wives or whatever.'

'I'm not police and I don't work for the papers.'

'Myrtle thought you did. That's why she pointed you at me. So what do you want, *Paul*?'

This girl was giving me a hard time. I was right on the back foot and I felt ridiculous, but I asked the question anyway. 'Tell me how you got here.'

'I paid someone fifteen thousand pounds to get me to England and get me false papers. Well, he lent it to us. We knew we had to pay it back. When we arrived, me and my friend, they showed us some jobs. Waitress, cleaner, and this one. How long does it take to make fifteen thousand as a waitress?' She snorted and opened her hands wide. 'So, I chose this job. I don't like it, but it's quicker. So what?'

'What about the other girls?'

'You like questions, don't you?' She blew smoke and shifted from one hip to the other. 'They all chose this, far as I know. I don't talk to them much. I just do my shifts and go home. I've been here two months and I've paid back three thousand pounds. I made a choice. So?'

It didn't sound like much of a choice to me, but who was I to say. In any case, she understood money. And I was out of time.

I pulled out a couple of fifties and held them up. She eyed them for a moment, opened her bag and let me drop them in. I nodded *thanks*. 'How did you end up here, Holly? Who showed you the jobs?'

'There was some guy. He's been here a long time. Speaks good English. He met me at the airport, showed me my new British passport and took my Croatian one.'

'What did he look like?'

'Tall, thick black hair, kind of heavy.'

I felt a door creak open. 'Was this guy Croatian?' I asked.

'No. Serbian, I think.'

'Do you have a name?'

She looked at the clutch bag for answer. Another fifty went in.

'He called himself Adrian,' she said. 'I stayed in a place he owns when I arrived.'

Adrian. The tension cracked up my spine. 'Can I have the address?' I said, and held up another fifty.

This time she shook her head. And glanced at the door. Now she looked anxious. Maybe she thought I would get nasty. At that moment I saw it all, despite her confidence and her calm. Men were different to her. They paid her and she fucked them. And sometimes they fucked her over. She might have known what she was getting into, but a set of lousy choices is no choice at all.

I laid down five hundred quid in fifties on the bench. I counted them out slowly, one by one. Then I shifted away from the cash and looked at her.

'Please,' I said. 'I think he's got a friend of mine.'

There was a long, long beat. Then she picked up the dough, folded it and stuck it in her bag. And gave me an address in South Kensington. After that, she glanced at her watch.

'Time's up,' she said. 'If you want to stay longer, I'll have to go upstairs and give them another thirty.'

'One minute.' On impulse, I pulled put the snap of Predrac Bassam from Korda's stash and held it out. 'Seen him before?'

She looked at it. I tried to read her face but there was nothing there.

'Yeah,' she said carelessly. 'Adrian. That's him.' She looked up, saw the surprise in my face. 'He's a guy with fingers in a lot of pies.' *Exactly*

Harry's words. 'Connected to everyone but works for himself. The address I gave you, he has a flat at the top. The rest of the house is for working. Girls, plenty of girls. That's where to find him.' She snapped her bag closed. 'Time's up.'

I followed her up the stairs. Denis was stood with a guy in a business suit, helping him choose a woman to take downstairs. She glanced at Holly and their eyes met. Holly gave her the tiniest of nods. I split.

Walking quickly down Caledonian Road I felt the fear. Adrian was flavour of the month for doing Devorty. And Adrian's smudge was in Korda's stash. And Korda had fucked off. With Korda's track record I didn't know whose fucking side he was on, but it started to smell like he was buddies with the Serbs.

I saw another plot, with Korda pulling the strings. One where he got into bed with a Serbian crew. Gave up a witness for execution, then called in the favour. And sorted it with them to fuck Devorty and Monty for the Heathrow dough. There were bits that still didn't fit, but this looked very fucking bad.

It came on to rain. Big heavy rain. I started to run.

19

I was back at the Metropole with Monty half an hour later.

The old guy had managed a meet with the Green Lanes Serbs. They'd named Adrian. They knew him well and they did a lot of business with him. He ran a bunch of working flats and he organised work for women who'd paid to get here from home. They reckoned he was a reliable guy.

'I'll bet he is,' I said grimly.

'Yeah,' said Monty. 'He's not the guy to go to if you want to bring someone in, but he takes over at the port or airport, sorts things from there. Most of the girls end up as prostitutes.'

I jammed in a fag and glared down at the traffic on Edgware Road. 'Anything else?'

'Adrian used to work with a big crew. They got nicked a while back for bringing in girls. Filth thought Adrian was connected but he slipped through the net. One of the crew went Queen's Evidence, went on witness protection. He got shot, murdered.'

'Frankie Korda's trial,' I said quietly. 'Surprised you didn't know about that already.' Monty just shrugged. I pulled out the snap of the geezer we found in Korda's gaff and thrust it out towards Monty.

'Remember this?' I said. 'The cunt might have been born Predrac Bassam, but these days he calls himself Adrian.'

The old guy didn't take it in. 'What do you mean?'

'One of the girls identified him just now. This is Adrian. Adrian, who we're hearing did Devorty. Adrian, who might have Noriko. And his snap's tucked up in Frank Korda's bolthole.'

Monty's face fell in. 'Maybe Frank was after him,' he spat. 'For fuck's sake, the gaff was turned over. Fucking rubble. Someone's after Frank, that's what it is.'

'No, Monty. I think Frank Korda's been on earners from this lot for years. Frank Korda gave that witness up, and now they're returning the favour. Frank Korda and Adrian are Fat Blackmail.'

Confusion piled into the old guy's face. He slumped on a bed. 'What about the girl, Carmen? He was in love with her.'

'He was or he wasn't, what does it matter? Frank Korda was playing you, Monty. Right from the start. He set you up.'

'No!' He was half shouting. 'Frank wouldn't do that to me. He couldn't! We were that close.'

'Yeah,' I said. 'And look at the difference that makes.'

I turned my back and leant on the window. From behind I heard the rattle of his pills and a long, raw cough. Then nothing. The silence built. I turned back and looked at Monty, hunched over and staring at the deck. He looked pretty much done in.

'They're setting a trap for us,' I said. 'Tomorrow won't be about no million quid for Noriko. It'll be about getting your numbers. For Noriko.'

'Depends if Bob Devorty talked before he died,' said Monty quietly.

'He talked,' I said.

My phone rang a few minutes later. Marcus. I looked down at Monty. He was lying on his bed, face to the wall. I could feel his despair. I told

Marcus I'd call him back from outside. I took the lift down to the street and punched in his number.

'Good news, mate,' he said. He sounded like there was a sale on at Damart. 'We housed one of the jurors last night. And it's in the right part of town – he dwells in Cheetham Hill. He'll need a visit tomorrow, latest. They're due to go out the day after. Can you do it?'

I'd almost forgotten about Casey. I felt guilty. 'I'll go tomorrow night. I'm in the Smoke right now, but I'll be back in time.'

'You sure?'

'Yeah.' We hung up. I had no idea when I'd be back; I'd have to organise someone to go in my place. Not Marcus. The juror would get edgy if Marcus turned up, with him sitting in the public gallery every day.

The phone rang again. It was Dave Craze.

Craze took some persuading, but he eventually agreed to meet in a coffee shop off Warren Street. I left Monty at the hotel, still rolled over on the bed.

Dave Craze was already tucked away in the corner of the gaff when I got there, nursing a vat of coffee. I nodded, bought something for myself as rent and sat down at his table. He was watching the door.

'Let's be quick,' he said. 'You know what happens if I'm seen with you.'

'Where's Harry?' For a second, I thought he'd get up and walk.

'She went back up north this morning,' he said. Sounded like she'd taken my advice, at last.

I took a sip of coffee. Fucking hot. 'How long have you been down here, Dave?'

'About six months, like it's your business. I transferred in the spring. My dad's ill, wanted to be closer to him.'

I grunted and slid the photo of him and Korda across the table. His face changed like it had been wiped with a sponge.

'Where the fuck did you get this?'

'Never mind. Who's the woman?'

He leant back in his chair and stared at me. 'Do you know where Frankie Korda is?'

'No,' I said, truthfully.

'Did you have anything to do with him going?'

'No,' I lied.

'Then where the fuck did you get this picture?' He looked right on edge. Fuck knew what scenario was running through his skull, what pieces of his past he was putting together. Dave Craze was bent, this I already knew. And I had a smudge that put him with another bent copper. Bad for him. He tugged at his moustache nervously. But because he was bent, he gave it up.

'The girl is called Carmen Pinto,' he said. 'That *was* her name, anyway. I don't know what she's called now. But there's a full scream out for her.'

I leant forward. 'Why?'

'Because she was on the witness protection programme,' said Craze, slowly.

'And?' I said.

'And she disappeared two weeks ago.'

I walked back to the Metropole trying to put together the full schmeer in my nut. Carmen Pinto, Craze said, had been a prostitute's maid. That meant she took the phone calls and the money for the girl selling her body. I already knew this, but I let him give me the chapter and verse. Carmen, Serbs, police, witness protection, Frank Korda. Dave Craze said the pair were properly loved up.

Craze told me how witness protection – WP he called it – worked. New identity, wired-up flat linked by alarm to WP HQ. Alarm sounding every time you walked in the door, no coded call from the witness and the local filth would be round in minutes. Location and details only known to a handful.

That was why Frank Korda was a nap for the bloke on WP who got killed. The circle of knowledge was very tight. And, said Craze, Korda was well known to hate pimps in general. And having sat through the evidence, he hated this one in particular.

And now Carmen Pinto had disappeared. I walked faster, hoping to fuck that Frank Korda really did love her.

Monty was stood at the window when I got back to the room. He looked like he'd just woken up – nothing on but a shirt and a pair of trunks. The kecks were baggy and loose. Showed the weight he'd lost.

'Monty?'

He turned at my voice. 'Come here, quickly,' he rasped.

I stood at his shoulder. 'What is it?'

He flicked back the net curtain and pointed down across to the corner. 'Look.'

Six floors down, there wasn't much to see.

'By that tree outside the Starbucks,' he said. 'Look.'

'It's a fucking tree,' I snapped.

'The young lad, leaning against it,' he said. 'Smart suit, sharp. Smoking a fag.'

'There's no one there, Monty.'

I turned away. He stayed put for a second, then he let the curtain drop and pushed past me. Rolled onto the bed, stretching for his pills on the cabinet as he moved. He shoved a couple down, drank from a glass. 'See them everywhere,' he said. 'Always the same, smart suit, white shirt. Sharp-looking. They've been following me since January.'

'We've not been bottled off, Monty. I'm sure of that.'

'Not you, me.'

The lad in the mod suit at his funeral. The snappy dresser at the hotel. I shook my head and the pictures went. Meant nothing. Then from nowhere, I shivered.

'Are you on the gear again, Monty?'

Lying on his side, he twisted his head to look at me. 'I know what I saw. Fuck 'em. All this time, I thought they were following me.' He rolled over, showed me his back and chucked his last words over his shoulder. 'I just understood, mate. It's the other way round. I've been following them.'

I took off my jacket and kicked off my shoes. Stretching, I lay down on my bed.

'This is bullshit, Monty,' I said. 'We need to focus on Adrian.' I looked at my watch. Ten past four. 'His gaff opens up for the evening. We'll go round then, see if we can do any good. Try and get some sleep till then. But whatever you do, don't fucking disturb me. I need the kip.'

I set the alarm on my mobile for six and drifted off.

20

The address Holly had given me was round the corner from the Science Museum in Kensington. It was three storeys and double-fronted. The door was red with a half-ton brass knocker hanging off it, and beside the bell was a discreet brass plaque engraved *Bassinger's* in tight copperplate.

I had a quick scout round the back before we parked up. There was a black metal fire escape down into a small garden at the back. Useful for the offmans, if it came to it. The plan was for the pair of us to go in as punters. Monty was to kick off in his room to draw some attention and I would go on the creep.

By half six we were parked up in the motor thirty-odd yards down on the other side. Monty was lying back in the passenger street, and from the sound of his breathing, he was asleep. He looked bloody awful, but he'd held my eye at the hotel and told me he was coming. And that was that.

I had my minces firmly on the door. We weren't in the best-hidden spot on the planet, but if there was going to be trouble it would come from there. I hoped that anyone checking the street for moodies would put me down as a nervous first-time punter, trying to summon up the courage to ring the bell.

The street was busy and well lit, and I had a good view of the action in and out. There had been a mini-rush of suits just after we arrived at seven, most of them dropped off in cabs right to the front door. I imagined this was the after-office crew, getting a quick punt in before they schlepped home. Then it had gone quiet.

Half seven, some movement. A grey Volvo pulled up. Someone got out on the road side, carrying a Sainsbury's bag and a bottle. The car moved off. The man moved quickly up to the door and reached for his keys. I caught him in the street light: jaw like a paving stone, thick black hair, two days' stubble showing even from here. Adrian. Holly was telling the truth. We'd got him housed.

I nudged Monty awake. 'Adrian's here.' He grunted. 'Your Serb mate's chum.'

Monty rubbed his eyes and sat up on his elbow. He didn't move the seat. 'You sure?'

'Yup. Just gone in looking like the main man.' Monty didn't seem that interested. He slumped back, a few beads of sweat on his nut and forehead.

'How are you doing?'

'Don't ask. I'll tell you when I can't handle it.' He rubbed at his chest and closed his eyes again.

I gave it till nine. By then there'd been plenty of footfall in and rather less out, much of it dropped off by black cabs. I guessed this was the kind of venue taxi drivers got a bung for every punter they recommended. Either way, I reckoned the best little whorehouse in Kensington would be busy enough to hide us in the crowd by now.

We climbed out of the Saab and stretched, strode across the street and rang the bell. A bald bodybuilder in a black coat that made him look like a bell opened up. He eyed us up and down suspiciously. I reckoned he was the kind of guy who did the up-and-down suspicious thing to anyone. Probably thought it made him look hard. Amateur.

'We've just come from a table-dancing club up west,' I said. 'The cabbie thought we might like to continue our evening here.'

'Membership is fifty pounds each, gents,' said the bellman, sweetly. 'Come in.' He swung the door open and we did.

We stepped into what looked like the reception of a boutique hotel. The only light came from a fake log fire and a couple of bankers' lamps stood on a wood-panelled counter, which nestled in the curl of a wide gold-carpeted staircase. The bellman shepherded us across a Persian rug to the stunningly attractive young redhead sat behind the counter. She was dressed like a porn version of a cocktail waitress: white bow-tie and a black waistcoat with nothing but a lacy red bra doing a lot of lifting and separating underneath. I slid two fifties across to her and scribbled a couple of names on her form.

'This way, gents.'

The bellman led us along a warmly lit, thickly carpeted corridor and down six wide stairs. A small foyer, then a pair of heavy mahogany doors and we were in what looked like a busy, red-lit nightclub about the size of Old Trafford. Except there was no dancefloor and the music was playing low. There were red leather button-upholstered chairs and couches slotted around low tables. The room was crowded with men talking to women in cocktail dresses. All the women were gorgeous and all the men were punching above their weight. On the far side there was a long bar lined with more women, each with a clutch bag.

'If you'd like to go upstairs, the ladies will show you the way,' said the bellman. 'Would you like me to introduce you to a few of them?'

'No, thank you.'

He hovered. I pushed a bulls-eye into his palm and he split. A podgy little guy in Michael Caine glasses followed him out the door with a pair of tall blondes shimmering along behind. I leant into Monty's ear.

'Up to the bar, five minutes and then we go upstairs with a couple of the toms,' I said. 'Give me another ten and then kick off.' He nodded. Even in the red light, he looked pale.

'OK,' he said.

We wove through the tables. The line of cocktail dresses shifted as we moved; a couple made eye contact. By the time we were leaning on the woodwork, we both had two women hanging off our shoulders. Another five and I was leaving with a Hungarian in her twenties called Eglatina. Monty followed with a tall Pole called Kim.

Eglatina and Kim stopped at reception to pick up a couple of keys. The bellman caught my eye and nodded approvingly. I felt sick. We went up and the red lighting went with us. The staircase was broad and wound up to the first floor past big black and whites of toned nudes. A long wide landing with half a dozen panelled doors. Kim opened one and stepped in. Monty followed. Eglatina led me up another curl of staircase to the second floor. Six doors again. At the end of the landing a red rope barrier and beyond that another, narrower, set of steps.

'What's up there?' I gestured at the rope.

'Offices, darling.' Eglatina smiled, unlocked a door and pulled me in.

The room had a king-size bed with a deep red throw slung over it. There was a big white towel laid on top and pinched at the centre so it looked like a bow. Flat-screen TV on a stand next to a stack of DVDs, a pile of neatly folded towels on a low cabinet and a shower unit built into the corner. It smelt of baby oil and wet wipes, like the dive in Kings Cross.

Eglatina arranged herself on the edge of the bed and flicked her dress at the split to show a bit of leg. She gave me a warm wide smile, then tapped a piece of card lying on the bed.

'Price list,' she said. 'You can choose.'

'Toilet,' I said. 'Where is it?'

She shrugged and waved a hand. 'Left, end of the landing, darling.'

I nodded thanks, then made for the door and padded quietly down the corridor. The bog was white on white with a shower in the corner. I locked up and tried the window. Painted shut. I whipped out a screwdriver and stuck in the gap between frame and ledge. A couple of good levers and I felt the paint crack and the window opened easily. It was big enough to crawl through, and gave directly onto the fire escape. Ideal. I stowed the tool back in my pocket, flushed the toilet and went back to Eglatina. She was still on the bed, same spot. I pulled out a couple of hundred quid and dropped it in her lap.

'Why don't you go and get us some champagne from the bar?' I nodded at the corner. 'I'll have a shower while you're gone.'

She shrugged and left. I gave her a few seconds then cracked the door an inch to see her nut bobbing downstairs and out of sight. Couple of steps out, drop the rope barrier, wait. No noise from the floor above, no light on the stairwell. I crept them two at a time, ears straining for noise. Voices somewhere, muffled. At the top, three doors. Dead ahead, a closed door with light coming from under it, and voices. The door on the left was shut, no light. The door on the right was ajar; a slice of street yellow dropped through the gap.

Then Monty's voice, shouting and screaming in a room downstairs. A door banged open on the landing below and his voice belted up the stairwell. Kim's voice, screaming back at him. I darted through the open door, snapped it closed and flattened against the wall just as the middle door was torn open and two sets of footsteps thumped to the stairwell. A quick coat confirmed my room was empty, thank fuck.

Outside, the floorboards creaked. A low voice came from the landing, muffled and indistinct. More of Monty's shouting, bouncing up the walls. More shouting, some other guy joining in. Another murmur from the landing. Sounded like a question.

'I don't want to wait,' said the other guy loudly. 'I just want the merchandise.'

I closed my eyes, jammed my nut right up against the wood, held my breath. *Shrink, flatten, try to disappear.*

It was Frank Korda.

'Give it a moment.' The other fella. I heard the trace of an accent. 'Let them get rid of him first.'

A roar from downstairs, more shouts, movement. Then a chirp from a mobile.

'Is he out?' The accent was speaking. 'No, is he out? OK, give the other guy some booze on the house. And finish.' I heard the phone clip shut. 'OK. Let's go.'

They started down. I cracked the door an inch in time to see Adrian disappear, with Korda just behind. My mind was racing.

I fucking knew it I fucking knew it I fucking knew Korda was behind all this.

I needed out and fast. I pulled the door open and listened. Monty was still roaring, but it sounded like he was being shunted slowly down the stairs. Up here, all quiet.

I stepped out onto the landing, and stopped. The door opposite caught my eye. It was padlocked from the outside. *Something to hide.* I had the screwdriver out and the lock off in ten seconds. Squatting, I listened for noise from below. Still nothing, good. Push the door open. Enough light from the office to see.

It was a tiny attic room. There was a single bed just inside the door.

I saw Noriko's long black hair spread across the pillow. Her face was twisted into the blankets. I bent over and shook her.

'Noriko?' I shook harder. 'Noriko!'

She was slack, lifeless. I shook her again. Nothing.

Then, from the darkness on the other side of the room, there was a groan. Another bed, someone trying to sit up, groaning. I swung the door wide open for the light.

It was Noriko. *Noriko* in the other bed.

What . . .

Noriko was trying to sit up. Her face was pure white, she was dribbling and shifting in slow motion. She looked drugged.

'*Please . . .*' I saw the bandage on her finger.

What?

Time started to swallow itself in big gulps. I scooped up Noriko, light as a breath, and darted down the stairs. I elbowed the bog window and pushed her out. Fire escape, across the garden, over the wall at the back, screaming into the phone for Monty. Then the Saab was there, and Monty, bleeding from the lip. I half threw Noriko onto the back seat. *I'll catch you up, just fucking go, there's another woman, I have to go back.* He called something but I was gone. Back up the metal steps and in the window, pause. All quiet, no one about. Along the landing and up.

Back into the room. Still quiet. I shot to the occupied bed. She wasn't moving. No sound. Was she breathing? Her face was turned to the wall. Was she breathing? I didn't think she was breathing. I reached to take her pulse. And then I sank into quicksand. Her pale wrist. The rose tattoo, in blue outline. The one she was going to get finished when she retired. I rolled the woman onto her back. It was Harry. It was Harry.

Movement downstairs, footsteps on the landing. I shot to the door and cracked it shut, left a tiny gap.

Boots creaked up the stairs. Someone talking into a phone. Adrian flicked by.

I felt Harry's body in the dark behind me. Her body. Harry was dead. Then I opened the door quietly and stepped onto the landing.

Adrian was in his office. Stood in front of a desk, muttering into his phone. English, Serb, Albanian, I wasn't listening. He looked up as I made the door.

The rest I saw from a hundred miles away.

I was on him, rolling him back on the desk. He clawed at me but I was too fast. The screwdriver was already in my fist, it punched down and stabbed Adrian in the neck. Someone heaved their full weight on top and pushed hard. The metal pierced his windpipe and sank in. Then there was a crack as his spine broke.

I was on the fire escape on Adrian's gaff, trying to get down the stairs. I couldn't move. A clank above me, I turned and looked up. Someone at the top, following me. No face, all in shadow. But the light picked out his collar and cuffs, young lad, smartly dressed. He took a step down.

Snap awake in the back of the Saab. Monty driving, fast. Lights, cars, buses flick past. My head lolls against the window.

Random images. Adrian flopped over his desk, neck snapped. Monty behind me, I was shouting, the old guy gathering me up, hustling me down the stairs. Gaff in uproar, punters all over, half-dressed girls scrabbling for the door.

Monty's talking now. Something about the hospital, Noriko. Must have called an ambulance. Yes, an ambulance.

We drive on. I feel the car switch and lurch as the old guy winds a route. We stop. Houses. He hustles me out the motor, up some steps. I'm indoors, maybe a bedroom, yes a bedroom. I'm on a bed.

Eyes open and closed. Dim light. I try to sit up. Monty in the chair next to me, talking, soothing. Couldn't hear what he was saying.

Then the door opens and someone steps in, turning on the light.

'Hello, Joker.'

Frank Korda.

I roll off the bed and lunge, throw him against the wall.

Then I smell the fags. Sixty a day, you stink of them.

And there's Monty behind me, his arm curled round my neck and squeezing. I flail but he's too well tucked in, not as strong as he was but he knows what he's doing. And I have no strength left. He's crushing the breath out of me. A tingle spreading up my body.

'Sorry, mate. I'm so sorry.'

Monty rolls me on my back and keeps squeezing. Black dots blurring my vision. Over his shoulder I see three tall, hooded figures, white robes dragging the deck. They flicker away. In their place I see a trio of sharply dressed lads: smart suits, black ties, black boots.

21

I gasped awake. I was in bed. Blankets and a soft mattress. Not my bed, then. And not the bed at the Metropole. My throat hurt. I stroked it gingerly. It felt like I'd swallowed a rock. There was some light coming through the half-open door. It picked out a wardrobe, a bookcase jammed with papers and stacks of books on the floor.

Voices a way off. Where the hell was I? I flicked back the blankets and swung my feet onto the deck. *Harry.* My head thumped and I felt dizzy. Harry was dead in Adrian's whorehouse.

I went cold, slumped forward, head down. *All my fault. Oh Jesus.*

The nausea came and went. I pulled myself into the present. I was woozy, but I was OK. But where the fuck was I? I heard voices, away in the house, and stiffened. Then I noticed I was naked except for a pair of old-school striped pyjama trousers.

There was a jumper thrown over a chair. Pulling it on, I looked for a weapon. A couple of cricket stumps leaning up against the wall. Have to do. I made for the door.

I crept out onto a landing, light coming from the floor below. The voices were coming from below. I started down, fingers brushing the wall, the wood in the other fist. One flight and round to another. The stairs were cluttered with papers and files, pushed up against railings.

Books and bits of junk piled up on top. Three bikes in the hall at the bottom. I was in Jenna Pleasing's house.

The voices were in the basement. I went down past the racks of leaflets and on into the kitchen. As it came into view, I saw two women perched on stools at the counter and talking. Frank Korda stood opposite, pulling slices of bread from an upended loaf and flipping them on the counter with a flourish. He scooped butter out of a dish, looked up and saw me.

'Here's the man now,' he said. 'How are you feeling?'

The two women turned round and Jenna Pleasing smiled at me. The other had a black bob and big eyes. I recognised her from the photograph: Carmen Pinto.

'You don't need to worry,' said Jenna, nodding at the stump. 'You're quite all right now.'

'How did I get here?' My voice was croaking.

'Monty brought you,' said Korda. 'While I was taking the women to the hospital. Why don't you sit down?'

The kitchen had been cleaned up and cleared out since the last time I'd been here. Most of the clutter had gone. There was an empty stool by Carmen Pinto. I sat down, still holding the cricket stump. Korda stood a mug of tea in front of me.

'The first thing you should know,' he said gently, 'is that Harry is alive.'

I looked at him like he was speaking Welsh. I grasped the stump tighter. 'What?'

'She's in the same ward as Noriko, Joker,' said Korda. 'Adrian pumped her full of Largactil – more than he needed to. Sedative. The amount he gave her, it slows down the heart, mimics a coma.' He watched me as I tried to take it all in. 'Adrian told me a woman had come sniffing around. He'd already had a couple of calls that morning, about people asking questions. He was very jumpy. So he took her. I didn't know she was your friend until Monty told me. I'm sorry.'

'Where is Monty?' I said.

'In a minute,' he said softly. 'You hungry?'

'Not really.'

'Why don't you try and eat?' Carmen Pinto. She had a warm, sweet voice. Spanish maybe. Or Portuguese.

'I'll make you something anyway,' said Korda. He started slicing cheese, talking as he went. 'Well, Joker,' he said. 'What's been going on? OK. Make yourself comfortable.' And then he started his story.

Carmen Pinto: maid, flat, Kilburn. This I knew. After a while, she realised she was maiding for a bunch of people-traffickers. She was a good woman, so she went to the police. As I also knew.

'She decided to give evidence,' said Korda. 'She knew the dangers, but she also knew it was the right thing. These people are the worst, Joker. It's like slavery, trafficking. It *is* slavery.' He looked at Carmen warmly. 'And that's where we met, while I was minding her before the trial.' She smiled back, and he reached out and squeezed her hand.

'Carmen was the reason I did Heathrow with Monty,' he said.

I shot a glance at Jenna Pleasing.

'It's all right. Jenna's an old friend.' He went on. 'There was another witness on WP. One of the crew, turned Queen's Evidence. Fifteens all round. Adrian was connected to them, so he made himself busy. He found out where the lad who'd given evidence was holed up, had him killed. Because of Heathrow, and not being able to account for my movements, I ended up in the frame. And so I got nicked, just as the money got clean.'

'I know.'

Korda looked across at his woman and his jaw tightened. 'Then Adrian went looking for Carmen,' he said. 'Whether he paid someone, or tracked her down or just happened to see her in the street, we don't know. But he found Carmen about two weeks ago, and took her.'

Carmen bargained for her life by telling Adrian about the Heathrow job and the three sets of numbers. Monty was dead so he went to the funeral to see if he could pick anything up. Then he tracked down Devorty and sweated him.

'I don't blame Carmen for talking,' said Korda. 'He would have killed her otherwise. And Adrian was a greedy man. Fond of money. So he put revenge on hold.'

'Did he get the numbers from Devorty?' I asked.

'Adrian told me not.'

I snapped my head at him and gripped the stump. 'When was that?'

'In a minute,' he said. 'In a minute.' He spread his paw on the counter, rapped a tattoo with his middle finger. Then he went on. 'Well; Devorty had a weak heart and he died on the chair. But not before Adrian got the full deal on Monty's scam. So he went down to Fulham and got lucky. Monty was out – on the way to Devorty's as it happened. So Adrian took Noriko, and became Fat Blackmail. Tore her fingernail out to show you he was serious.'

Korda didn't know Carmen was gone until I got him out of Strangeways. Witness protection phone-lines are barred for all prison numbers, to stop villains threatening witnesses. He'd rung her from the service station on the way down to London with the change I'd given him for the sandwich. Payphone on the wall by the toilet. And again in Jimmy's restaurant while I was on the dog to Harry. No reply.

The copper had recognised the Serb handiwork on Devorty, and he knew Adrian had beaten the rap. He started to get nervous about

Carmen. He used the phone I'd bought him to call a mate in the Met, found she'd vanished. That's why he split.

'Sorry about running out on you like that, Joker,' he said. 'I was worried about Noriko, but Carmen had to come first.'

His woman looked down at the counter. I couldn't see her face.

I noticed a cheese sandwich in front of me and forced down a bite. Couldn't taste it. 'So what were you doing at Adrian's place last night?'

'Buying back Carmen,' said Korda, simply. 'I had some money kept safe up in Manchester. I reckoned as soon as he knew Devorty had no successor, Adrian would want to cut his losses and run. He was a cunt, but he was a businessman as well.'

'I only cost twenty grand,' said Carmen.

I dropped my head into my palms. 'Twenty grand,' I said. 'He'd probably have traded Noriko for the same. All this shit, for nothing.'

'I was going to call you as soon as I had Carmen,' said Korda. 'Tell you about Noriko. But Adrian was a businessman, as I say. I didn't have enough for both of them. You'd have done the same, Joker.'

I let that one hang in the air. 'Anyone got a cigarette?' I said. 'I don't seem to have one on me.' Carmen found a pack and we both lit up. Jenna clunked a heavy glass ashtray in front of us.

'I saw your car when I came out with Carmen,' said Korda. 'Found Monty inside. Now that was a surprise.'

'I'm sure it was,' I said.

Then I'd screamed for Monty and come out with Noriko. Korda and the old guy followed me back in, found me with Adrian's body and got me out. Korda took Noriko to hospital, Monty drove me up here. And Korda called Dave Craze, who sent round a bunch of jam butties. The coppers found Harry.

'Dave called about an hour ago to say Harry was all right,' said Korda. 'She'll be in hospital for a few days.' He cracked a smile. 'Dave said the paperwork on this one will be a bastard.'

Monty knocking me out. I was too tired to be angry. 'Where is he now?'

All three of them looked down at the counter, almost in time.

'Well?' I said. 'Where's Monty now?'

There was a long silence. When Korda spoke, his voice was tight. 'There was no stopping him. I had to let him go.'

'What?' I said. 'Where?'

'He knocked you out to keep you safe,' said Korda. 'We stripped you, and he shredded and dumped your clothes. For the forensic.'

'What?' I said. Hammering in my ribcage. *Jesus.* 'Where is he?'

'Monty knew Adrian's crew wouldn't be quiet till they had a scalp for whoever killed him,' said Jenna gently. 'He didn't want you looking over your shoulder for the rest of your life.'

A chill swept up me. 'Tell me what he did. *Just fucking tell me!*'

'He went up to see them,' said Korda. 'To tell them he did for Adrian.'

I stood up, the stool flew against the wall and smashed something. Carmen jumped. 'Where's he gone?' I shouted. 'I've got to get up there. Where's he gone?'

Korda laid a big hand on my arm. 'He went about four,' he said quietly. 'It'll be over now.'

There was a clock on the wall. Five to seven and an early December dawn was starting to show. There were birds singing out in the garden. I hadn't noticed them before.

*

I went at two that afternoon. I'd gone back to bed after we were done in the kitchen and when I woke around midday, Korda and Carmen Pinto had already split. I didn't know or care where they'd gone. Jenna Pleasing made me scrambled eggs and I ate them without tasting. I just needed the fuel.

The Saab was still outside. Jenna gave me some of her husband's clothes to wear. When I went into the kitchen to say goodbye, she was at the counter, putting food on a plate.

'It's Gerald's lunchtime now,' she said. 'Just as well he doesn't remember much of what goes on around here.'

'Why did he do it, Jenna?'

She shook her head. 'I suppose he felt he had to. He wanted to make it right with you.'

Then she reached into a drawer and pulled out a long white envelope. 'Monty gave me this for you just before he went this morning.'

'I don't want it.'

'Take it. He went and scribbled it on the landing outside your room. I sat and watched him. When he'd finished, he stood at the door and looked at you for a bit. And then he left.'

I took the letter and stowed it. 'Why did he lie to me, Jenna?'

'I don't know. He never lied to me.'

'Maybe you weren't important enough to lie to.'

She smiled. 'Maybe. Who knows?' She poured out some tea and put it on a tray. Then she looked at me and said, 'Fat Blackmail. When Frank told me the name, I recognised it. It was one of Monty's old stories. All about a kidnap.' She blinked furiously. 'I've got it somewhere. Do you want it?'

'No thank you,' I said. 'I've had enough of Monty's stories.'

There was a silence. I wanted to go, but there was something left to ask. I knew I'd never come this way again.

'Jenna,' I said. 'What were you to Monty?'

Something danced in her eyes.

'Jenna is my middle name,' she said. 'Hardly anybody knows that.'

I knew the answer, but I asked anyway. 'So what's your first name, then?'

'Elspeth.'

'Of course it is,' I said.

Monty's letter sat on the passenger seat until I got home. I dropped in at Amy's to leave the dough from the hotel in her loft and made the flat by eight. I changed, made tea and sat in the chair by the window, the one where I read the papers on Sunday.

Hello mate,

I'm sorry for all the shit I brought on your door. I shouldn't have set you up. Maybe it was the cancer, the dope, maybe just the fear of going. I couldn't take the risk you'd say no. I should have known you'd say yes. I see that now.

Please make sure Noriko gets my share of the bank. And, please, keep an eye on her when she gets out of hospital. I don't think she'll hang around long, though.

I'm off to see these geezers now. Don't worry mate, I'm OK about it. I'll only lose a few months, let's face it. And you'll get a lot back, that's the main thing.

Try and forgive me for all the crap, mate. I've tried to balance the books.

Love,

Monty.

I burnt the letter over the sink and washed the ashes away.

Later that night, I rang Marcus for the address and went across to see the juror. He was called Billy Twine and was about twelve years old. I propped him and he said yes before I'd finished speaking. The jury went out next day and took twenty minutes to bring back a verdict of not guilty.

When I went to pay him off, Billy Twine told me he wasn't surprised at the result. Everyone remembered Casey from the teatime wrestling when they were kids and he'd made them laugh. He'd always been one of the good guys then. When the foreman took the vote, not a single paw went up for guilty.

22

I picked up Monty's ashes from Golders Green Crematorium a fortnight later and drove south.

I'd been the only mourner at his funeral a few days before. Noriko was out of hospital, but she didn't come. She was staying in St John's Wood with a friend of hers and barely moved across the front doorstep. She didn't fancy having words with the police over Monty's fake death and the whereabouts of his brother, Ted. She was flying to Japan on Christmas Day next week. She hadn't been back to Chalk Farm at all.

I'd only seen her once, to give her the two hundred and fifty grand from King Street, and to explain about Monty. Ayumi had answered the door, dressed scruffily in a baggy black sweater and footless tights. The air was thick with dope and I waited about twenty minutes for Noriko to come out of her room, sitting with the holdall of cash in front of me.

She emerged looking pale, with dry patches of red skin on her cheeks and neck. Ayumi brought us apple juice and I told her how Monty had died, and why. She listened dully and then asked if I would open a bank account and launder the money for her. I said no, and left.

Harry was back home but not intending to work again for a while. I gave her fifty grand off the bank and I saw her two or three times a week. She'd given me a message from Dave Craze: as far as the Met were concerned, Monty had killed Adrian over money and then Adrian's mates had killed Monty in revenge. And that was it.

A teacher walking his dog had found the old guy on Hackney Marshes the day after he went missing. He'd been stabbed all over the shop and shot twice. Jenna Pleasing identified the body.

Some Serb gangster washed up on the sand at Tilbury a few days after. He'd also been stabbed, and his throat was slashed. Looked like Monty had taken one with him.

The three million quid that made Monty Fat Blackmail rotted where it was, useless without the numbers. A forgotten and pointless prize, locked in a bank strongbox in Zurich.

I'd tried to occupy myself by doing little things. I met Sara and the kids when they came back from America and taken them out to dinner. I'd started to teach Lou to drive. I'd written a few emails to Italy and got a couple in reply. I'd had Casey round for fish and chips one night.

Keeping busy seemed to be working. The memories of the last few weeks were starting to recede, and every time I managed something normal, I imagined a little more distance between me and the past. That was the idea, anyway.

Now I was driving south with Monty's ashes. I took the Brighton road and Monty's face hung in front of me as I drove. I tried to describe him to myself, but I couldn't focus. His image and character kept slipping away and darting round corners like shadows.

I thought of Ted, lying in Highgate with a marker saying Montague Lee. I was glad I didn't have to sort that one out.

I came off the main and took the road for Devil's Dyke. A few minutes later, I pulled into the hotel car park and sat with the urn on my lap for a while, smoking a cigarette.

It was getting overcast when I finally left the motor, heading out across the Downs. There was a path as far as the little fort about half a mile on, then it was just rough grass. The ground was still damp from rain earlier in the day and I felt the wet stripes across my strides as I moved. Another ten minutes or so and I got to the level patch where Monty and the kids from Wishwood used to play football. The slope dropped away steeply here, just like he said. Looking down, I saw it fall sharply for several miles, all the way to a skinny road with tiny cars.

Loosening the cap, I held the urn above my head.

'Goodbye Monty,' I said. 'Be seeing you, some time.'

Then I threw the urn as far out as I could. It hit the deck and started to roll. Bang, bang, bang, hitting stones and mounds, bouncing higher and rolling faster.

Suddenly, it hit a rock and flew right up into the air. The cap spun off and Monty's ashes whipped out into the wind. The empty jar hit the deck and bounced slowly and lazily, finally flipping up on a clump of grass and disappearing out of sight into the trees.

I turned and made for the car. It was starting to rain.

AN EXTRACT FROM THE PREQUEL TO
FAT BLACKMAIL

THE LAST STRAIGHT FACE

NOW AVAILABLE IN PAPERBACK

It was a Chinese croupier who found Tomas face down on the steps of Manchester's Royal Infirmary at four o'clock on the Tuesday morning. She'd been kicking around in casualty with a suspect fractured wrist since ten and was making her fags last by smoking them one an hour, on the hour. The paper said she'd thought Tomas was a drunk at first, only he didn't answer when she called across to see if he was OK. Then she saw his shirt was covered in blood from neck to waist and there was a thick sugary pool dripping from the step he lay on down to the next, and the next step after that.

1

I got out of Strangeways at half past eight on the Friday morning and Terry met me at the gate.

He walked up to me, stopped a couple of feet away then shifted from one foot to the other. Either he was nervous or he wanted a piss. 'Hello, mate.'

He'd put on some weight and there was more colour in his face than when I'd last seen him inside eight months ago, but he still looked pretty fit and hard, and his fine brown hair was clean and recently cut and getting flicked at by the breeze. He was wearing crisp designer jeans, ironic seventies shirt and jacket and new trainers. And none of it copy gear, I'd bet.

I looked past him down the slope to Bury New Road. Cars and the good noise of traffic, straightgoers on the pavement doing that brisk efficient stride they use on the way to work in the morning, the quick-step one where they stretch their legs a little bit further, moving with purpose in anticipation of a new day – bang, bang, bang, I'm a straightgoer.

I looked back at Terry. 'Fuck off.'

'What?'

I was already past him and down the slope. I heard him skip shuffle behind me and his breath as he caught up. 'I thought we were mates.'

'We're not.'

'I thought –'

I stopped walking. 'Just fuck off.'

I did the straightgoer stride down the hill, looking for a cab on the main drag. Off the slope by the car lot, I glanced over my shoulder to see the little shit yapping along behind me. 'I just wanted to meet you out of the nick. What's the matter?'

I grabbed his mile-wide seventies collar and slammed him up against the chainlink fence. Then I leant right in so we were nose to nose, and now he was frightened.

'Hey, mate –'

'No. No mate. Not since you stuck us in it.' I shook him with each word. 'Captain Cocaine.'

'I told you, there was no malice.'

I jabbed a finger at the nick. He thought I was going for his eye and flinched. 'Eighteen months. In there. Down to you. Because you took some charlie. Coke, Terry, on work. On a piece of work.'

This time, his nut made the fence sing.

'Going on a piece of work means to burgle and to thieve, Terry. It means chopping up the prize and then going home and spending it out. And living to tell the tale. It does not mean getting nicked and doing time, down to you. And your charlie. Coke to keep you going. Which got found. By filth. And got us nicked. Do you understand?'

He nodded a quick and frightened yes.

'Today is about seeing my son and my daughter, Terry, maybe going for a walk where I want to and smelling air without the stink of piss in it. This is my ordinary world, Terry. Not yours. So fuck off.'

I let go of him. But I didn't walk. Nor did he. Instead, I saw him sold and branded and wearing a scold's bridle.

'I've been chucked out. Janey chucked me out. I've got no money. And nowhere to go.'

So that was it. Girlfriend slings him, he's got no dough, he comes looking for me. I thought it was meant to be the other way round when you got out of the nick. You came out, someone gave you money. Not like this.

Terry's dad was a peterman – a safebreaker – we used to call Yoda, and he'd been a very good friend to me, even saved me from a ten stretch once. Yoda was dead now, so his son had his father's credit and I didn't have the choice. That's why we walked to Victoria station together and went into the buffet and I told him to sit down, and went up to the counter to buy tea and biscuits. Then I looked at the shelves and thought, *All this choice*, so I scooped up a plate and went back along the food counter opening little plastic windows and metal lids and putting food on to a plate, just because I could. Eggs, bacon, sausages, tomatoes, chips, baked beans, hash browns, toast, butter portions, jam and marmalade, more eggs, bacon, eggs, pig's knuckle, hip bone, thigh bone, knee bone, ankle bone.

Now hear the word of the Lord.

I wasn't hungry. I'd had my porridge in the nick. Have your porridge on the last morning, or you'll come back for it. That's what they say. I paid and walked the tray over to Terry. 'Here.' I banged it down. 'Just stay here.'

I looked round for the toilets. A few seconds later I was standing in one of the pissy cubicles going through my cash. They give you a week's social when you get out of the nick. Fifty quid. Leon had sent me in three hundred a couple of weeks ago, and I still had most of that. So I counted out two and trousered the rest.

There was a payphone just outside the bogs. I phoned Carol, an old mate who owed me a couple of favours. Yes, she said, Terry could stay for a few days. Then I went and dropped the dough on him. A tenner slipped off the fold and went on his plate, soaking up the baked beans. He looked up at me like a dog wanting a Bonio. I gave him Carol's address and the SP and told him to behave himself. 'None of your crap,' I said. 'No liberties. Understand?'

He nodded, then looked at the dough.

'A twoer. Against your half of our last parcel.'

'What about the rest?'

'I'll be in touch. If it wasn't for your dad, I wouldn't even be talking to you.' Then I stuck my face in his. 'Taking fucking cocaine on work,' I spat. 'You prick.'

He squirmed in his seat, half-twitched and half-smiled some sort of thanks. Then he picked the tenner off the beans and tried to smile at me again. I made for the door. As I pulled it open I glanced at him. He was sat there licking the sauce off the money.

I did the straightgoer stride again, away from Terry and the station, then I did a left, crossed over, glanced back to check I was alone and doubled back for Marcus's shop and my whip-round from the chaps. Marcus had sent me the postcard saying he was holding it this time round and I was to come and get it. A couple minutes more and I was there: six massive, carved wood thrones and an equally heavy-looking table on the pavement. The street doors were locked back. He was open.

I went in and down a thin gap between a pile of office chairs and a stack of bathroom cabinets. I turned left at the last cabinet and walked past three lifesize copies of the Venus de Milo, except the last one had arms. Marcus popped out from behind this, brushing Brillo-pad grey hair out of his eyes and tugging at one end of a large brown thing.

'Need any help, Marcus?'

He looked over his shoulder, then straightened up and stuck his hand out. 'Do you want to wait in the office a minute? Sort us out a brew?'

Now I could see a young lad at the other end of the brown thing. About twenty, spotty and with John Lennon bins on his nose. A student, probably. Straight, definitely.

'When you're ready, Marcus.'

I slid past him and turned left at a stack of fake Louis XV chairs and ducked into the little cubbyhole of an office. There were two gas burners standing in the corner and, as usual, it was incredibly hot. I pulled off my jacket, tugged out my shirt and flapped it around to get a bit of breeze up my chest. Out in the main shop there was thudding, scraping and puffing as Marcus and the kid dragged the brown thing out on to the pavement. I ferreted around for the teabags and reached a couple of mugs down from the shelf.

Marcus wasn't an out - and - out villain, but neither was he straight; he dabbled, and he'd buy a parcel when there was something going. But he knew most of us and because he was half and half he was usually out, which is why he got given the whips when they came. I turned at a scrape to see him kicking at a stone lion doorstop.

'Leave it open, Marcus. Please. I've lost three pounds since I walked in here.'

He was in a long black winter coat, furry scarf and gloves and showed no sign of taking them off.

'You hot?' The way he asked, you'd think we were druids on Salisbury Plain celebrating the winter solstice by dancing around naked.

'Yes, I'm hot. I'm always hot here. Everyone's hot here. Name me one person who comes in here and says they're cold.'

Apparently genuinely bemused, Marcus stopped prodding the lion with his toe and made a thinking face. 'I can't think of anyone offhand.'

'Of course you can't. Because there isn't.'

He considered this for a second, then shrugged. 'Anyway, I've sent the lad away for half an hour so we can have a rabbit. I suppose we can leave the door open.' He nodded at the CCTV above my head. 'If any customers come, I'll just have to nip and see to them.' Then he went deep inside his coat and pulled out a thick roll of notes. 'Six hundred and forty five.'

'Thanks, Marcus.'

'Whatever, mate. You're welcome. You and a few others, always welcome.'

A beat.

'Jack sends his best.'

'Jack?'

'Jack Keane. He's out.'

Jack Keane. Haven't seen him since . . .

Marcus waved a finger at the dough as it went into my pocket. 'Very generous on that. Sit down.'

I crackled onto an office chair wrapped in plastic as he slid past for the kettle. 'I didn't know he'd come home.'

'Told me to tell you he's away for a couple of days and he looks forward to a drink with you when he gets back. You and Jack go back a long way, don't you?'

'All the way to Foston Hall. Were you ever there?'

'I managed to avoid detention centres.'

'Christmas Day, it was. Jack and me down the block. Other people remember Johnny Rotten, punk and space hoppers that year. I just remember PE at dawn, the kids who couldn't read and the smell of piss. And Jack. How did he look?'

'Fitter than a butcher's dog.'

'He always kept fit.'

'And it's been a long stretch.'

'Yeah, eight years.'

We trailed off. He looked in his mug. I knew what was coming.

'I was a bit surprised to hear about the brown, pal.'

'It wasn't mine, Marcus. I don't go near heroin. Someone planted it on me.'

'Didn't know you had any enemies.'

'Well.' I got up and started to pull on my clothes. 'Thanks for everything, Marcus. Good to see you.'

'And you pal. Are you going to be in the club tonight?'

'No, I'm taking the kids out. Next couple of days, I suppose. Just need to get myself sorted. Fancy slipping back into things quietly. Know what I mean?'

Marcus nodded. 'OK, pal.'

I could have dwelt on the heroin that got me the extra eight months, but instead I went to Market Street and bought kecks, T-shirt, socks, shampoo, soap and deodorant. And a towel and trunks. Then I walked to the metro, bought a ticket to the swimming pool at Sale but got off at Stretford. My licence said I had to check in with probation, might as well do it now.

The place was a car-park from the out and a right feel of the nick on the in, especially the woman on the desk who looked me up and down like a dog screw. Pam Beresford was sick, she said, so I'd be seeing Mr Kingsolver. Just then a door opened and a tall guy in his fifties stuck his head through, calling my name. He waved me in and went through the script at a rattle. I sat and tried to look attentive and nod at the appropriate times. It was all *yammer yammer yammer* automatic parolee supervised till the two thirds point of my sentence *yammer yammer* report once a week for the first couple of months *yammer yammer* Pam ill *yammer*

Kingsolver away next week *bunny bunny* next visit wouldn't be for a fortnight.

A touch.

Yammer yammer behave myself at all times any nonsense and I'd be breached – back inside, that meant – *yammer yammer*. Prick. Then he flicked his hand at the door. The gesture said, *You can go now. And a bit lively*. I split.

There was a payphone outside on the corner, I dropped in some shrapnel and tapped out a number. Lou and Sam had been down to London on a trip with Sara last weekend and we'd not spoken since. I'd been running images of seeing them again in my nut for the last few weeks. The answerphone picked up. Of course, half term, and with Sara at work, they'd be in bed. Where else would two teenagers be this time of day? I left a message and went for the metro. I spent the tram journey on the way to the pool fantasising about wide expanses of blue water, imagining how I would dive and roll at the deep end, changing direction under the surface and swimming round in circles, just because I could.

I pulled myself up and down the bath twenty times in all. There was no rush.

Apart from a loud knot of ten-year-olds in the shallow end, I had the place to myself. I made the swimming slow and powerful, felt the chlorined water splash over my shoulders, face, ears and mouth. I spat water out every other stroke, and kicked harder than I needed to. At each end of the bath, I flipped over on to my back and looked at the foaming wake I'd kicked up behind me.

After I'd done the twenty, I did one more to bring me down the deep end again. Then I dived under the water and kicked my way to the bottom. I swam a full width and emerged gasping for air at the other side, went down again and barrelled underwater, came up for a quick breath, kicked myself back under. This time I went right down to the blue-tiled bottom and rolled over on to my back, holding my nose and looking up. Cheeks bulging with air, I could see vague shapes of light above, hear my heart beating through the blood vessels in my ears. I came up and swam to the corner.

The kids had cleared out and now I had the place completely to myself. I swam a few more lengths, slapping the water hard with my feet and churning up a line of white horses behind me. Then out and into the changing rooms, which smelt of disinfectant. Not the sort they use inside – there was a flower in there somewhere.

A few seconds later I was standing naked under a hot shower, soaping myself up and starting to scrub the stink of nick from my skin. I lathered up face neck shoulders arms stomach arse thighs and legs, stood on one foot then the other, working the soap round ankles, across soles and between toes. The water clicked off and I lathered my ears till they squeaked. I hit the button and felt the water again, then the creamy lather loosened on me and started to slide down to the tray, swirled round my feet and schlepped down the big steel plughole. Head tipped back, I opened my mouth, feeling the shower jet rain on to my face, sluice out my pores, run off my chin and fall on to my chest. Endless steaming hot water. And no one to keep an eye out for.

A shower is a good place to do you if you're stripped off and they're dressed.

A pack of boy scouts ran and skidded into the changing room a few minutes later, and it popped up that if I stayed here much longer someone would try and do me for loitering, so I stepped out of the jets and wound the towel round my waist. Then I went across to my locker, pulled out my gear and the new stuff I'd bought. The kids weren't looking my way, so I squatted down quickly and pulled my money out from under a bench where I'd stuck it in the space between a support and the wall, twisted up in a plastic bag.

There's a lot of thieves about, you know.

Into a cubicle and locked the door behind me. I could still hear the kids outside, but at least I wouldn't be nonced off by Brown Owl.

I towelled dry, then emptied the M&S bag onto the bench and flicked through the stuff I'd bought. I pulled on the socks first. They stretched over my toes – clean, fresh, new. The boxers were snug and the T-shirt was soft, a perfect fit. Strangeways was off my skin.

I pulled the rest of my clothes on, then bundled the towel and bits into one plastic bag and the old underwear into another. I opened up and stepped out. The scouts had gone, leaving berets and green and yellow cravats and woggles hanging all over the shop.

I sat down on the bench for a moment. The fact was that if I wanted to strip off and swim again, I could. If I wanted to go and sit up top and listen to the kids laughing and larking around, I could. If I wanted to buy a paper, and read it or not read it, or go into a shop and change my mind about what I'd come in for, I could. No more doors where someone else had the keys. I was out, I was having dinner with the twins that evening and I'd be paying. There was a half share in a decent parcel coming my way. I had some plots on the back burner, and that would be more money. And I knew more work would be coming my way; it always does when you've got a good reputation. And – without giving myself too much of a reference – I did have a good name. The swim had reminded me I was pretty fit. The divorce had been half civilised and Lou and Sam had taken it well.

The main thing for now was that Strangeways was lifting off me. I walked out through reception and on to the street, jammed the prison gear into a bin on the pavement and walked for the metro. I had an appointment with a brass I knew up in Altrincham called Harry.

Harry was not that pleased to see me. She'd been busy since breakfast, and the punter now sitting in her work bedroom was over-running; he was having a cry because he was cheating on his wife *and* his girlfriend.

'Didn't expect you for another hour.'

'Do you want me to come back?'

'No – kitchen and keep quiet.'

She prodded me in and closed the door. I made myself a brew and spent half an hour taking the tops off her washing liquid and fabric stuff to smell the lemons and flowers, looking in her cupboards and unscrewing spice jars for the thyme and oregano and chillis. I found some coffee beans and dropped them into my palms and crunched them together and stuck my face right in for the crisp bitter scents. I breathed them all in deep – proper smells, healthy smells, not the antiseptic nose of the nick.

'What are you doing?' Harry was standing in the doorway. I'd not heard the front door go.

'Sorry, Harry,' I dusted the coffee bits into the sink. 'You don't get good things inside.'

'I guess not.' She flexed her arm and winced. 'I hate it when they keep themselves from coming. You can feel them tensing up. So they can get an extra few seconds of me touching them. Little tick.'

She took a couple of steps as if to touch me, then mugged she'd forgotten something and swung away to the sink, arm outstretched like a Dalek, and washed her hands with the Fairy.

'How are you, anyway?'

'I'm fine, Harry. Just fine.'

Harry's father and mother were both Thai. Her real name was something that started with Arayatera and went on for about fifteen minutes. She'd been here for a ten stretch and her English and accent were near enough perfect. I'd known her for years, but it still surprised me when I got her wholesome Manchester tones.

'Just fine? Just out of the nick and just fine?' She dried her hands on a kitchen towel, then flipped up a blue pedal-bin lid, balled the paper and slung it in. She folded her arms and leant on the sink. 'You'll be wanting your phone.'

'Did you get the chance?'

'It wasn't difficult.' She went into a drawer and brought out a slim silver model. 'I charged it up first thing and stuck twenty quid on it as well.' It came across with the charger.

'Thanks.'

'And this.' She held out a card with an eleven digit number on it. I glanced down and up again, but I didn't reach out. 'Don't you want it?'

I reeled it off to her.

'I keep forgetting your memory for numbers.'

'Police can't look inside your head.'

'Anything else I can do for you?'

'Just wanted to be in a non-nick place, Harry. For a bit.'

She nodded. Then her eyes fixed on mine and moving slowly, she slid her bare feet the couple of steps she needed to be right in front of me, one foot either side of the chair. She put her hands on my shoulders and bent at the waist, bringing her cheek and neck up close to my face. I felt the warmth of her skin an inch from my nose, breathed in her perfume, strong and sharp. All flowers and fresh air with the edge of alcohol. She moved again, and the motion seemed to release a fresh cloud of scent from her skin. She almost brushed her cheek against mine and I felt her eyelashes tingle against my temple. Then she straightened up and took a couple of paces back, her eyes fixed on mine as she sat down opposite at the table. The kitchen seemed very quiet and restful, the only sound was a gentle ticking from the clock on the wall. She held my gaze a while longer, looked down and the spell was broken. I noticed I was very tired, the swim had taken it out of me. I yawned.

'Sleepy?'

I nodded. 'Just a bit. I had a dip on the way here, to lose the smell.'

'You want to go to bed?'

What was this?

'To sleep.'

Oh. 'No. No thanks.'

'OK, I'll make us something to eat then. Go and lie down in the living room. I'll call you.'

She sat back and stretched her arms above her head. This made her left breast half slip out from under her satin wrap. She looked down, then at me and pulled it closed.

'You'll be needing some money too, I suspect.'

'No. Thanks though, Harry. I've got my whip.'

'You'll be through it by lunchtime tomorrow. Especially if you go and spend it on another tart like me.'

I let that one hang in the air.

'Some of us are expensive,' she went on. 'Pay us enough money, and we'll give you so much time and attention . . .' she tugged at her belt, 'you'll hardly notice we're a whore.' She threw her long black hair up and it fell over her shoulder like a horse's tail.

'Will five hundred do?' she asked. 'I owe you some favours. You haven't forgotten, have you?'

'No.'

'Six hundred with the phone and time on it. Give it back to me when you can.'

It was easier to say yes. 'Thanks, Harry.'

'Don't mention it.'

She went to the corner of the kitchen and, squatting down sideways to me, pulled up the lino and lifted a floorboard. She was a good-looking woman, not much more than thirty. I got a glimpse of her right breast this time as she pulled out a roll of notes from the cash box under the floor, straightened up and stood it on the table in front of me.

'Stick that down your pants or wherever you're keeping your money these days.'

'Thanks.'

'OK,' she said, and shooed me towards the door. 'You know where the sofa is. Go lie on it.'

Down the corridor I went into the living room, took off my jacket and shoes, then lay down on the soft grey sofa, punching a cushion into shape under my head. In the kitchen, I heard cupboards being opened and pans moved around.

Harry was a brass, but she did it solo. That's pretty unusual – even the expensive ones like her usually end up with a pimp. Not Harry. She didn't need anybody for anything. She even ran her own website from the computer squatting on a desk in the corner. She was also a trained kung fu nutter, able to break arms and legs at twenty paces. No need for a maid, then. Another difference was that she planned to get out before she turned thirty-five. Lots of girls say that. What made her most unusual of all was that she probably would.

Twenty minutes later, we were sitting at the kitchen table finishing off the bacon and eggs she'd whistled up. The eggs were slightly burnt round the edge of the whites and the bacon was crispy and done under the grill. The salt came out of a mill and I could feel each individual crystal on my tongue. I clinked down knife and fork and Harry whisked the lot away, replacing it with a bowl of chocolate pud from the microwave. She'd got changed into jeans and sweatshirt and was now leaning on the counter crunching her bare feet as her own pudding heated up. The machine pinged and she sat opposite me again. 'So what are your plans for the rest of the day?'

'Couple of people to see, drop in at my place, then I'm taking the twins out for dinner. What time is it?'

She twisted round in her seat, spoon poised at her mouth. 'Clock says half past. But I keep it twenty minutes fast.'

'Why?'

'Hooker time. The punters always take their watches off. The later they think it is, the more in a hurry they are to leave.'

'Clever.'

'If I was really clever, I wouldn't be a whore.'

I became fascinated by my chocolate pudding.

'Anyway, I'm finishing early today. I'm studying.'

'Studying?'

'Open University course. History of Art. I've told you before.'

'I remember,' I said. 'Can I use your phone?'

'Go ahead.'

I picked up the handset, punched the number in and got the machine. I left another message saying I'd ring again later.

'No one home?'

'Half term. Teenagers.'

'They won't be up yet.'

'Seems not. Thanks for the food, Harry. And the dough.'

'No problem.' She picked up a cloth and started to wipe off the table. When she got to my cup she wiped round it, then lifted it and handed it to me. I carried it into the living room and put my boots on there. By the time I was back in the kitchen she already had her books out on the table and was leafing through a pile of notes.

'Thanks for everything, Harry.'

'I'd like to chat. But I've got to work.'

I nodded and scooped up the bag with my swimming gear. She walked me to the front door, we said our goodbyes and I left.

Harry lived in the Downs, one of the better areas of Altrincham on the outskirts of Manchester. Quiet, broad, sloping streets with trees, leading to parades of shops and restaurants.

I took out my new phone and punched in Leon's mobile as I walked. Leon was my best friend and my teacher. It was Leon who introduced me to proper villainy more than twenty years ago and showed me how to make a proper pound note. He was also my ex-wife Sara's current lover.

The call went straight to voicemail. I hung up. I don't trust answerphones. Come to that, I don't trust texts or emails either. Or most people.

Then I rang Casey, my fence. He'd been shifting the stuff I nicked for years and was currently holding a parcel for me. I asked if I could drop by. He said yes, so I grabbed a taxi at the station and gave the driver the name of a hotel about fifty yards away from the big man's gaff. In the car park, I handed a tenner over the back seat and asked him to wait. Then I went in the main entrance, walked through the lobby and slipped out the side door off-show from the front. A couple more minutes and I made Casey's front door. It started to rain as the hall light went on the other side of the glass, and I saw him glide down the corridor towards the spyhole. He opened up and leant on the frame in outline. 'You were quick.'

'Hello, Casey.'

'We're in the back.' He waved me in, locked up and then sort of danced down the corridor in front of me singing *Fly Me to the Moon* in the club style. Casey was six foot five and a slightly fat version of the wrestler he'd been when he picked up a bronze at the Commonwealth Games sometime in the seventies. He flicked the dining-room door open, spun on the ball of his right foot and went 'Ta-da!'

'Are you taking something, Casey?'

'Just glad to see you on the street, that's all.'

It was getting dark now and the only light was a lamp on the dining table, papers spread its ten-seat length. The room smelt of fresh polish.

'Hang on a minute.' He *dooby-dooby-doed* to the corner, switched on a lamp and spun round. He'd grown a beard. Shaggy, flecked with grey.

'You've grown a beard, Casey.'

'Clever boy.'

'It makes you look like a wino.'

He gave me the sort of look that had probably once been a signal to Giant Haystacks that he was about to start bouncing off the ropes before he was very much older. 'I thought Orson Welles.'

'Sherry commercial Orson, perhaps. Not *Citizen Kane*.'

'I know you're trying to wind me up. It's not going to work.' He launched into the chorus, snapping a finger and thumb in time to some chat about Jupiter and Mars.

'Casey. A man could die of thirst in this house.'

He stopped and looked at me. 'Sorry. Forgetting my manners. Do you want a brew?'

'Please.'

He schlepped out into the kitchen and was back a few seconds later with a tray of coffee. He tried to jive and pour at the same time, but it slopped into the saucer so he gave the Rat Pack moves a body-swerve and settled for humming *Volare* while he served up.

'How was the Big House?' he asked.

'Pretty much the same.' I made space among the papers for my cup. 'Terry was my main problem. On to me all the time. Sorries and apologies right and left.'

'And rightly so. Did you know he was on the charlie?'

'No, so he can't have been on it for long. He met me this morning on the steps. Bird's chucked him out, so he says.'

'Did you fuck him off.'

I took a mouthful of the coffee. It was pus.

'You sorted him somewhere to stay, didn't you?' He chuckled and pulled at his beard. 'You bloody soft lad.'

'I did it for his father.'

'Course you did. You really are a straight face, aren't you? Keep the code, stick to the rules. I think you're the straightest face I've ever known. So what does Terry actually have to do to get struck off your Christmas card list?'

'He's got his dad's credit for now. And that's it. Now, let's talk about something else. How did you do?'

'All right, then. Sixty grand. Cash Wednesday, if that's all right.'

'It is.'

Just then, two small pairs of running feet belted from one end of the house to the other above our heads. I looked up and back as Casey thumbed at the ceiling. 'Au pair's playing with the kids.'

'Au pair? You getting respectable, Casey?'

'Well, wife wanted one. Marta she's called. Spanish. Nice girl.'

Suddenly the beard and Sinatra tribute made sense.

'How is Stella?' I asked tactfully.

'Huh?'

'Stella. Your wife, Stella.'

'Watching telly at the front.'

'Get on with this Marta, does she?'

'Yes.'

'Who hired her? You or Stella?'

'You want more coffee?'

I flicked him a quick grin. 'No thanks, one of those is quite enough.'

The feet pelted back again, and I glanced up at the ceiling. When my eyes flicked down I caught Casey examining me over the rim of his cup. 'All right, Casey?'

'Yes, I . . . er . . . ' He tailed off, then leant across the table and fished a thick white envelope from among the papers. 'There's a grand there. I had it about me when you rang. Thought you might need some exes. I'll take it off the sixty.'

'Thanks.' I stowed the cash and sat waiting for what I knew was coming.

'So are you seeing the twins, then?' he asked after a pause.

I looked at him; he couldn't meet my eye. 'The brown was planted, Casey,' I said. 'I don't know why, but it was stuck right on me.'

'Of course, right.'

I'd known Casey for ten years, and for the first time I was uncomfortable in his company. 'What else did you hear?'

'Nothing more than the spin. I was a bit surprised, that's all.'

'Yeah, so was I. Eight months surprised.' I drained my cup. 'I've got a taxi waiting, Casey. Got to go.'

He walked me to the front. No dancing this time.

The door swung open and there were two screws in the narrow gap. 'Routine search,' said the youngest, a spiny toerag of about twelve. Thin-faced and wearing heavy specs. 'On your feet.'

Just behind him was an older screw called Katz who I'd known on and off for years. He seemed to be on a watching brief, minding the YTS boy. YTS took a couple of paces into the cell then stood face to face with me and said, 'Is there anything in your cell, or do you have anything on you, that you shouldn't have?'

I took in his anxious spotty face and white rubber gloves. 'Of course,' I said. 'I've got a blade stuck round the s-bend of the karsi, and a quarter of blow up my arse.'

What I actually said was: 'No. Nothing.'

And I didn't. Not only was I too careful for all that caper, I only had two weeks left to do.

I emptied my pockets of snout and lighter and pulled my shirt and vest off and handed them to the bespectacled youth who fingered them uncertainly, then handed them back to me. I pulled them back on, then slipped off my strides and skids for their inspection. I wasn't being modest, the routine was for their benefit, so they couldn't be accused of springing a spin just to see you naked. For the sake of a little voyeuristic fun. Not that I have anything against gays, mind.

Strides and skids were fingered and returned. Then socks and shoes came off and went up for inspection. Katz looked a bit weary by now, but the kid was starting to get into it. He checked the seams on my socks and the seams on my shoes. Then he checked them again. Rather disappointed, it seemed to me, he handed them back and told me to take my bedding outside and shake it over the landing. He followed me out as Katz started to run over my peter.

'We're not picking on you,' said YTS. 'This is routine. Just routine.' He made such a point of saying it that I almost expected something to slip out of my blanket and fall the ten foot or so to the suicide net.

Then Katz shouted me in. I turned, went back into the cell, and saw him standing over a sheet of newspaper spread out on the cell floor. On it were the contents of my wastebin. An old *Guardian*, scraps of paper, toilet rolls. Katz looked straight at me. In his upturned palm was a wrapper from half an ounce of snout. In the middle of the flattened foil was a cluster of neat little handmade envelopes about half an inch across.

'What's this then?' he asked.

'We both know what that is,' I said.

'Twelve ninety, boss.' The driver was twisted round in his seat. 'We're here, boss. Twelve ninety.'

I got out and stuck the money through the window. He snorted and drove off and I crossed the road into the cul de sac. My place had been empty while I'd been away and the twins had kept an eye on it for me. The upstairs windows were lit, so the Wessons must be in. I wanted them to think I was still off 'on business', so I let myself in quietly, crept up the stairs to the first floor, opened my flat door double quiet and kept the lights off, standing for a moment to let my eyes adjust to the gloom. There was a pile of letters on the hall table, stacked up neatly by one of the kids. A couple more crackled under my boots. I squatted, dropped them next to the answerphone, called Lou and Sam again and got the machine.

'Lou, Sam, it's me again. Ringing about dinner tonight. It's about half four and I'm at home. Give me a bell as soon as. Bye.' I hung up. There was something wrong here, but I couldn't work out what.

I pushed open the lounge door as the streetlamps came on and window shapes of pale yellow light were thrown across the deck and up the walls.

Everything was the same as eighteen months before: widescreen telly in the window, red leather chairs, red leathertop desk and chair in the corner, white marble fireplace and fake gas fire. Eight twelve-foot shelves down the walls either side of the bay window, some with books, some with pictures, some empty. A club chair by the fire. Low stack of *Cosmo Girl* and *Heat* and other Lou mags on the table. I pressed my foot into the Persian rug, felt it give into the red Chinese carpet underneath. The place smelt a bit musty, but it felt OK.

Leaving the lights off, I went into the bedroom and the bathroom. They were also fine. In the kitchen I put the kettle on and went back into the bedroom to change strides, shirt and shoes. A black leather jacket came out of the wardrobe and I transferred everything from the other. Still in the dark, I went into the kitchen and made black coffee, carried it along the corridor and stopped dead at the hall table as I realised what was wrong. The answerphone light wasn't flashing. I hadn't got a message from the twins.

I left the flat immediately, moving fast on to the main drag to look for a cab.

Buckingham Road is a quiet residential slice of Heaton Moor – speed bumps, bay windows, the lot. I bought number forty-five on a mortgage when Sara and I got married, but it had been in her name for years now. When we split up, the twins stayed with her – she offered them stability. My deal could involve prison waiting rooms.

I took my finger off the doorbell and listened, then rang again. A few steps back and I saw the downstairs curtains were drawn; the bedroom curtains were back, but no sign of life. Back to the bell and I kept my finger on it till the end went white. Certainly long enough to wake sleeping teenagers.

Maybe they were due back from London tonight, not yesterday. But they knew I was out today, they knew we were going out. They wouldn't forget that, wouldn't miss it without letting me know. Lou even left me a message if she knew I'd been away for the weekend, just to welcome me back.

Gas. I'll say I smelt gas.

I nipped down the side entry and dropped over the wall to number forty-five. I found the spare key under the ledge and had the kitchen door open in a few seconds. Inside it looked a bit tidier than usual. Fridge humming quietly in the corner, clock on the cooker green in the dark. Down the corridor to the front room. I paused for a second and let my eyes adjust, then pushed the lounge door open. What I saw in the glow from the street hit me like an iron bar across the face. Breaking the habit of a lifetime, I turned the light on.

The room was completely empty. Not a stick of furniture.

I swung round, slammed on the hall light, took the stairs two at a time and tore the bedroom doors open.

Empty, all of them.

I slapped on the bathroom light and saw empty shelves. I opened cupboard doors, looked in the bathtub. Nothing. Nothing nothing nothing.

I half-ran, half-jumped down the stairs, noticed the lampshade had gone in the hall but the answerphone was still plugged in, shot round the house, looking behind doors, checking in cupboards, like I was expecting them to be hiding. Then I ran round again switching the lights off, slumped in the dark at the foot of the stairs and tried to think.

My ex-wife and children had gone and taken everything with them. And, it seemed, my brain had been replaced with handfuls of cotton wool. Trying to get my thoughts into line was like building a wall with this cotton wool, but whatever had happened here, I'd been turning lights on and someone could have seen and dialled three nines. I was on parole, and not in the mood to argue the toss about whether I had the right to be here or not. Get out, and swift.

I locked the door and stuck the key back, then went over the wall and I was on Buckingham Road again, walking fast. What the hell did I do now? Leon. Try Leon again. Straight to voicemail. What the fuck was going on?

Sara worked about half a mile away on the main drag. I started running, it started raining again and I was damp and sweating as I made her building. There was a courier in leathers just coming out, I slammed past him and took the stairs two at a time to the third floor where Michelle, her PA, was just pulling on a long blue coat to go home.

'Where is she?'

Michelle was in her late twenties and slim with a mop of dyed-red hair. She took a second to recognise me. 'Oh, hello . . . ' she broke off, eyes dancing round the room. Then, 'she phoned in yesterday, said she had to take some time off.'

'They're gone, the house is empty, Michelle, where is she?'

A door opened and a tall meaty neck with five o'clock shadow came out, whisking it shut behind him. 'What's the fucking noise for?' said the neck. 'I've got Japs in there.'

'It's Sara's husband, Mr Bryant.'

Bryant turned, six foot of *I'll deal with this* white-collar aggression. 'Do you understand what a fucking office is? Sara's ill, she's at home and *you* are out of order, so leave right now.'

I was still on prison time, and you don't let someone talk to you like that in the nick. I stepped towards him and he bristled up. Big and beefy, he probably fancied his chances, I could see it running through his brain. *This guy's a villain, probably a bully too, I've heard enough about him from Sara, he doesn't frighten me, the prick.* He jerked his thumb at the door. 'Go on, piss off.'

I made to leave, then swung round and slammed an open palm into his face. The move knocked him back hard against the wall which actually shuddered. I grabbed him by the throat and made a fist. 'Whatever you know, tell me now.' I was thinking nick. I couldn't stop it.

He gave it up in a beat. 'She phoned in sick, then she phoned in again and said there'd been a death in the family and she needed some more time off.' His tongue shot out and worked round his mouth. 'That's the truth. That's all we know.'

It was. Still on prison time, and I knew. I dropped him, his legs gave way and he slid down the wall to the deck.

'I'm sorry, Michelle.'

I took the stairs three at a time going down. If Bryant gave it three nines I was completely fucked. On my kind of licence they hardly needed an excuse to recall you and I'd just given them plenty – they'd have me back inside without the option. I hit the bottom, tore open the door and out on to the pavement. A few blocks down and I slowed, then managed to flag a cab for the centre. It was a black London-style. I slammed the divider shut and called Sara's mobile. Straight to voicemail.

'Sara, it's me. I don't know what's going on, but just call me – please. I'm on this number.' I left it and hung up. The twins didn't have mobiles; Sara was worried about brain tumours.

I called Leon, broke a rule and left a message. 'Leon, call me back as soon as you get this, whatever the time. Here's the number.' I rattled it off and saw we'd hit Deansgate. 'Stop here.'

I chucked some money at the driver and went into a bar. It was heaving and smelt of sex, there were bright lights and loud music, likely lads with gel-chopped number four crops and girls with plunging necklines, pierced navels and strappy sandals. Kids enjoying themselves. Of course, it was Friday night.

I pushed to the counter and got lucky. The barman – who'd been flipping bottles around like a circus juggler – stopped and clanked them down on the metal counter in front of me.

'Beer, any beer,' I shouted.

'These are on promotion,' he shouted back.

'Fine, whatever.' He flipped my glass into a double somersault and I dropped some coins on the counter.

The first drink when you get out is usually very important, you take time over it. Right now, I didn't even notice the label. It was just the rent. I took the bottle and pushed my way through damp bodies to a corner where I could watch the door. A couple got up off a bench where they'd been kissing enthusiastically. I slid into their seat, lit a cigarette and burnt it halfway down on the first drag. I tried to think but I couldn't,

I felt like something had been torn out of me; Lou and Sam were just seventeen and they'd gone. The twins were my life, the most important thing that I knew or had ever known. Even though they lived with their mam, I saw them both as often as possible; they had keys to my place and came and went as they wanted. Sometimes I'd go home and find one of them on the sofa because they'd had a row at school or home and wanted to be away from it all, with me. Or just because we hadn't spoken in a few days and they missed me. And now they'd gone and I didn't know why. What if I never saw them again? The tear inside me got wider. If that happened then my life was over. Might as well just walk out of here and go and top myself now.

No, come on, think. Remember the rules: get knowledge. The first thing was to get knowledge. What did I know from seeing the house? I saw them all dead for a second, laid out on slabs, tags on toes. No, push that down, that wasn't it. And it didn't make sense. Murders would mean police tapes, a watch on the house, a screw at my cell door at three in the morning. No, think about what you saw at Buckingham Road. It was empty, but it was tidy. Looked like they'd packed carefully. And the answerphone was still there to take messages, make people think they were just out or asleep. You'd have to get inside to find the truth.

Who might know? Leon, but I couldn't find him. Had they all gone off together?

Who else? Her friends, they must know – and Steph. Her sister Steph. Steph was very close with Sara, her son virtually lived round Buckingham Road when he was a kid. No way she wouldn't know something.

I pushed out to the street and found a quiet shop doorway just off the main drag. Steph was engaged, so I tried a couple of Sara's friends. No answers. I left messages with my new number on a couple of machines, then tried Steph again. Jan, her husband, answered immediately, like he was sitting over the phone.

'Jan?'

There was a pause. 'What do you want?' He sounded like a man who'd been up all night.

'What's wrong, Jan?'

With the silence, I thought he'd hung up.

'Jan?'

'We don't want to talk to you. We have nothing to say. Just leave us alone.'

The line went dead. I dialled back and it was engaged. What was his fucking game? Well, whatever it was, he wasn't on. I'd lay money they knew more than me right now. I'd find out what their fucking problem was.

Fifteen minutes later I was on their road. I kicked open the gate at number sixty-three, went up the path and buzzed. The door opened and Jan was there in silhouette. Couldn't make out his face, but he was wearing an overcoat like he'd just come in. Steph was slumped on the stairs in a long grey mac. She looked up to see who it was.

'What do you want, you fucking bastard?' Then she screamed and launched herself at me, thudding into my gut and punching and slapping my face. 'Get out you bastard, get out!'

She carried on hitting me, I covered my head with my hands and let her do it, Jan did nothing to stop her. I felt him standing to one side, letting his wife do what she wanted. There were slaps and thin fists on my head and shoulders, the backs of my hands, then it died away and I looked up. She stumbled back a couple of steps, dissolved into sobs and slammed her face into Jan's chest. He stared at me over her shoulder, and now I could see his eyes were red from crying. I took in the hall, saw Tomas's cycling helmet and his bike leaning up against the wall. I started to guess, the question was burbling out, but Jan spoke over me.

'Tomas is dead, and the police say it's because of you. You filthy dirty evil bastard. You killed Tomas, our son. You.'

I was in another cab. Lights people streets shops crowds clubs pubs cars buses street signs traffic lights flicked by the window. From a distance, I heard the driver ask where I was going. I heard myself mumble something to do with the city centre.

These are the facts. Jan and Steph had been out all day. They'd been out because they'd been organising the funeral of their only son,

Tomas. This is Tomas, who used to play football with Lou and Sam and sleep over with them in a tent in the back garden at Buckingham Road. Somewhere I have a picture of Tomas with Lou and Sam and a bird's nest they found when we all went walking in the country one Sunday in spring. Before I made them put it back, I took a photograph. It's about six in the evening, the children are tired after an afternoon's walking and running down hills and chasing each other. The sun is low in the sky and the shadows are long. The twins are seven and Tomas is nine. He's wearing a red jumper Steph knitted for him and he's stood in the middle of my two, giving a gap-toothed smile and holding the nest out to the camera, showing the eggs unbroken.

These are the facts. Tomas said he'd be staying at a friend's Monday night. The police rang the door about six Tuesday morning, Tomas was down at the Infirmary, shot. He was dead by the time Jan got down there.

The copper who stayed with them for the statements was a DC from Bootle Street called Sommerfield. He told them that Tomas had a couple of wraps of heroin in his pocket. Sommerfield said he'd had words with his boss, a chief superintendent called Hamilton Jacks.

Keith Hamilton Jacks. I knew him all right.

Sommerfield said Hamilton Jacks knew I'd been dealing seriously for some time, and that Tomas worked for me. Easy enough to get hold of a mobile phone inside, that would be how I pulled his strings, said Sommerfield. Must have been working for me when he got shot. Post-mortem said Tomas was a regular heroin user. Sommerfield told them that dealers like me try to get their people on the brown to control them. Keeps them on a string, Sommerfield told them.

Jan and Steph hadn't known Sara and the twins had gone, but they weren't surprised. Sara knew about Tomas, and Steph had told her what Hamilton Jacks said. I guess she didn't want Lou and Sam near me any more.

This was when Jan reminded me that I was a lousy father and a lousy human being. Then he slammed the door in my face and I heard them both crumple into sobs as I waded down the path. The noise followed me along the road and stayed in my head while I wandered, looking for a taxi. Now I was thinking of a nine-year-old Tomas playing with the twins. Then the shots came in like a baseball bat and the tears started up. No. There'd be time for that later. Stick with the here and now.

I was in trouble. Tomas was my nephew and Tomas was dead and the police had told his mam and dad that I was involved. And I was on parole and I'd slapped Sara's boss around so the filth could be knocking on my door to take me back to Strangeways any time. I'd be no good to no one back there. I couldn't go home.

We were coming up Portland Street opposite the old Queen's. I told the driver to pull in, chucked a note over the back seat and jogged across the Gardens to Mother Mac's down Back Piccadilly. I bought a drink and sat in the corner watching the door.

Just after nine Marcus came in, still in the winter coat and scarf but with a double-thick black beanie on his head this time. I wove through the boozers and grabbed him at the bar.

'Aye aye. Thought you were out with the kids tonight?'

'Are you driving?'

'It's down the side.'

'Let's go and sit in it.'

Marcus's red Merc was tucked down the side street with a table wrapped in plastic strapped to the roof rack. We got in and he turned on the heater.

'Are you going to the club tonight, Marcus?'

'Later.'

'I've got some proper trouble, Marcus.' I took a deep breath. 'My nephew's been murdered.'

'Oh, Christ.'

'He was shot and dumped at the Infirmary early on Tuesday morning. I need your help, Marcus. I need you to ask around at the club for me tonight, someone must know something. Don't mention my name, don't say he was my nephew, but can you see if anyone knows anything? Names, rumours, anything at all. Please.'

'What's his name again?'

'Tomas Warzyniak, nineteen years old. Royal Infirmary, Tuesday morning, early. The filth say he was dealing brown, but I don't believe that.'

'Was he on the gear?'

'They say so, I don't believe that either.'

'OK, I'll see what I can do.'

I was sweating from the heater, so I cracked the window a couple of inches. 'Have you got a pen?'

'In the glovebox.'

I opened it, found a pen and wrote my new number and Tomas's name on the back of a flyer for a car dealer in Hyde. 'Call me on this number, no other.'

He folded it away in his wallet. 'You should call Jack. If there's class A in there, he might know something.'

'I know what Jack's game is, Marcus. Call me as soon as you've got something.'

'OK, mate.' He nodded outside, it was raining again. 'Do you need a lift anywhere?'

'No. Thanks, Marcus.'

There was one cab left on the rank in the Gardens. I slid back the divider and asked for the Alex Park Estate. 'One of the avenues off Quinney. I'll give you a shout.' The guy clocked me hard in the mirror. The Alex was bandit country. I managed to haul up some calm. 'Just come from the hospital, need to talk to a relative.' Which meant *I'm not at it*.

Fifteen minutes later, we pulled up on the main drag where it cut into Benny's close. 'It's just down there.'

'Yeah, and I'm stopping here.'

'Okay, will you wait then?'

'How long?'

'About fifteen minutes.'

He looked at the meter. It clicked three fifty. 'Fifteen and I'll stop here for you.'

It was only spitting now. I jammed a score through the divider and got out. 'Fifteen minutes,' I said.

I got out and slapped a few paces away from the cab. Then I heard the motor fire and the slag shot off as a waterfall broke on my head, thick sheets building almost immediately to hail. Pressing into the shelter of some bushes, I snapped up my collar and saw a sudden movement down the street. Other side, a few houses along, a guy bobbed out into the light for a moment and it was Tomas, the sharp-boned body, the long hair like curtains. I wiped the water out of my eyes and peered through the hail again. He was gone. The rain stopped.

I jogged the hundred yards down the street and hit the bell. It rang somewhere away in the house and I heard the old guy wheezing and sliding up to the glass. Movement behind the spyhole, then clanking and bolts and keys as he opened up.

'Good to see you on the street again, mate.'

'Can I come in, Benny?'

'Yeah, yeah, course.'

The only light in his lounge was a chipped anglepoise on the coffee table shining on a Swiss Army knife, a tobacco pouch and some rectangles of blow a couple of inches long.

'When did you get out?'

'This morning.'

'And you want something for your head?'

'In a minute. I need a favour, Benny.'

Benny was an obsessive United fan, he listened to or watched every local news bulletin and read half a dozen dailies in case there was something in about the Reds. And because of all the lads in and out buying blow, he had a pretty good idea of a lot of stuff that never made it into the papers, local or otherwise. I told him about Tomas.

'Christ, I'm sorry mate.'

'OK. Have you heard or read anything about it?'

He blew out over his teeth. 'I read something, I think. Couple of days ago, young kid. Shot in the belly, dropped at the Infirmary. I think that was it.'

'Are you sure, Benny? This is important.'

'I know it's important, it's your nephew.'

'I need as much knowledge as you can get, Benny. Mainstream, or off the street. I've got a new number.' I wrote it down on a newspaper and laid it on top of the pouch and cubes of dope. 'Tomas Warzyniak. But keep me out of it, OK?'

'OK.'

'Soon as you can, Benny.'

He wrapped me an ounce and a half of rocky. I paid him and went looking for a cab. Bad area, bad time. *Get out of sight.* I jogged for Stretford, scanning the roads for a paid lift. It started to rain again.

Half an hour later and piss-wet through, I was checking into a B&B on Chester Road round the corner from Old Trafford. The room was a box with a coat hook on the back of the door. I pulled my jacket and shoes off, opened the window, rolled a joint and lit it, then rang Leon again. Voicemail, again.

'Call me, Leon. It's urgent.'

Then I thought of Leon's mam, Judith. He never gave her number out as she was getting bad on her legs and he didn't want her running for the phone. But I knew her well. She answered on the eighth ring. I tried to sound relaxed.

'Hello Judith, it's me. Sorry to trouble you, love. But I got out today and I've been trying to get hold of Leon.'

'I know it was today, I told him to bring you out here to lunch, but it was business he said. It's always business with you, I told him. I asked him who was going to meet you, but he said you'd be happy on your own for a bit. How are you?'

'I'm fine, Judith. It's just that I've been ringing his mobile and getting the answerphone.'

'He's got a new one a couple of days ago. Which one are you ringing?'

'Must be the old one. Can you give me the other?'

'Just a minute.' I heard the phone laid down and a drawer being opened. Villains change their mobiles as often as they can afford it, but normally he'd have told me. 'Here we are.'

I wrote it down, then called it back. 'I'll give him a bell right now.'

'He has it off half the time, anyway. He's a mystery to me, that boy. Always has been.'

'Can you take my new number, Judith? And ask him to call me?'

She wrote it down. It took a while.

'Sorry to be a trouble,' I said.

'Trouble indeed,' she was all mock indignant. 'When are you ever trouble to this house? Goodnight and God bless.'

We hung up and I rang Leon's new number. Voicemail. 'Ring me the minute you get this, Leon. It's urgent.' I spewed my number and hung up.

I'd been tugging so hard on the joint it was nearly gone. And I'd stuck plenty in it. Suddenly I felt dizzy, then the blow whispered at me. *They've all done a runner. Sara, Lou, Sam, Leon. He's taken them all away to his place in Spain. To start a new life together.*

What about the twins?

Plenty of language schools there, probably all been planned for months. That's why he didn't give you the new number. You've been away a year and a half, remember.

Fuck off. They don't need to run from me. Not together. And Leon wouldn't do that to me anyway.

Wouldn't he?

'No,' I kicked at the voice. 'And he wouldn't do it to Judith, and she can't tell a lie to save her life. Except to the filth.'

I laid the spliff in the ashtray, leant back and closed my eyes.

The cold woke me and I didn't have a clue where I was. Then it was, oh Christ blue bed cover grey curtain flock walls single bed Tomas twins Christ no Jesus Christ.

I got up and closed the window, my watch said 03:15. I picked up the phone to check no one had rung, tried Leon again. Nothing.

I undressed, crawled between the sheets, reached out and flicked off the light. Curling up in a ball, I tried to sleep.

Acknowledgements

We'd like to thank everyone who gave up their time to read, comment or otherwise help out on *Fat Blackmail*. The names in the frame here are Matthew Birchwood, Tony Burrows, Anna Cocozza, Gabriella Francis, Michelle Gribbon, Rae Howells, Jo Johnson, Maurice Kirk, Julie Klavens, Richard MacAndrew, Jerry Pass, Jack Pearson and Helen Zaltzman.

Special thanks to Cap, for advice on technical matters; to Martin Clark for help and advice on police and police procedures; and to John Devlin for advice on some of the legals. Any mistakes in any of these areas are down to the authors.

Thank you also to Becky Senior, Ben Yarde-Buller, Francesca Yarde-Buller and Tom Viney at Old Street for reasons, various. Certainly too many to go into here.

Finally, Leslie Gardner at Artellus for all the usual help and support as *Fat Blackmail* was written. On behalf of us all, we thank you.